Jungle Rules

Paul Shemella

PAGE PUBLISHING, INC.
New York, NY

First originally published by Page Publishing, Inc. 2018

ISBN 978-1-64298-114-8 (Paperback)
ISBN 978-1-64298-116-2 (Hardcover)
ISBN 978-1-64298-115-5 (Digital)

Printed in the United States of America

For Betty

Chapter 1

Mamoré

B *olivia, August 1998.*
        He had forgotten how dry the jungle could be. Dust covered his boots and fatigue pants as he walked along a dirt trail toward the river. The dry season he had known in Panama was easier to remember, he guessed, because the American colony was so familiar to him. Here—at the edge of the thirsty forest, with savanna stretching to the horizon—he and his three comrades could not have felt more alone. It was midafternoon. He was anxious to get it over with.

His men followed, as they always did, allowing him to set the pace and pick the route. AKs covered fields of fire. When he stopped, they squatted in place, straining under the weight of their equipment. He surveyed the landscape and checked the map. They were still about a kilometer from their goal—the edge of a slow muddy river, separating the authorities of two countries.

The Mamoré.

He pointed to a conspicuously large tree laden with epiphytes and made a lariat motion in the air. This would be a rally point if they got ambushed or separated and had to regroup. They each acknowledged with a silent head nod, stood up, and prepared to walk again.

The walk was always the hardest part of the mission. It was even worse than the night free fall from twenty thousand feet into an unfamiliar drop zone. Adrenaline had gotten them through the jump but, like any drug, it had worn off too soon. The heat had become unbearable. Sweat mixed with camouflage paint on their faces and carried it, stinging, into their eyes. He was looking forward to getting in the water.

In front of him walked the two Bolivians. He didn't need them. He hadn't wanted them. His briefers had insisted on including them, almost certainly for political reasons. But the Bolivians had marked the drop zone correctly, and the linkup had gone well. Still, he ordered them to stay ahead of him. He wanted them to know they would be the first seen—and the first killed—in the event of a compromise. Trust took a lot more time than they had.

He wondered—and worried—about the people who knew he and his men were in Bolivia. Starting with the president, there were at least five Americans who could burn him. But his real concern was the government that owned the soil on which they walked. Corruption in Washington was limited by the rule of law and a lingering morality; here, it was hard to find laws, let alone morality. There was more money near this border than anywhere else in the country. It came with violence and death. Bribery was always the first step. The "*fuerzas especiales*" had been certified clean, but he did not know the certifiers, or where they had been.

Looking back, he felt a surge of confidence. In Grenada, he and his men had survived a long gunfight with unexpectedly capable Cuban forces. In Panama, they had sunk enemy patrol boats in the canal, coming underwater in the night. They had gone into the bush after that, searching for dead-enders bent on taking revenge for the *Yanqui* invasion. Before combat, years of dangerous training had forged within them a bond stronger than love. He knew that ordinary people could never understand that, people who had not routinely risked death, those who could not, through sheer will, perform impossible feats of strength, endurance, and courage.

The Americans had field names of two syllables, along with at least two tactical specialties (shooting was a given). Behind him walked Bosco, the team's medic and resident sky god. He was the shortest of the four, but he could outrun all of them. Although he did not expect to use it, Bosco carried the satellite radio. The Latino looked worried. On patrol, Bosco always looked worried.

After the medic came the big man. His teammates called him Butkus for his intimidating size. Though the big man's specialties were heavy weapons and diving, it would be his formidable strength that would be needed this night. He was more than just big. Butkus could carry heavy loads for days without stopping. And still do the job. Whatever job needed doing. In spite of his awesome physical presence, Butkus had the face of a boy. A very big boy.

Last in line came a cocky southerner they called Tinker. A world-class rock climber, he was also astonishingly good with a knife. But Tinker's highest-value skill was as a gifted boat mechanic. He seemed to have a permanent grin on his prematurely wrinkled face. Anyone observing him would have seen that the young man was glad to be where he was, looking for trouble in a faraway place.

Years earlier, the three of them had nicknamed their leader Carlos, after the famous terrorist. It had been a gesture of respect. Like a cat, Carlos moved slowly through the heat, hesitating often as if to sniff the air. His lanky build seemed spring-loaded. A camouflage flop hat covered wavy black hair that grew thick to his collar. With average height and olive features, he could navigate a crowd in Turkey without being noticed. Or in Bosnia. Or Bolivia. His Spanish was flawless, almost as good as Bosco's. Carlos was the best any of them had ever seen, with great field instinct and no fear. They felt safe with him in charge—even here.

Stopping again to mark their position with a satellite fix, Carlos noted with pride that he could still dead-reckon. He didn't need electronics. Just like the old days. But simply getting to the target was not the mission. He had a plan, and they were on track. He took a long pull from his canteen, motioning for his men to do the same. The water tasted of iodine, but it felt good flowing through his tired body, all the way to the prominent veins in his arms. He squatted several times to get the blood out of his legs.

Glancing behind the patrol, Carlos noticed a scarlet macaw glide into the forest. Even though he didn't have the time, he noted that the bird was at the extreme southern end of its range. Nothing wrong yet, but he had learned through long hours of observation that, in these places, birds have better senses than men. Tuning into nature had saved his life before. Looking ahead again, he noticed the Bolivians were getting too far in front of him. He took a few quick steps forward to warn them, then hurriedly led the patrol into the trees.

In the next instant a low-flying airplane appeared from out of nowhere! Snapping his head up, Carlos watched a Cessna 206 eclipse the sun, barely a hundred feet above the thin jungle canopy. There was no time to hide. Instinctively, they froze in place. The plane was so close, he could see the pilot looking down at them through the tops of the trees. As long as they remained frozen, Carlos knew his team would be invisible from a moving plane. But the face overhead unnerved him.

This area, he knew, was a major air corridor for small planes loaded with cocaine base headed toward final processing in the jungles of southern Colombia. His boss in Panama had called them scud missiles with chemical warheads in selling the drug war to a skeptical Congress. Carlos understood where the refined cocaine would be going; he wanted nothing more than to bring the plane down in flames.

But that was not the mission.

A few minutes later the patrol came to a perpendicular tree line, and Carlos realized why the Cessna had flown over them. The plane had been following the Mamoré. The river had cut the jungle in half. Flowing north, it was the only landmark between horizons. Carrying silt from the high Andes, the muddy water headed for a distant sea looked more like chocolate milk. They reached the bank, set a security perimeter, and finally took off their packs. It was five o'clock in the afternoon. The tropical sun would drop out of sight soon, and there were weapons to clean. The Bolivians departed to find the boats they knew would be upstream; the Americans prepared themselves for action. When the equipment was ready and the rations finished, they took turns sleeping.

Five hours later they were ready to cross the river. The water was low but still deep enough that they would have to swim. They were good swimmers. The boats would come afterward to speed them away. What they needed now was stealth. They had not been seen, and Carlos was responsible for keeping it that way. There was nothing else he could do at this point except rely on his training. And the training of his men. And the return of the Bolivians. He worried that he and his men might die. He didn't care about the Bolivians.

It felt good to be wet. Carlos always felt safer in the water—even this water. He adjusted his fins and led Bosco into the current while the other pair watched up and down the bank. Four Americans. He expected to be outnumbered anyway, and fewer men made less noise. Carlos and Bosco, no more than six feet apart, moved across the gaping hole in their universe. A very black hole.

Rucksacks had become floats to be pushed across the two hundred meters of smooth water. Adorned with branches, the packs resembled the many clumps of grass dotting the edge of the river. The men swam snakelike, scanning with their night vision goggles as they stroked beneath the surface. Without making a sound, they approached the opposite bank. Carlos knew exactly where he was. With a red flashlight, he signaled the others to cross while he and Bosco held fields of fire. It wouldn't be long now.

When they had assembled again, each man stowed his fins, donned his pack, and sloshed off into the tree line. The water, mixed with sewage from countless peasant villages, poured from their fatigues. Minutes later the water had drained off, but the men still smelled of human waste. They made no noise. Sneakers had replaced combat boots. They needed to leave civilian tracks. Footprints that Carlos wanted someone to find.

Intelligence had located the compound at five hundred meters from the river. Carlos was confident they had made the right decision to infil by parachute, walk, and then swim. As always, he had listened to his men. Carlos liked to plan by consensus. But during execution he was guided by instinct. After all these years, the four of them had the same instincts. Combat was like a pickup game of basketball, fluid and efficient.

They walked along a narrow path until they saw the road. Carefully pacing the distance, Carlos followed the edge of the road until he saw something that did not belong to the forest. It was the villa they had studied on the satellite photo.

He led them to a vantage point from which the team could survey the target. It was after midnight now and, although the house was mainly dark, the fence lights were blazing. No night vision goggles needed here. Experience had taught them that anyone looking into the jungle would have zero night vision. There were four armed guards walking the perimeter inside the cyclone fence. This would be the easy part, thought Carlos, and he wondered why anyone would want to be a guard.

On cue, the others took their posts at assigned corners of the fence. The loud broadcast of the diesel generator masked what little sound they made. Carlos had wanted to put the guards to sleep with dart guns but realized early in the planning that it would be too risky. They would have to kill them. Not many governments—and certainly not the cartel—could be expected to spare human life. Such a senseless act of mercy would be easily attributed to the Americans. His orders had been clear—"plausible denial" above all else. Carlos understood without being told that he and his men would be on their own after the operation.

The team was linked together with squad radios but, until now, there had been no reason to use them. Now the plan called for a simultaneous takedown of all four guards. As soon as they were in position, Carlos donned an earphone and got the word he needed from each man. They were in place, aiming at their targets with silenced barrels. He took a deep breath, centered the red laser dot on his own target and voiced the order into the boom microphone in front of his lips. He squeezed off one round and watched the unknowing head snap back, exploding as it disappeared from the scope.

Carlos's target thudded to the ground in unison with the others. He exhaled forcefully, feeling the exhilaration. The revulsion and remorse would come later.

Tinker ran to the fence, cut a flap, and held it open for the others as they moved quickly from their sniper positions. The informant had been right; there was no alarm. This was a hastily fortified hideout for a very desperate man on the run. Tinker counted three heads going through the fence, then stayed to cover their backs.

Showtime.

Carlos dreaded the next ten minutes, not for the raid but for the wait. Ten minutes out here seemed like ten hours. It wasn't as safe as being in the water. The three men put on their gas masks and checked each other for leaks. Butkus took out a can of sleeping agent and opened the valve. They were in a tight perimeter at the air-conditioning fan, still in the shadow of the garden wall. The gas was sucked into the house as they watched in every direction for signs of movement. Anything that moved would put them in mortal danger. They counted on Tinker to see what they could not—and to deal with it.

They watched, but mostly they waited.

Precisely ten minutes later, Carlos motioned to Butkus to follow him and ran to the front of the house. He was a bit surprised to find the door locked but quickly stepped aside as the big man's boot almost took the door off its hinges. Stealth was no longer necessary, at least inside the house. There were three filthy-looking Latin men passed out on the floor of the living room. Two others, just as dirty, were sprawled unconscious over the bar. A skin flick was still playing on the oversize television. Carlos led Butkus down a long corridor to the farthest bedroom door. He opened it carefully and turned on the lights.

A fat middle-aged man and a stunning young woman lay together under satin sheets. Butkus walked quickly to the bed, ripped away the top sheet, and hoisted the man onto his shoulders. Without slowing down, he followed Carlos outside while Jose covered them from behind.

In less than a minute they were all back in the trees, having left nothing but sneaker tracks. Carlos had arranged for the boats to meet them at 0200. It was now after 1:00 a.m., and they moved as fast as they could with the extra weight. Though there is nothing heavier than a limp body, Butkus was strong enough to keep up with the others. Later, when the effects of the gas wore off, the fat man would be able to walk, but for the next four hours he would be a cadaver.

Someone wanted the fat man alive. Gas had been the only way to make sure they got him out that way. They could have planned to shoot their way into the house but, after much debate, Carlos had decided it would be too risky. He hadn't been too worried about their quarry; he'd been thinking about his men. He didn't want one of them wounded or killed so far out on a limb—with no medical backup and no diplomatic status. This was a risky business, with life-and-death decisions at every turn; Carlos had always bristled at the standard bureaucratic caveat "Safety is paramount." Aggressive training and sound operational procedures would put them in the safest position, no matter the circumstances. If safety were paramount, they would have stayed in Virginia.

They had started out together as patriots. Even though the motive was now money, they were still Americans. Still his men. He would protect them as best he could. They had the fat man, and they were getting close to the river again.

He smelled it before he saw it. During the day, it looked like a tourist poster; by night, it was just another dirty South American river. They waded to the edge of the current and waited in waist-deep water. He adjusted his night vision goggles and locked his gaze upstream. Bosco and Tinker covered the rest of the compass. Butkus knelt and shrugged the prisoner off his shoulders to let the river take the weight, controlling him with the muscle memory of a former lifeguard. Butkus was aware that the life he now guarded—as despicable a life as he could imagine—was extremely valuable to someone. He wondered who, and why.

Carlos spotted the boats long before they saw him. His gut had told him they would be there, but his head had prepared him for a long swim. He gave the signal, and they floated closer. The Bolivians were polling in the shallows with the engines down, ready to fire. Years ago, when he had served in the Navy, Carlos had known the flimsy craft as bonka boats, always clogging Third World harbors, a nuisance to US warships. Now they were his primary means to get out of Brazil. And Bolivia. The big man lifted the prisoner and plopped him onto the lead boat like a trophy fish.

"*El pez gordo*," said Carlos to the night. The kingpin is a fat fish indeed, he thought, climbing into the boat. It was the first time Carlos had spoken since giving the order to shoot the guards.

The rest of the team got into the boats as quietly as they could. They floated for ten minutes longer, listening to the night. When Carlos felt secure enough, he told the Bolivians to start the engines. As the forty-horsepower Yamahas bit into the water, the team cruised downstream toward the next phase of the operation.

Carlos took off his flop hat and relaxed for the first time in twenty-four hours. He had not been able to sleep before the snatch, and now the fatigue tugged at him. His men noticed he was dozing off and increased their own vigilance. This was the most dangerous time of all; they had hit the objective, but the operation was not over. There was a lot of river between the team and the clearing where the helicopter would meet them. A lot of opportunities for sudden failure, and death. They had taken every precaution but, as always, uncertainty stalked them.

An hour later they rounded the large bend in the river. The rendezvous. Carlos took Bosco and went up to scout the landing zone. The others waited with the boats, preparing for exfiltration. They had agreed that the Bolivians would not leave until the team was airborne (if the helicopter failed to come before daylight, they would need the boats again). In that event, it would be a long and dangerous trip out, even with the Bolivians. Carlos had already decided that before continuing all the way to Riberalta he would kill the fat man and leave him floating in the river. At that point it would not matter to Carlos if his briefers did not get the drug lord. They had already paid him half the money, and he wanted his team to survive to spend it.

Rallying at the river's edge, Carlos briefed everyone again. When they all understood the plan, he motioned for Bosco and Tinker to go back to the LZ and place the lights in the middle of the field. They did it quickly—a little too quickly for Carlos's critical eye—and returned with two thumbs up. Leaving Tinker to watch the boats, he brought Bosco and Butkus—still carrying the fat man—to a layup position to wait with him. Carlos thought that if he let the Bolivians stay with the boats alone, they would be too tempted to run. He wondered if they thought the gringos would kill them. If Carlos had been in their position, he would have thought that. Butkus handcuffed the prisoner and checked the duct tape that kept the man's mouth shut. The limp body would come alive soon.

And again, they waited.

They heard the helicopter, but they could not see it. Although the whine of the engines was getting closer, it was impossible to tell where the bird was coming from. It was several long minutes before the large machine materialized almost directly overhead. It was enormous and—for men who had not made an audible sound in a long time—very loud. The prop wash, laced with the memory-inducing aroma of jet fuel, forced them to lean toward the aircraft as it eased to the ground.

Carlos wanted one more look at the prize before they left. He walked over to Butkus, took out a flashlight, and thrust it toward the prisoner. There was panic in the face even before the fat man opened his eyes. The captive did not know where he was, but he understood—probably better than his captors—why they had taken him alive. He would be interrogated—perhaps tortured—until he revealed the names, locations, and account numbers the US government could obtain no other way. He did not know, however, that he would also be hidden away for a long time. And that dangerous rumors would echo through the Amazon Basin.

Carlos waited for Tinker to release the Bolivians, and one by one the Americans boarded the helo. After a head count, he gave the "OK" sign to the young Air Force pilot. The tailgate came up as the helicopter rose above the trees, inclining its nose to the southwest. As he began to relax again, Carlos examined his mixed emotions about the mission. He was proud of the way his men had performed—the tactical execution had been virtually flawless—but he was glad their part was over. It had been easier to kill when he had done it for his ideals. Carlos was tired of killing for himself (and for money) especially when he wasn't sure it was good for his country. He told himself it was not a moral issue—the men they had killed were just scum. But he asked himself if the operation would make any difference at all.

Carlos looked again into the frightened eyes that stared at him. Feeling nothing, he closed his own eyes and slept through the first leg of the long ride home.

Chapter 2

Potomac

C arl Malinowski ran along the Potomac. If his legs hadn't hurt so much he would have had a smile on his face. The towpath was his favorite run, but he wasn't doing it for fun. It was not quite light yet, but he could smell the trees and hear the birds. Running in the dark was good training, but August heat was the real reason he was out so early. He preferred the steamy heat of the jungle to the smoggy oven of Washington. It was a great feeling to have the mission behind him, his men in one piece, and money in his pocket.

The ride home had been long indeed. After the helicopter had delivered the team to a remote airstrip in southern Bolivia, a COD aircraft had flown them over the Andes to the USS *Vinson*, transiting north from its Chilean port call. With the prisoner secure—and alone—in the brig, Carl and his men had relaxed for the five-day run to San Diego. Once in port, they had turned the fat man over to an FBI official with the proper code words before flying commercial to the East Coast. His men had gone back to Virginia Beach while Carl returned to Washington for two days of debriefings and a return to normal life.

He gritted his teeth and raced up the steps to the Key Bridge. Racing up stairs and hills was the only way he could deal with them. It was the training again.

Always the training.

He eased up on the span and, with sharpened senses, felt the river emerging from the darkness to either side. His future was not so clear.

He coasted downhill and stopped at the traffic light in front of the Marriott. A slow walk to the condo would cool him down properly. He hadn't decided yet if he would go back into the field, but he couldn't afford an injury. He needed to be *ready* to go back. At forty-four, Carl knew he was near the end of his operational effectiveness. But he was still a warrior. A good contract might come his way, and old habits die hard.

A mercenary with a midlife crisis, walking the streets of Rosslyn at dawn.

The neighborhood was coming to life as he walked uphill. He noticed an attractive blonde woman in high heels walking carefully down the hill, briefcase in hand. A professional. Someone with class. Understated but sexy. She didn't see him staring. As he waited with male anticipation for the distance to close, he noticed something else. His guard was down, so it took him a few seconds to realize what was happening.

A crouching figure came out of the bushes just behind the woman and fell in behind her. The man took three long strides and lunged for the purse hanging from her shoulder. The mugger pushed her to the pavement, grabbed the leather bag, and took off across the street! Without thought or hesitation, Carl was off like a missile to intercept the thief.

He didn't see the car coming right at him.

The driver saw a blurry figure leave the sidewalk, headed for impact. Like a squirrel coming out of the forest. Carl didn't even have time to slow down. The driver braked and swerved; Carl hurdled onto the hood of the vehicle and pushed off in a running leap. Somehow, he managed to stay on his feet. He was back in the jungle, focused on the quarry; nothing was going to stand in his way.

And the gap was closing fast!

The fleeing youth was now looking back, gasping and grunting, pain on his Hispanic face. Carl, with arms pumping and legs burning, was close enough to feel the kid's strength ebbing away. Then he executed a flying tackle that brought the guy down hard, bouncing off the sidewalk. Carl could feel the skin being torn from his fore-arms and elbows as the two men skidded to a stop.

The force of the tackle had subdued the mugger temporarily, but Carl could see that he was hyped up on drugs and still danger-ous. Working on top of his opponent like a wrestler, he gathered the scrawny elbows behind the man's back and pulled him to his feet. The attacker still clutched the purse in his right hand. Carl snatched the prize away and hung it around the guy's neck. He ran his free hand all over the filthy clothing and found no weapons.

"Cabrón! Vamos!" He shouted the only Spanish that came to mind.

Inflicting as much pain as possible, Carl pushed the guy back to where the woman, now on one knee, was still trying to get up. A police car was coming into view when he wrestled the man into posi-tion just in front of his victim. Carl's arms were a bloody mess and he felt like throwing up. He was pissed off and still breathing hard. Foaming at the mouth, he shouted at the man again.

"Tonto! El bolso . . . a la dama!"

With his left arm now free, the exhausted attacker lifted the purse over his head and gave it back to the woman. She stood up and put it over her shoulder, looking gratefully at Carl. She was bleeding from the knees and her suit was badly torn, but she was more beau-tiful than any woman he had ever seen. Carl was proud to have been able to help—especially her. Still shaking, she managed a smile.

"You must be my guardian angel!" she gushed. "I don't know how to thank you." She kept smiling.

Even in his pain, Carl felt more blood rush to his head. If he hadn't been red from exertion, Carlos the warrior would have been caught blushing.

"My pleasure, miss." He smiled like a schoolboy, almost forget-ting he had one thing left to do.

He looked over his shoulder for the police car. As it skidded to a halt, Carl shoved the prisoner against the door. He was back in the field again, and the rush of pleasure was undeniable. The officer came out of the driver's seat with handcuffs at the ready. Carl helped his captive painfully into the cuffs.

"Looks like you've done that before," said the cop. "You have law enforcement experience?"

"No," Carl responded. "I just watch a lot of action movies . . . What happens now?"

"We all go down to the station . . . I need statements," said the man in uniform. "And thanks for nailing this scum. There's been lots of robberies in this neighborhood lately. It's all drugs. They need the money for crack cocaine. It's not safe out here anymore. This place used to be a refuge from the high crime on the other side of the river . . . Christ, even the mayor uses drugs! I got another car coming to pick up you and the victim . . . See you later." And the cop raced away with Carl's prisoner.

Carl turned around as the police car left. The woman was still standing there, as tall as he, beautiful and bleeding. She had picked up her briefcase and, for an instant, he feared she might just walk away.

"I think we both need some medical attention, miss . . ."

"Bach. Gabriele Bach," she answered in a steadier, pleasing voice, with just a trace of an accent. "You more than I."

"Gabriele? What a beautiful name! I'm Carl Malinowski . . . very pleased to meet you—even under these circumstances." He was still breathing too heavily for normal conversation.

"The pleasure is mine, Carl, but you really need to see a doctor." She looked up the street toward the Metro. "Here comes another policeman. He can take us to the hospital." Taking charge, she raised her hand and waved the speeding car to a stop.

"We have to go to the police station and make a statement first," said Carl. "I can wait with these," he continued, nodding at his bloody forearms. "As long as they give me a towel so I don't bleed all over the desk." He was beginning to relax.

Gabriele took off her silk scarf and started wrapping it around his right elbow. "This is all I have . . . I'll make sure they give you first aid before they make you write anything."

He was impressed by her presence of mind. And her unselfishness—especially after being violently attacked. After all he had been through, Carl Malinowski was not easily impressed. As he opened the car door for her, he was glad they had both been summoned by the cops.

They sat together in the back of the police car. He wasn't a talkative man, but suddenly all he wanted to do was talk.

"So, do you work here in Rosslyn, Gabriele?"

She shifted her hips to face him on the seat. "Just up Arlington Boulevard. I teach German at the Foreign Service Institute. I was on my way to work when all this happened."

"Do you always go in so early?"

"I was trying to catch up on some things." She raised her blonde eyebrows. "Do you always patrol the streets so early . . . looking for damsels in distress, no doubt?"

It was the contours of her face that intrigued him the most. Her features were prominent yet subtle. Instead of marble, the sculptor had used something close to silk. "I have to get my run in before the heat gets too bad," he said, breaking into a smile. "I'm glad I decided to walk back through the neighborhood, though."

"*You're* glad? My whole life is in that purse!" Then she added, "And watching you run my attacker down was very exciting stuff . . . You live nearby?"

"I live on the Fort Myer side of this concrete island. I can see the Marine Corps Memorial, as well as the monuments in the distance. That makes up for the concrete."

"I guess that makes us neighbors!" she said with another smile. Carl's elbows were killing him, but his heart felt like it would float out of his chest and into the air.

Cutting their conversation short, the police car came to a stop in front of the station. Carl slid out and opened doors for her all the way to the squad room. Once inside the chaos of the office, Gabriele went into action.

"Excuse me," she said to a passing female clerk. "Can you tell us where this man can get some medical attention?" The clerk stopped and looked at Carl's bloody arms.

"Follow me," she said. "We have a small locker where he can get some bandages . . . but that's about it, I'm afraid."

"We just need to get him patched up a bit so he can fill out a report," said Gabriele calmly as they walked down the hall. "That's all we need right now . . . thanks."

After the clerk was gone, Gabriele began washing his arms, taking out the bits of gravel embedded in his skin. Carl wanted her to work for hours, but she was finished in minutes.

"What about you?" asked Carl, looking at the top of her head as she bent to apply the second bandage.

"I'm fine," she replied, glancing up at him with matted hair hanging over her eyes. "We'll both live, I think!"

They went back to the maze of desks and made the required statements. Carl knew it wouldn't do much good. This guy would be back on the street soon . . . and sooner or later he would get a gun. There were thousands more like him out there. America was falling apart, and drug violence was a big factor. He wasn't sure if his own activities had made an impact, but at least he had done *something*. Getting Gabriele's purse back had felt almost as good as taking a monster from the jungle.

"Those arms of yours will be fine," said Gabriele as she adjusted one of his bandages. "If nothing is broken, you should be back in business in no time." She hesitated, then looked him right in the eye. "By the way, what *is* your business?"

"I'm a very small defense contractor," he said evenly. "I write doctrine for the Army and Navy."

"That sounds dreadful," said Gabriele. "It must be better than it sounds!"

"It's all right," he explained. "And it pays better than you think . . . You teach German to diplomats?" he asked, changing the subject.

"Yes . . . and it's not as good as it sounds. Most of my students are brilliant but arrogant as the devil. I have some military attaché students, not as well educated but easier to work with. The pay is OK, though, and I like Washington."

"You're native German?"

"Yes, I was born and raised in the little town of Waldenbuch, near Stuttgart. In Stuttgart they make Porsches. In Waldenbuch we make chocolate."

"I prefer chocolate," said Carl without missing a beat. "Why did you come to the States?"

"To go to college. I liked it so much, I stayed."

"And I'm glad you did," replied Carl. "Is there a . . . Mr. Bach?" He couldn't believe he was flirting. Carl had never flirted with anyone.

"Johann Sebastian is the only Bach I know of other than my father," she said with a grin. "The composer reportedly had twenty children, so I'm probably related to him somehow. Is there a Mrs. Malinowski?"

"Not anymore. I'm divorced with no children," said Carl carefully.

They arrived at the hospital at that moment, and Carl was glad they had. He did not enjoy talking about himself. It wasn't just having to hide his real job; out of the field, he was genuinely shy (his own men didn't know how shy he was—and he didn't want them to ever find out). He had already opened up to Gabriele more than he wanted to. That was a slippery slope.

The stitches didn't hurt because the pain in his elbows was still roaring through his head like the drone of a C-130 cargo plane. Thank God for Motrin, he thought. It was for people like Carl that Ranger candy had been invented.

They were out of the emergency room in thirty minutes. Gabriele's cuts were minor, and she was trying to keep Carl's mind off the pain.

"We were talking about marriage," she said.

"I think it's a little soon for that," he quipped.

When she laughed, it seemed to come from her soul. The sound simply burst into the room—a brief explosion of joy, muffled quickly by years of social training.

"I'm sorry it didn't work out, Carl," she said, suddenly serious. "I've never been married, but it seems as though it would be one of the most difficult things to do. People are so complicated, so unpredictable! It's hard to know what you're getting into. I have had some good male friends, but I have never met a man I wanted to marry. It's a lonely way to live, but it's safe."

"It wasn't too bad," he said. "I was too young, and so was she." He didn't want to go any further, so he changed the subject. "Would you like to have dinner with me?"

Gabriele's face lit up again. "That would be wonderful, Carl . . . but I insist on paying. I owe you big time."

"Tomorrow, say at seven?" He knew intuitively that this would be the most important date of his life. "Do you like good American food?"

"That's one of the reasons I stayed! German food is good, but not for a whole lifetime," she said with an exaggerated wince. "Too much saturated fat!" Gabriele retrieved a business card from her slightly battered purse. "Here is my address. Just drive up in front of the building. I'll be there."

Carl looked at the name rather than the address. "I see you spell your name differently than the tennis player. I used to think of her when I heard the name. Now I'll think of you."

"I'm glad to hear you've dumped Ms. Sabatini for me, Carl . . . Do you have a restaurant in mind?" That smile again.

"*Chick's* has the best hamburgers . . . Sorry for the saturated fat!"

"Good choice, Carl. I love that place! It's wonderful for people watching." She lowered her head and glanced up at him. "Now I can concentrate on one person."

Carl stayed home all day after the policeman dropped him off. It wasn't until he'd had a long hot shower, taken with his battered forearms spread like a priest, that he finally looked at the *Washington Post*. Staring him in the face was the article he had expected but had not really believed he would see. It hadn't taken long.

> *Reuters*. August 11, 1998. Bogotá, Colombia. A powerful bomb destroyed the offices of Juan Espinoza Rojas early this morning, killing at least twenty members of his import-export corporation, generally acknowledged to be a

vast network of illegal narcotics suppliers to the
United States and Europe. The whereabouts of
Mr. Espinoza are unknown. Police are trying to
establish whether there is a connection between
this attack and the disappearance of rival cartel
leader Jorge Mena Velasquez, who hasn't been
seen in more than a month. It is rumored that
Espinoza's men have abducted Mr. Mena, an
action that could well have led to this morning's
bombing. Both Mr. Espinoza's and Mr. Mena's
crime syndicates have been battling recently with
Peruvian-based organizations for control of the
$10B/year US market. Jorge Mena Velasquez is
believed responsible for the downing of a US
airliner last year in response to the extradition
of his two sons to the United States. His sons
are being held in a Florida prison without bail,
awaiting trial later this year for the murder of two
US Drug Enforcement Administration agents in
a Bogotá bar.

It was happening! Carl quickly scanned the rest of the paper but
found no other articles regarding the drug war. The *Post* was not running any analysis pieces yet; they would come later. He had always
understood the strategic reasoning behind his mission to capture
Mena, but he had not been convinced until now that it would inten-
sify cartel violence in Colombia. The president had wanted Mena,
the terrorist, for killing 283 Americans. The State Department had
wanted to pressure the Colombian president to dissolve his (widely
accepted) ties to the illegal narcotics industry. The CIA and the
Pentagon had wanted the cartels to destroy each other. Thanks to
Carl and his team, it seemed they had all gotten what they wanted.

What had been a half-hearted conflict with waning public support had taken on warlike characteristics with the terrorist attack the
previous year. The government of Colombia had been less and less
supportive of US goals since the extradition of Mena's sons. Colombia

had become, in the administration's view, one big drug cartel. Life in Colombia was becoming intolerable—even for Colombians inured to violence by their own history. But life on the streets of America was also getting worse; Carl had just witnessed another example. He sat in his living room, looking at the Washington Monument, and tried to imagine where it would all finally lead. He thought about whether he would be asked to participate in this war again—and he wondered if he would.

The following evening, Carl drove his white pickup truck around the corner and down the street to find Gabriele standing outside her apartment building. He double-parked the truck, got out, and waved to her in the evening light. She walked toward the truck and met him halfway.

"Hi, Carl! What a nice truck! Is it bulletproof?" She wore snug white pants with an emerald-green silk blouse. Light blonde hair fell to her shoulders without a curl.

Carl appreciated the pants. He had never seen legs as long or as lean in his life. He suddenly wished he drove a Mercedes.

"I used to drive a car, but it wasn't tough enough for these Washington streets," he said apologetically. "If you still want to go to dinner with me, the truck is more comfortable than it looks. I even polished it . . . just for you."

"I feel safer already."

"It's great to see you again, Gabriele," he said more confidently. "You clean up pretty well!" Quite unconsciously, he took her hand. He suddenly realized that he was touching her and, in the same instant, sensed that she didn't mind. Still sporting the bandages that symbolized their meeting, he led her to the refuge of the cleanest truck in Washington.

Carl closed her door and walked around to his side. He took a deep breath and, out of habit, checked up and down the street. He sat down and eased the vehicle into gear, merging into traffic for the twenty-minute ride. He was relaxing again. He felt so comfortable with her that it made him *un*comfortable. He would have to be careful. It would be impossible to open up completely, but he hated to start out with lies.

"So, how are all those diplomats getting along in German?" He felt better asking questions than answering them.

"Not so good, Carl. German is an awful language. I'm glad I learned it as a child. Americans have a lot of trouble with it, even though English is derived from German." She was more serious now but still warm. "How was *your* day?"

Without a trace of hesitation, he explained half of his professional life. "Boring. I really enjoy writing, but I hate the business end of it. Dealing with the government is always frustrating. They have to get several bids on every contract, even if they know you and have used you before. I spend a lot of my time just sitting around waiting for something to happen." *Boy, is that the truth!*

"What kinds of things do you write?"

"Mostly technical stuff—tactics, techniques, and procedures."

She looked at him with sincerity radiating from her face. "What about?"

"I write what I know." He hesitated. "I was in the Navy for a long time." He almost cringed, waiting for the inevitable next question.

"Interesting . . . what did you do in the Navy?" asked Gabriele, not sensing his growing discomfort.

"I was mostly on ships. I was what they call a gunner's mate, and then I became an officer." All true so far, but he was getting into shoal water and needed to change the subject. "What did you do before teaching at State?"

"I went to Georgetown University. I loved it." The million-dollar smile again. At that moment Carl wished he'd become a stockbroker.

"You speak with only a trace of an accent," he ventured, trying to keep up the momentum.

"Yes. I've been here a long time. I'm older than I look!" She didn't look a day over thirty, but he guessed she was about forty.

"I guess you are!" Carl responded easily. "You look like you could still be a student."

Gabriele rolled her eyes. "You're very kind but terribly blind!"

They sat on the second floor of an old warehouse. It was completely refinished with shining wood, ceiling fans, and Leroy Neiman lithographs. It was packed, as usual, and they almost had to shout over the din. It was indeed a great place to people watch but not a great place to talk. It was perfect for a man who wanted to talk but was afraid of what he might say. They did talk but, to his relief, it was not about work.

"I've wanted to tell you what a nice name you have," said Gabriele. "It's not corruptible . . . that is to say one cannot put a 'y' on the end of it like most Americans seem to prefer . . . Do you have a nickname?"

Lying through his teeth, Carlos the warrior said, "No." *Here we go . . .*

"Here, everyone wants to call me Gaby," she said.

"Naturally . . . can I keep calling you Gabriele?"

"That would be great, Carl." She hesitated, then asked him another question. "How did you get your chiseled Latin face with a name like Malinowski?"

"My mother was Italian."

"Ahh . . . you *are* Latin! I noticed the other day that you speak some Spanish." She wasn't interrogating him, but her curiosity forced him to think on his feet.

"*Si, Senorita* . . . and I hope you didn't understand what I said!" he said, laughing. "I also speak Italian, but I have no desire to learn German!"

"Smart man. Between us, though, we could get by almost anywhere in the western world." Gabriele had a brief mental picture of herself and Carl lying on a Mexican beach, sipping tequila sunrises. It scared her. She was falling in love with a man she barely knew. It had happened before; it had almost ruined her life.

They finished their meal and went downstairs to the bar. Surprisingly, it was quieter there. Carl decided to steer the conversation toward something totally benign. "So, how are things in Waldenbuch, Gabriele?"

"Beautiful. I love to go back to visit, but I couldn't live in Germany again. When I'm there, I practically live in the forest . . .

and in the coffee shops, where I stuff myself with German cakes. It's wonderful, but there's not much else to do. And German men are such assholes!" She stopped for just an instant, and Carl had the impression she regretted the remark. He thought maybe he wasn't the only one trying to be careful.

"I couldn't wait to get away when I got out of *gymnasium,*" she finished.

"You were a gymnast?"

She laughed. "No, no . . . but how would you know? German children have two education tracks, *folksschule* and *gymnasium.* We had to take tests at age eleven to determine which track we'd follow—for the rest of our lives. *Gymnasium,* which is the equivalent of high school and junior college here, prepares you for the university. *Folksschule* prepares young people for the nonacademic professions . . . and they are considered professions. Sometimes I wish I'd been a baker."

Though a child of immigrants, Carl had not thought much about the differences between Europeans and Americans before. He was, himself, a case study of the difference in education systems. He had enlisted in the Navy right out of high school, served for eight years, and then gotten his college degree by going to night school. He had been commissioned at thirty, the age when many German bakers were becoming master bakers—and earning a lot more money than naval officers.

"That's fascinating to me . . . I came up through the ranks."

"Yes, the American system is much better at giving second chances . . . Were you—how do you say it—a late bloomer?"

"Not really. I grew up on the north side of Boston in a blue-collar neighborhood where almost nobody went to college. None of us had the money, and most of us didn't know any better. I knew I was smart enough to go, but I couldn't have done it at age eighteen . . . even if we'd had the money. There was too much other stuff I wanted to do. The Navy was a great place to start my adult life."

"I am still somewhat of an elitist about education, but I do like the American spirit of equal opportunity. I mean . . . one can do anything in this country!" She took a quick sip from her beer. "That's the real reason I stayed."

"But do you *feel* at home here?" he asked cautiously.

"Yes . . . and no," she responded thoughtfully. "I still have one foot in each country. I suppose I always will. When I'm here I feel German. When I'm in Germany I feel American. It's pretty confusing sometimes." What she could not say—not yet—was that she was terribly lonely in both places.

"Do you have a hero, Carl?" A safe question, as well as an interesting one.

"Actually, I have two," said Carl. "Jacques Cousteau and D. B. Cooper."

"Who's D. B. Cooper?"

Carl looked at her with a twinkle in his eye. "He hijacked an airplane over the Pacific Northwest about twenty years ago. He took a lot of money, then stepped off the tail ramp of the plane and parachuted into the forest. He was never seen again . . . a genuine folk hero."

"You're joking, no?"

"Not completely," said Carl, laughing. "He had a lot of courage, and I admire courage. So, who are *your* heroes?"

"On the male side, it would have to be Schiller."

"The writer?"

"He was the best of the German poets . . . and a rebel to the core. At one point, he was thrown in jail for criticizing the local prince."

"Maybe he and D. B. Cooper had something in common."

Gabriele laughed at this, nodding. "You asked about my heroes, plural. Until you came along, I didn't have any *living* human beings to admire . . . We Germans are pretty careful about heroes after what Hitler did to our country." There was emotion in her voice, and then a quick recovery. "I don't have any female heroes."

"You don't have to admire *me*, Gabriele. I just did what anyone would have done."

"I don't believe that," she replied. "There's something special about you, Carl. You're different than the other men I've known."

"I hope to never let you down, Gabriele," said Carl, swallowing hard. He needed to change the subject again.

"Do you like baseball?" He gestured toward the television screen behind the bar.

"I'm afraid not. I grew up with European football. Baseball—to me—looks like a bunch of men, wearing pajamas, standing around waiting for something to happen!" She was laughing again.

"Lucky for you, Washington doesn't have a baseball team anymore!"

"I would go with you, but I'll never understand the game."

"That's OK, Gabriele," said Carl. "Baseball is a bonus feature of Americanization . . . You don't need the extra credit. I can learn to love soccer."

They paid for the drinks, and Carl drove her back home. They would both have to work in the morning. There was no place to park in front of her apartment, so Carl stopped the truck and turned to her with his hands on the steering wheel.

"Here we are," he said, trying to control his heart rate.

"Time flies when you're having fun . . . and I had fun," she said earnestly. "I haven't had that much fun just talking to someone in a long time. I am very glad we met, Carl. Thank you for a wonderful evening."

He thought he could see tears well up in her shocking blue eyes—wishful thinking . . . in the dark.

"It was my pleasure, Gabriele . . . Meeting you was worth every stitch!" He fumbled for something else to say, not wanting her to leave just yet.

"Call me if you need a bodyguard." He grinned.

"I'd prefer something less violent," said Gabriele, kissing him on the cheek.

Carl saw an opening. "If you're free on Tuesday, I can get us tickets to see Jane Goodall's chimpanzee lecture at the National Geographic building, downtown. What do you say?"

"That would be just great, Carl," she replied immediately. "Are you a nature lover too?"

"Yes . . . I like birds best," he said. "Especially jungle birds."

Chapter 3

In Between

T he next day was Sunday. After his run, he took the *Post* from the doorstep to the kitchen table. This was a morning to linger over strong coffee and catch up on the world. He sat down with a steaming brew and flipped to the editorial page. Suddenly, he remembered what it felt like to be shot.

Paul Henning
What Is Happening in Colombia?

In the past few days, violence in Colombia— already one of the world's most violent societies—has skyrocketed. The bomb set off in Bogotá on Friday is just the latest escalation in a war within a war. The Revolutionary Armed Forces of Colombia (FARC) have been trying to overthrow successive Colombian regimes since 1964. But having started out as an insurgency with revolutionary ideas, the FARC has morphed into a terrorist organization, as well as a drug cartel, competing for access to the American and European markets. It is difficult to tell the players without a program. While the FARC is still at war with the government, drug cartels— apparently tamed three years ago—are tearing each other apart. And where is the Colombian government? We have heard absolutely nothing from President Solano or his ministers, something that prompts speculation. Is the government itself compromised by the cartels? The president has been linked to Juan Espinoza Rojas, a close childhood friend and archrival of Jorge Mena Velasquez, the powerful "Pasto" cartel leader. Mena is believed responsible for the downing of a US passenger jet last year, a tragedy that killed 283 Americans. It is thought that Mena has been in hiding, but there are also rumors that he has been kidnapped. Did President Solano or his friend Espinoza have something to do with Mena's disappearance? That remains to be seen, but the price of crack cocaine on our streets is going down and the number of criminals is going up. What happens in Colombia does not stay in Colombia.

Carl put down the paper and, breathing a little harder than normal, stared out the window. Henning was a conservative columnist, well connected with both parties, who had written extensively about the drug war. He had sources, on Capitol Hill and inside the administration, willing to give him information—off the record—on sensitive matters. Carl wondered how much "help" Henning had received on this piece, as well as what *other* information had been leaked. He felt the chill of vulnerability go right down his spine.

His hand trembled slightly as he picked up the phone. He couldn't tell if it was anger or fear. He dialed the number for a local beeper, belonging to his CIA contact, known to him only as Jeff. As previously agreed, Jeff would call him back, and they would arrange a personal meeting somewhere in the area. Jeff usually proposed a restaurant or bar; Carl preferred being outside.

Ten minutes later, Jeff called back. "What do you want, Carl?" Jeff was clearly annoyed.

"I have to see you, and I have to see you soon. Haynes Point. Wear some jogging clothes. I already ran, but I could use a nice walk," said Carl steadily.

"OK, Carl . . . I'll be there in one hour. Same spot?"

"Yeah . . . at the statue. We'll walk from there." Carl hung up and drained his coffee mug.

Last night had been better than a dream. Today was off to a bad start.

Carl drove toward the Pentagon and across the Fourteenth Street Bridge to Haynes Point. He left his truck in the parking lot and walked down the road to the rendezvous location. He felt safe here, surrounded by water, with the National War College across the river to his left and the airport on the other side of the river to his right. Three ways out: one by running and two by swimming.

He was thirty minutes early. Enough time to recon the site before he exposed himself at the meeting. He also wanted to watch Jeff's arrival. That was how Carl had been trained all those years ago. The place was already filling up with tourists, adding another margin of safety.

It was hot. The ozone heat that made his lungs ache. After going through the motions of warming up—observing everything and everyone—Carl stood in front of the statue: a large man, lying on his back, half buried in the soil. The man's hands were reaching up toward the sky, one knee, both feet, and part of his face exposed. The statue bore the name "The Awakening" but, as he studied it, Carl couldn't tell whether the man was rising from the earth or sinking to his death. He knew the feeling well.

Carl sat on the railing and continued his surveillance. He spotted Jeff walking across the grass on the other side of the statue, waiting for the snake to come to him. As Jeff approached, Carl jumped to his feet and nodded. There was no smile and no handshake. They just started walking.

"Good morning, Carl," said the younger man with feigned enthusiasm.

"You bastard!" was the reply, delivered in a low, seething tone.

"Come again?" asked Jeff, managing to look surprised.

"You talked to Henning, didn't you?" It was a statement.

Jeff smiled the plastic smile that annoyed Carl so much. "I never said we wouldn't help the press start the rumors we want to spread, Carl. Yes, we talked to Henning. It's part of the plan."

"What exactly did you tell him?" demanded Carl.

"Not much at all, really. He got a call from one of our people, posing as a Colombian government official. Henning wanted to meet with him, but our man said he couldn't take the risk. Paul Henning knows a lot about Colombia, and it was easy for him to construct a conspiracy about the president and his criminal financial backer. It's not a stretch to assume that Mena's people attacked Espinoza's offices. The whole government enterprise is running scared. The ones who are not corrupt are leaving. The others fear for their lives. We have certainly stirred the pot."

Carl let out a long breath. "So there's no indication that the US might have been involved?"

"None whatsoever, good buddy. Did you think we'd sell you down the river or something?" Jeff was sickeningly—almost frighteningly—cheerful.

"Yes, as a matter of fact, I do," replied Carl coldly. "If we'd gotten in trouble down there, you weren't prepared to bail us out."

"Plausible denial was part of the mission . . . Why the fuck did you agree to do it?"

"I needed the money." Carl paused, sizing up the man walking beside him. Jeff and he were worlds apart, a bureaucrat and a warrior thrown together by the dynamics of political intrigue. Jeff was an arrogant but boyish product of the Ivy League. He'd never served a day in uniform and didn't know the first thing about what motivated men like Carl. Jeff operated on a different ethical plane.

"I also knew we could get him," Carl continued. "It was the ultimate tactical challenge. Do I think it was important for the national security of the United States?" He hesitated, then said with considerably less passion, "I've been back and forth on that one."

"Very high-minded, my friend."

"I'm not your friend . . . and you haven't told me everything I'm entitled to know."

"What else do you need to know, Carl?"

"Where's Jorge Mena now?"

"You know I can't tell you that. You want to try and break him out?" The plastic smile again. "Now *there's* a tactical challenge!"

Carl glared at Jeff with contempt. "I'm more interested in what you're *doing* to him. It makes a difference to me as his kidnapper. I don't have physical custody anymore, but I have a *moral* claim." He paused to emphasize the point. "I went to a lot of trouble to take Mena alive . . . It would really piss me off if you killed him."

"I can assure you that we're taking good care of him, Carl."

"That gives me a real warm and fuzzy, Jeff . . . Thanks for the meeting." He turned and walked quickly down the road to his truck.

Carl turned the key and unlocked the dead bolt on the door to his small office on Wilson Boulevard. The sign on the door read, "Malinowski Technical Writing." He didn't have a secretary. In fact—although he actually *did* write manuals on tactics, techniques, and procedures—he did not spend a lot of time in the office. With a powerful Macintosh at home, he did most of his writing there. The office was mostly a front—a place to get mail, and a place to receive visitors. When he was not out of town, Carl made sure to put in at least one appearance a week.

He sat down at the desk and went through three weeks' worth of mail. Defense contracting was a stable income. It was also a great cover. His fieldwork paid better, but it was completely unpredictable. He also knew that soon he would be too old to do it anymore. Increasingly, Carl thought he was ready to quit soldiering. He rarely thought about the odds of getting killed; he didn't have anyone who would miss him. Then he started thinking about Gabriele.

He was smitten with her. He had known enough women to understand that Gabriele was different. A once-in-a-lifetime encounter. He was not religious, but there was a spiritual feel to this. Was her kindness toward him just a way of showing gratitude? He wasn't sure, but he intended to find out. The problem, of course, would be to leave some things unsaid. He didn't mind lying to strangers—that was part of his business. Carl had never lied to a friend. With Gabriele, he would have to compromise. Or lose any chance to spend the rest of his life with her. If that was what she wanted. He enjoyed the fantasy while it lasted.

There was a letter from his uncle in Boston, reminding him of the second anniversary of his father's burial. His presence at the memorial mass would be appreciated. Carl didn't need to be reminded because he wasn't going. He would see his father's grave on his *own* time. He knew the motive behind the letter. Uncle Jerzy had been in the fishing business with Carl's father. A visit would not be about remembering Carl's dad; it would be about remembering his father's debts—all of which had fallen to Carl.

There was a letter from Major General Hatcher, thanking Carl for his excellent work on the *Handbook on Jungle Warfare* for the Special Forces Training Command. The general didn't have to do that, thought Carl, and he immediately felt better. Hatcher was just one of the great generals he had worked for. The Army, he believed, knew how to lead. Carl had found that each service brought something important to the table. The Navy knew how to think, the Marines knew how to take ground, and the Air Force—in addition to having some very good pilots—knew how to run a business. He missed working with all of them in the solemn commitment to keep Americans safe.

The rest of the pile was junk mail and old news magazines. He junked the mail and took the magazines with him. He drove to the mall and walked into the air-conditioned expanse. He didn't have any projects to work on, and he was grateful for the time off. It was only eleven o'clock in the morning, still an hour before he needed to be in the gym. It had been a long time since he'd had someone to shop for. He looked, smiling, at lingerie (way too soon for that), watches (too expensive), perfume (she didn't use it), and candy (nothing European). Then he walked into a nature store and bought a copy of *Virginia Birds*, asking the clerk to gift wrap it.

He was still thinking of Gabriele as he walked out of the store on his way to lift weights.

Carl got up the next morning and ran the tow path. The paper was waiting for him when he got back. It was on the front page.

Bogotá Bombed Again

Associated Press. August 15, 1998. Another powerful bomb exploded in central Bogotá this morning, killing dozens of members of drug kingpin Juan Espinoza Rojas' import-export business empire. The explosion was so powerful it blew the façade off a church across the street. Like Friday's bomb, yesterday's blast detonated at the peak of rush hour. The dead are still being counted, but the total is thought to be close to 200. There was no immediate statement from President Solano, who has been under pressure to step down, following strong allegations that he was funded by Espinoza during his campaign for reelection. The two men, who grew up together, are said to remain close friends. Mr. Espinoza appears to have escaped injury. H. Robert Harding, the outspoken American ambassador to Colombia, issued a brief statement calling for the president to use what power he still has to bring an end to the violence. Harding cautioned that the United States cannot do business with Colombia until the government becomes part of the solution to America's drug problem rather than the problem itself.

Carl turned to the editorial page. His concern deepened as he read the column.

Paul Henning
Harding Out On a Limb

The situation in Colombia has given new meaning to the word "corrupt." While the country's two major drug cartels destroy each other, there are growing indications that President

Solano has taken the side of his childhood friend, Juan Espinoza Rojas. Espinoza's biggest rival, Jorge Mena Velasquez, has not been seen in a month. It is rumored that Mena had been hiding in Brazil to avoid assassination at the hands of Espinoza's men. Why did Mena, among the toughest of criminals, leave the country to hide like a coward? Did he feel *that* threatened by Espinoza? Or, did he have a president—and his loyal army—out to get him for personal reasons? And the final question: Where is Jorge Mena now? The American ambassador, H. Robert Harding, is telling it like it is. His call for the Colombian government to solve problems rather than cause them does not have a diplomatic ring—but it is right on target. Harding is sticking up for what is right—at some personal risk. He has taken a professional risk as well, unless we assume that his harsh statements indeed reflect the views of his boss, President Ferguson. Was Solano's full-court press against Mena a demonstration of his desire to cooperate with the Americans? Or, was it cooperation with—and in support of—his friend Espinoza? Only time and more information will tell.

Carl put down the paper and launched out of his chair like a rocket. *Shit!* There was no need to confront Jeff again. There was nothing Carl could do. He was stuck with a situation over which he exercised not the slightest degree of control. As the little twerp had explained to him, feeding the press had been part of the strategy all along. Carl's part of the operation had not been disclosed, but he was becoming more worried with each iteration of Henning's public hypothesis.

Carl was standing in front of his high-rise condominium at 1900. He was looking up and down the street again, not just for Gabriele, but also for drug addicts lurking in the shadows. He knew they were there. There was nothing he could do that he had not already done. The taking of Noriega and defeat of his corrupt military, the training of security personnel all over Latin America, and, most dramatically, the snatch of Jorge Mena were all on the supply side of the drug war equation. The street where he waited for Gabriele was on the demand side.

And the demand side was winning.

Another development disturbed him even more. American border officials in the southwest were being paid off to let drugs into the United States. Corruption was not just a Latin American problem. He hated corruption; he held no mercy for those who practiced or tolerated it. But he also understood poverty, and he knew the difference between survival and greed.

Carl had killed more than a few times in his life—men who had been unlucky enough to face him in battle, or men who had just been in the wrong place at the wrong time. Some of them, he supposed, had been family men. His remorse was for the good men among them, and for the loved ones they left behind. The bad men he had killed were just gone. He didn't spend any time thinking about them; their families were better off without them.

Gabriele pulled up in a black Volkswagen Jetta. She honked the horn, leaned over, and opened the passenger side door. He climbed in, looked at her, and found his heart in this throat again.

"I see you made it to work this week in one piece!" he said cheerily.

"If I'd gotten mugged, Carl, I'm sure you'd have materialized from nowhere to rescue me . . . Where to, my guardian angel?"

She laughed the laugh he loved. It was not a girl's laugh, nor was it a man's laugh. When she did it, he felt better than he had ever felt in his life. Well, almost. Coming down from the high of a successful field operation was hard to beat.

He gave her directions to the National Geographic building.

"How've you been, Gabriele . . . other than staying out of trouble?"

"Same thing, day after day," she sighed. "I like what I'm doing, but it gets very routine. I hate routine, but I don't know how to break out of it."

"I've been lucky enough never to have a routine," said Carl. What he didn't say was that keeping to a routine invites ambush. Even the cultivation of chaos in his personal life was a professional undertaking. "I always try and do the unexpected," he continued. "It keeps me from getting bored."

"I'm afraid teaching is pretty much the same thing every day . . . I sometimes wish I knew how to do something else," she lamented as the District sprawled in front of them.

Carl had one eye on Gabriele while the other searched for M Street. "It's hard to change when you've been doing something for a long time," he said with unintentional irony. He didn't know any more than Gabriele did how to break out of a routine.

They spent the next two hours listening to Jane Goodall talk about her life's work at Gombe Stream in Tanzania. She was splendid, as usual, explaining how chimps live in the wild—and how closely their behavior resembles that of humans (Carl was most interested in the aggression piece of this).

"That was great!" said Gabriele as they stood to leave the auditorium. "I'm very glad you asked me to come here, Carl. I think I finally found a female hero."

"I wanted to give you someone besides Schiller," said Carl, laughing. "He's good, but he's dead!"

"Thank you for that," she said seriously as they filed out of the auditorium.

She looked at him in the dim light of the parking garage. She was trying not to show it, but tears began forming. Tears of sadness for all the wasted years she hadn't yet told him about.

"Thank you again," she said in a soft voice.

They spoke very little on the way home. She was afraid of telling him too much about her former life; he was afraid he would say too much about his current life. The result was almost total silence.

She rolled to a stop in front of his building and kept the engine running. His eyes were fixed on her as he mumbled for the right words.

"Gabriele, I have something for you." He pulled a small package from the breast pocket of his sport coat and handed it to her. It was wrapped with pink crepe paper. She said nothing as she opened it but kept looking up to make sure he was still there.

It was the bird book. As she held it in the dashboard light, a beautiful woodpecker looked at her from the cover. "Carl, this is wonderful! I don't know what to say!"

"Say you'll come birding with me on Saturday."

"That's an easy one . . . I will! Are there some good spots nearby?"

"Yes, surprisingly good . . . Wear some clothes you don't mind getting dirty . . . Pick you up at seven. Before the heat comes. Is that OK?"

"Perfect . . . I'll be ready."

"See you then." He leaned over and kissed her on the cheek and squeezed her shoulders with his big hands. He was out the door before she could react. As she sat there catching her breath, he turned around in the light of the doorway and waved. She rolled down her window and waved back, but he was already inside.

"See that?" said Carl, pointing to a large tree on the right, about twenty meters ahead. He passed her a pair of thousand-dollar Zeiss binoculars, prefocused. "That's a pileated woodpecker on the trunk, about eye level."

She leveled the binoculars at something moving, then exploded with joy. "He looks like Woody Woodpecker, Carl! Look at the size of those feet . . . and the red on his head!" She gushed. "I've never seen anything like it!"

The morning was off to a good start.

He led her around the swamp, pointing out king rails, musk-rats, great egrets, eastern bluebirds, and dozens of other species. It was like another world. He needed another world at the moment, and he was grateful to her for sharing it with him. Gabriele had a childlike fascination with the animals that rekindled Carl's spirit. She was a tonic. After a while, he had trouble concentrating on the wild-life. He was thinking ahead.

By eleven o'clock the baby carriages were getting in the way and so was the heat. The humidity had not sapped her enthusiasm, but it was time to go. Carl led her back to the parking lot.

When they got to the truck Gabriele turned to him with a huge smile and handed him the binoculars. Before he could speak, she reached out again and threw her arms around him, resting her chin on his shoulder.

"Thank you so much, Carl, for a wonderful memory!" she half whispered into his left ear. "I hope this isn't the last time you take me bird-watching."

"Thanks for being such a good sport, Gabriele." He didn't know if his knees would hold out until they sat down. "Not all women—especially beautiful women—would like braving the heat and the bugs."

"It was fantastic . . . I'm hooked!" She almost shouted as they belted into their seats. "I can't believe I was missing out for so many years!"

The ride to Rosslyn was a blur. He was sure he had glanced at the road once in a while, but he couldn't remember. Like driving drunk. Every time he looked at her she was already looking at him, her bosom heaving under the thin shirt. He parked in front of the apartment building and walked with her up the inside stairs. At the door, he bent forward to kiss her goodbye. Gabriele suddenly took the back of his head in both hands and pressed her lips hard against his mouth.

So much for goodbye!

"I think you should come in," she said.

"If I come in, Gaby, I might stay . . . Is that what you want?"

"That's what I want." It was a simple statement, delivered with no hesitation.

They kissed again as she tried to open the door. Stumbling over the threshold, she pulled Carl into her small living room. He drew her close and let his passion flow into her. Like lightning. She relaxed at last, surrendering to the sensation of falling. Holding him at the hips, she pulled back and looked into his eyes with the longing he had wished for. Her lips were quivering, and he thought she might cry. The sexual tension that had been building between them broke at once with irresistible force. He reached out and slowly undid the top button of her shirt. That was all Gabriele needed to send her over the edge. He could feel her trembling with excitement as she took his hand in both of hers and brought it to her face. Carl almost had to run to keep up as she turned and led him urgently into the bedroom.

They didn't come out again until it was dark.

For two weeks after Carl and Gabriele made love, they were inseparable. The only place she went without him was to the institute. He spent those hours on physical training and planning their activities. He couldn't get enough of her, his passion overflowing like a wild river. Gabriele was nearly insatiable, so hungry that Carl could tell it had been a long time since she'd had a man. But the sex was just a bonus. They more they talked, the more they found there was to say.

Carl was coming out of his shell, intellectually as well as socially. The knowledge he had gained from years of voracious reading, confined for so long, came gushing forth. He found that he liked the theater. He had never worn a tie so often in his life. He was beginning to feel like a gentleman, and it felt better than he thought it would. Best of all, the anxiety over what was happening in Colombia receded to his subconscious.

Gabriele was suddenly on top of the world. The cultural wonders of Washington she had so long denied herself were again part of her life. She was beginning to forget the physical and psychological abuse she had suffered at the hands of other men. She was now confident this man would protect her from that, and from the disease of disappointment. Not completely sure, but confident. She was in love with a man who obviously cared about her. All she had ever wanted to do was give. Now she had someone to give to.

She had discovered his scar right away. He had worried about that—about the questions it would bring—but it wasn't until later that they had talked about it. Explaining that he had been ashore in Grenada, Carl had confessed to being wounded in the shoulder while standing too near some Cuban engineers defending themselves. Gabriele had accepted that, demonstrating her understanding by kissing the ugly bluish knot on his otherwise smooth skin.

Something else she had noticed about his body surprised her. Carl was by far the fittest man she had ever been with. His baggy clothing covered taught, lean muscles, especially in his stomach. It hadn't occurred to her to ask him why a forty-four-year-old man kept himself in such good shape, but she was very glad he did—both in and out of bed.

It was Sunday morning, and they were both exhausted. Gabriele was lounging on the couch with the paper. She was humming to herself the music from an operetta they had attended the night before. It was another beautiful day in her wonderful new life.

Abruptly, the phone rang. She looked toward the bathroom where Carl was taking a shower. She had been in his apartment many times by now, but she didn't think she knew him well enough to answer his phone. *There is nothing more personal than a phone call!* She let it ring until the recorder came on.

"Carlos, this is Butkus. I know you don't like me to call you at home, but you haven't been in the office for at least a week. I need to talk to you soonest. Out here."

She had a brief moment of fear. It was the first time she had felt anything but confidence since she'd met Carl. She didn't know exactly what it was, but there was something strange going on. Carl came out of the shower a few minutes later. Still in a towel toga, he went to the living room and stood in front of her.

"Would you like some breakfast now, Gaby?"

She looked at him with a weak smile that revealed a trace of anxiety. "Someone named Butkus called while you were in the bathroom. He called you Carlos . . . I thought you said you don't have a nickname."

Carl suppressed his own anxiety and looked at her calmly. "He's a business associate of mine, honey . . . As you know, I've been on vacation!" Carl looked down and swallowed hard. "I'll call him back later."

43

"Carlos?"

"Butkus is actually more than a business associate," Carl continued. "He and I were in the Navy together. I used to listen to a lot of Santana, and my men started calling me Carlos." He took a deep furtive deep breath. "That was a long time ago."

"Best guitar player ever!" she asserted with obvious relief. "Can I call you Carlos?" She opened her arms to embrace him.

"Please don't! I like my name just the way it is, Gaby." He tried to sound playful, but inside he was angry with Butkus. Field names were for the field. It was a good thing the big man hadn't said anything else.

They had already planned to return to normal after Sunday. Whatever normal was. They were in love, each secure enough now to let go of the other for a while. As long as it wasn't for too long. Gabriele had suggested they spend every other night together. Carl had laughed at the notion of putting lovers on a schedule. *German organization!* He had reserved the option to see her whenever he needed her. She liked that idea, as long as she had the same option. They wanted to live together, but they knew it was too soon. They also knew that every other night would not be enough.

Carl picked up the phone that evening after Gabriele had gone home. He was feeling better about the slipup by the time Butkus answered. "Jerry, this is Carl. I can talk now. How's it goin' down there?"

"I'm fine," said Jerry. "Sorry I called you at home, but you just dropped out of sight on me."

"Yeah . . . I guess I lost track of the time," Carl answered carefully. He didn't want to go into his new personal life just yet.

"I talked to Lieutenant Colonel Nichols about ten days ago," said Jerry. "He gave me a new time window for Fort Sherman. It's earlier than we had wanted. I tried to bounce it off you before I got back to him. I couldn't get you, so I told him it was OK."

Carl's other life was now in focus. "So, when's the time window now, Jerry?"

"Next week." The big man waited for a reaction. When he didn't get one, he continued. "We start a week from tomorrow. They can't support us next month . . . They got a bunch of Rangers comin' in. Sorry to spring this on you, sir." Jerry still called him sir from time to time. It was a habit, but also a measure of his respect for the man who had saved his life.

"That's OK," said Carl, thinking it wasn't. "I can do that. I just have to hustle a little bit. Are all the ranges laid on?"

"We got everything we need . . . I also have the Draegers, so we can do some oxygen swims. All you need to do is show up."

"I'll be on the usual flight next Saturday," said Carl without conviction. "Can you pick me up in the Land Cruiser?"

"No problem, Boss. See you at the airport. The others will already be in the barracks when you get here."

Carl hung up the phone and thought about how he would present this to Gabriele. It was a critical time in their young relationship. He did not want to be away from her. Even for two weeks. He also fished for a cover story that would make sense to her. He couldn't tell her what he was really doing in Panama. Carl briefly considered calling Jerry back and saying he couldn't make it. He rejected the idea just as quickly. They were a team; after so many years and so many miles, he couldn't let them down. At least not yet. He had been doing some serious soul-searching since the Mena snatch, but he wasn't quite ready to give up his fieldwork. He knew that the longer he spent with Gabriele, the closer he would be to making that decision. But, for now, he was stuck. The timing sucked, but the training ritual could not be avoided.

He picked her up the next evening. They began their date by walking across the bridge to Georgetown. They would finish it in the early morning, with Carl slipping silently out of bed to let her sleep. He would finish the night in his own bed to preserve the façade of their freedom. He had rehearsed what he was going to say, but he was still afraid. It was not the *intoxicating* fear of his field addiction. He was on the knife edge of an alpine summit; he could fall in either direction.

They stopped at the middle of the bridge and leaned on the railing. Upstream, the river was rough and full of rocks. Downstream—behind them—the water was calm. Carl thought that, if he were to fall in here he would be carried into the calm water. It made him relax to think about calm water. Taking her in his arms and brushing her face with one hand, he began, "Gabriele . . ."

Then he hesitated.

"You haven't called me that in two weeks, Carl." A confident smile.

"It's a beautiful name that you will hear often. I want you to hear it for many years." He spoke from the heart, and he found that his heart had a lot to say. But there was no time, so he skipped to the bottom line.

"In just one month, you've changed my whole life. I will never be the same, Gabriele." He drew a breath. "I love you."

This was not getting any easier.

"I love you too, Carl." Tears were now streaming down her cheeks.

This was not the time or the place to mention Panama. Gabriele's emotions were very close to the surface. Carl knew intuitively that she had been hurt before, maybe more than once. It had been his observation that beautiful women were especially vulnerable to the dangers of falling in love with uncaring men. He was determined to be a caring and devoted man.

As they sat down to eat dinner, Carl realized that this would be his last trip to Fort Sherman. Nothing after that would get in the way of his new life. He was still on the knife edge, though, looking for a way to get down without falling. Sitting there over a plate of seafood pasta, he carefully began the descent.

"How would you like to go to Panama?"

"Carl!" she burst out. "I'd be thrilled . . . You could show me all those birds you always talk about . . . When do you want to go?" She sat forward like an attentive student, hands clasped under her chin.

"In two weeks . . . I have some business at the American bases down there that I just can't get out of."

"That soon?" Surprise without skepticism. "What kind of business comes up that quickly?" A wrinkled brow. "Don't get me wrong," she continued. "It would be fantastic . . . but I *will* have to talk to my supervisor."

"Here's the plan, then," said Carl quickly. "I have to conduct interviews with military personnel involved in something called Foreign Internal Defense." That much was true. Carl had a contract to write a manual on FID but had not worked out an interview schedule. "I was hoping to do the interviews next month, but now I have to do them next week. I'll have to fly down on Saturday and work until Friday of the following week. Come in late Friday. I'll pick you up at the airport. We'll stay at one of the great hotels in the city for a couple of nights, then I'll take you to a guest house on the Caribbean side. Great wildlife . . . sultry tropical heat . . . pretty romantic. What do you say?"

Gabriele didn't know what to think, but she knew what to say. She also knew it would be a good opportunity to see what it felt like to be without him for a while. "I'll make it happen, Carl . . . What a great way to spend our first vacation!"

Chapter 4

Panama

He ran headlong underneath the night. Distant harbor lights, reflecting the speckled sky, did not penetrate the black veil of his consciousness. He ran without seeing. Like prey in the jungle. Not looking back. Rocks underfoot, his body bursting with sweat in the humid void. Fleeing his memories into nothingness. Not looking ahead. Not thinking. Fast, then slow. Higher, then lower. Crouching and leaping forward, he scrambled along the jetty.

The rain had come and gone a few hours before. The rocks had dried in the afternoon heat, though he knew they would be slippery where the tide had been. He tried to run the high ridge but surrendered often to the even darker rocks below. Only the horn at the channel entrance broke the rhythm of his labored breathing. Order in the distance. A sound to restart his hearing. A pattern to steady his heartbeat. Then a light, occulting every four seconds. The return of sight. A sudden blast of stack gas. Machinery throbbing. A giant shape passing quickly through the darkness.

He stopped abruptly and sat down hard. Reaching behind, he unfastened the life jacket strap and fumbled for his fins. Sliding into the choppy sea, he pulled them over his boots. Wet fatigues pressing against his skin. Back to the void. Kicking, stroking, gliding forward. Relentlessly. Looking behind and above. Safe within the womb. Briny waves moving under and through him. Like blood. Rising and falling toward the unseen shore. Stars pointing the way, he swam on.

Thunder ahead. Booming across the space between. Lightning stabbing the horizon. Coral below crashing water. Froth glowing in starlight. He stopped kicking and watched the wall of white. An opening. Shallows, then sand. The edge of danger. Crawling from the sea, he stowed his fins and stood looking back. Nothing behind. The warm breath of tropical air. Surf and sound outside, jungle silence inside. Beach curving ahead, beckoning in the dark.

He was running again. One soggy boot in front of the other. Sloshing through salt spray. Floundering in soft sand. Sprinting over rock. Weaving up and down across the sloping shore. Gulping air. Stabbing pain and more pain. Not giving in. Pulling away from the past. Searching for the end.

Lights ahead. Buildings. Three shadows forming in front of him. Full circle now, he ran faster. Familiar voices. Then he was there.

"Fifty-six, thirty-seven." Butkus pressed a cold beer into his slippery hand. "Welcome to Panama, Carlos . . . Good time!"

They sat in a small aluminum boat in Lake Gatún. The sun was only halfway to its zenith, but the humid air was already hot. The gray carcasses of tropical hardwood trees rose from the glare of the smooth water. It was dead quiet and they were completely alone. The fish, starving from overpopulation, grabbed everything put in front of them. The four men had more than they needed and were now throwing them back. It was not just the tasty meat of the peacock bass that had brought them to the lake; it was a tribal gathering. The main reservoir of the iconic canal. A place to talk freely. A place to relax before their two weeks of intensive combat training.

Carlos was sitting in the stern with Tinker. Billy Joe Barnes was a good old boy from southwest Florida who had grown up in and around boats. His father, like Carl's, had been a fisherman. Unlike Carl, Billy Joe was a gifted mechanic. He had fixed every engine of every boat his dad had owned, plus a few of his own. Often working the boats instead of going to school, he had become an accomplished seaman before he joined the Navy. He had finished high school but—since it seemed he had never attended class—no one could figure out how. But Carl knew. Billy Joe was much smarter than his heavy drawl made him sound. He was also street-smart, with a wild streak that had gotten him into a lot of trouble early on. Carl had taken the kid under his wing and made him a professional sailor. Billy Joe was completely devoted to him.

Butkus sat in the middle of the boat. If he had been anywhere other than dead center, the boat would have listed that way. He was 220 pounds of muscle and looked taller than his six feet, three inches. Jerry Tompkins had grown up on the high plains of Wyoming in a town with a population much smaller than its zip code. He had played tackle football at the district high school thirty miles away, but even there they'd had only enough boys for seven-man teams. Jerry had played every position, both offense and defense. Although not ready for college, he had gone to the University of Wyoming to play real football. But there was something missing. Jerry had wanted to see the world beyond the plains, and he'd dreamed of putting himself in danger. Thanks to Carl, he was still living that dream. Everyone looked up to Jerry Tompkins. His coolness under pressure was admired as much as his size. And he got things done. Carl never went anywhere without him.

In the bow sat Jose Rios. He had gotten the name Bosco as a kid in New York City where he'd consumed large quantities of milk and chocolate syrup. His mother had immigrated to Queens from Colombia to join her sister when Jose was only three. Jose had grown up fast, faster than he should have. New York had been no picnic, but it was paradise compared to Medellín. He had joined the Navy to get out of the city. There was nothing else—nothing else legal—for him to do. He was poor and swarthy, but the Navy had given him a level playing field on which to excel. Jose had become a hospital corps-man—one of the best in the fleet. But he thirsted for action, and the modern warship just didn't have enough of it. He had volunteered for special operations. There'd been plenty of action after that.

All three of his men were now civilians. Like Carl, Jerry had put in twenty years. The others had made the break at fifteen years, getting smaller pensions. They had left the Navy to work for Carl, and he was keenly aware that they depended on him to supply them with danger and money. They all lived in Virginia Beach, working jobs that could be put on hold when the call came from Washington. The irregular fieldwork had been lucrative enough to make up for the interruptions to their normal routines. Billy Joe had been married twice. Jerry and Jose had each done it once. Carl was not sure if divorce was a cause or an effect but, in the teams, it had been a way of life. All of them were single now, and they liked the freedom. They didn't have time for families anyway.

The fish had stopped biting and there was more time to talk. They would be headed back to camp soon to continue preparing for their training. Jerry looked at Carl and asked the question they all had on their minds.

"So when's the next gig, Boss?"

Carl had thought about the answer to that one for more than a month. If he'd been the only one in the boat, the answer might have been different than the one he found himself giving.

"It's too soon to tell, Jerry, but there's a lot of potential down south. You guys have probably been reading about what's happened in Colombia since we got Mena. I don't know where that situation is headed, but you can be sure the Company will want to have some influence. It's getting pretty nasty down there."

"Not as nasty as *we* are, Carlos!" It was Billy Joe. He had a great big smile on his leather face. "That last op was awesome!" He pumped his fist and cackled as the others nodded. Carl smiled as *he* nodded, but it was lecture time.

"We did well, Billy Joe." He hesitated. "But good tactical execution isn't the same as being nasty. I don't have to tell you guys how brutal the drug traffickers are. We read about the bombings, but there's a lot of shit going on in between. Bogotá has more than thirty murders a day . . . a *day!* The barons don't care who dies or how they die. They kill whole families to terrorize people into behaving like robots. Those who are just shot to death are the lucky ones. Many of them are tortured as slowly as possible . . . You better hope they never snatch *us*."

"They won't get us, Boss," said Jose to everyone. "We have confidence in you . . . and I definitely don't want to die in Medellín, man. It would really piss off my mother."

Carl let them laugh and then looked at three smiling faces. None had the slightest trace of fear, pain, or guilt. They were committed, and they were optimistic. At that moment, he realized that he was the only one having doubts about their future as a combat team. A combat team on a roll.

He would have readily given his life for any of the three. He almost had, many times. Bravery was not the issue, though; they were all brave. But, as the leader, Carl kept a protective instinct in focus. With the trust of these men came extra responsibility. The burden of that responsibility weighed heavily on him as they talked.

"What about Yugoslavia, Boss?" asked Jerry. "The Special Forces guys are hunting war criminals. Can we get a piece of that?"

"Right now, they don't need the help, Jerry . . . but I'm looking and listening for opportunities. Just be glad you don't live over there. Nothing will be settled for a long time."

"And you think the drug war will be won anytime soon?" asked Billy Joe.

"It's not any less violent, but it's more important to us," said Carl. "That is, to the United States. If Bosnia goes down it's no big deal. If Colombia goes, the rest of Latin America may go with it. But the biggest reason to fight the drug war is that our streets are full of the stuff. If we didn't help the government stop the shit from coming in, crime back home would be even worse than it is. If I didn't think it was doing some good, I wouldn't take these contracts."

"What do *we* care, as long as we get paid?" said Billy Joe.

"But *I* care," said Carl a little too emotionally.

"We're mercenaries, Boss." Billy Joe looked at the bottom of the boat as he challenged his mentor.

"Speak for yourself," Carl continued, trying to control feelings he couldn't explain. "As long as I'm working for Uncle Sam, I don't consider myself a mercenary." He took a deep breath. "Do we kill for money? Yes. But we did that in the Navy, too. Now we're doing it for the Company—but it's still for Uncle Sam." Carl silently wished he still believed that.

"Well, Boss . . . now that you put it that way . . ." Billy Joe looked up at Carl, shaking the blond hair out of his eyes. "I guess it's not the same as working for *Preferred Outcomes*. I mean, they go in and kill for any government willing to pay them. That would be OK with me, ya know, but I hear ya."

Jerry chimed in with his booming voice. "A mercenary is a warrior without a country. I agree with the boss . . . I like the money, but I want us to make a difference—for the USA. I can't say we do that every time, but it's nice to think so . . . like the tagging ops. No doubt about those."

Carl and his men had penetrated Colombian waters the previous winter on two separate occasions. The first had been at Buenaventura on the Pacific side, where they had placed an electronic tag on the hull of a small cargo vessel bound for the States. Carl and Jerry, treading water, had been compromised that night and forced to shoot two security guards on the wharf. Several months later, they'd gotten into Barranquilla harbor in a leased fishing boat and tagged a submarine the cartel had bought from the Russians. A week later, the sub had been busted by the US Coast Guard off Florida. Tons of cocaine that didn't end up on American streets. Carl was sure there would be more tagging operations if they wanted them.

Jose gave the others a sarcastic look. "Any of you guys know what happened to Jorge?" he asked, referring to Mena. "I mean, who has him, and what are they doing with him?"

"I tried to find out, Jose," said Carl with a frown, hidden by dark Oakley sunglasses. "The Company won't tell me. I told those guys they'd better not kill him. I said that *we'd* earned that right, not them." He paused. "Actually, I don't think they will kill him. He's too valuable to them alive."

"That's good, Carlos," said Jose, grinning. "Remember, he could be my father!"

Billy Joe scratched his head and squinted through unprotected eyes. "Let's see now . . . Terrorist, international criminal, good at business, loves women . . . Yep, that's you all right. I noticed the resemblance when Butkus carried the fat man out, but I was too polite to ask about it."

They laughed so hard, they almost capsized the boat. Another serious discussion turned into a joke. Humor in the face of danger made room for courage. Finding humor in the consequences of their actions made them comfortable. Carl wished he could still do that.

When the tiny vessel stopped rocking, Carl looked at his watch. Cumulus clouds were building into thunderheads. It was time to go. He signaled to Billy Joe to start the engine, and they headed for the base. Serious work lay ahead.

Jerry had taken care of everything, as usual. Carl had long ago delegated to him the task of setting up their training days in Panama, working all the details directly with Lieutenant Colonel Nichols. Mac Nichols, the commander of the base, was a friend of Carl's, but that wasn't the reason he let them train there. Jeff at CIA had negotiated a memorandum of understanding with Major General Hatcher, Nichols's boss at Fort Bragg. There were only two copies of the memo, and one of them was in Nichols's safe. The paper would protect him in case something happened and it could not be covered up. He was glad to help Carl and his men, but he knew what they were doing was political dynamite. He didn't want to know *exactly* why they needed to train at his base every few months. It was better not to know.

The first week was devoted to weapons and explosives. Shooting skills, if not reinforced through practice, eroded quickly. They wanted to be ready when the mission came down. Gun clubs—even in the United States—did not give them access to most weapons of war. Jerry made sure there was plenty of ammunition in the storage bunker, and they would shoot up everything they had before leaving Fort Sherman.

After physical training, they started at the pistol range. Although pistols were secondary weapons, they were very important to the team. Carl and Jerry had proven that at Buenaventura, shooting .357 Magnum revolvers from the water. The Sig Sauer P226 was their standard handgun, especially since the nine-millimeter rounds were interchangeable with the MP5s. Billy Joe still preferred to carry a .45 in the field, claiming he could knock a man down by clipping him in the earlobe. It was almost true. Pistol shooting was, to them, a personal experience of almost religious intensity, and no conversation passed among the men for the next three hours.

After lunch in the field, they moved to the sniper range where, for the rest of the day, they sighted in and test-fired the .50-caliber M88s. The weapons were heavy and difficult to carry in but, for sabotage, there was nothing more useful. One individual sitting on a sand dune could take out an oil refinery without penetrating the fence. Jerry could hit a circle the size of a man's head from a thousand yards in practically any weather. The others had some trouble getting the thing into position but, though none were as good as the big man, they could all hit with it.

At the end of the day they returned to the barracks and relaxed. Nichols had put them in an old building not used by the conventional Army soldiers when they descended on Fort Sherman for jungle training. There were no Army students on the base now, but Nichols didn't want anyone on his staff to ask questions. The barracks were run-down, but Carl and his men worried about security more than comfort. For two weeks, it was better than sleeping in the mud. They took most of their meals in the barracks because Carl had placed the base club off limits and there wasn't much to do in Colón. They would drive to town later in the week when the very thought of another fish fillet made them sick.

The second day was all Kalashnikov. The AK-47, whether manufactured in Russia, China, or somewhere else, was still the ultimate people's weapon. It didn't take a lot of expertise to break it down, and it didn't need to be cleaned all that well. Any ignorant part-time guerrilla could drag it through the mud all day and it would still fire. When it did fire, the AK was accurate—with the punch of a 7.62-millimeter slug. But there was another reason Carl often had the men take it in the field. If they were caught carrying non-gringo weapons, he and Jose had a reasonable chance of talking the team out of a jam. As always, worst-case planning.

The next three days saw them testing Austrian knee mortars, firing a variety of man-portable machine guns, throwing hand grenades, and conducting live-fire immediate-action drills. They spent a lot of time with the German MP5 submachine gun, Carl's weapon of choice for close-quarters battle. By Friday afternoon, they were ready for an all-night patrol. Returning to the barracks for lunch, they prepared for the jungle and got some sleep. At sundown, they were picking their way through dense foliage, headed toward the beach near Piña.

"God damn black palm!" Billy Joe blurted out in pain from the rear. He pulled his hand quickly away from a thorned tree. "Jesus . . . I feel like Jesus," he said to himself, staring at the barbed needle sticking out of his camouflaged hand.

"Shut up back there," warned Jerry. "This may be training, Tinker, but it ain't no joke . . . You're gonna feel a lot more like Jesus if you don't quit cryin'."

"Sorry, Butkus . . . Hey, Bosco, pull this thing outa my hand!"

Carl paused the patrol, went to one knee, and held his field of fire.

Jose closed the gap with Billy Joe. "Shoulda worn gloves, man." Putting a red flashlight in his mouth and pliers in his hand, Jose yanked out the thorn, along with some of his friend's pride. It was dark now and—finally—quiet.

"Let's move!" said Carl in a loud whisper. And they were off.

The team struggled in silence for ten kilometers, with the jungle sucking body fluids faster than they could replace them. The team came out exactly where Jerry had built the target hootch. Carl was grateful for the satellite and happy to see the moon rising though the trees. After some quick on-site planning, they rigged the structure with C-4, set fuses, and withdrew. The explosion sounded good, but they went back to inspect the ground for unexploded ordnance and fire.

They took a different route back; by dawn they were in the barracks. At midmorning the weapons were clean, everyone had eaten, and they were all in the rack.

The first week had gone well, and the men wanted to blow off steam. Billy Joe sat on his bunk looking through the pages of a worn girlie magazine. "Where d'ya wanna go tonight, Boss?" he called across the room.

"I have to go see a friend about my other business, Billy Joe," said Carl with a tinge of guilt. "I'm doing a manual on FID doctrine, and I need to learn more about what's going on in SOUTHCOM. I'd rather go with you guys, ya know." That wasn't really true anymore, but Carl couldn't leave without saying it.

"That's OK with us, Carlos . . . We can suffer through this town on our own. Not much to do out there, but I need to get off the base for a while." Billy Joe looked around at the others. "Right, guys? Y'all ready to go steamin' with me?"

Jerry and Jose nodded together. "We'll try and keep you away from the Panama whores, little brother," said the big man.

Billy Joe took the bait. "I know this one . . . lives out by the old hotel. She could suck a golf ball through a garden hose!"

"Whatever you do, don't fuck her," warned Jose. "I'm a great medic, but I can't help you with AIDS." Billy Joe didn't always like having a corpsman for a running mate.

"I know better than that, you dickheads . . . I jus' wanna look," joked Billy Joe. "Besides, I've had enough of Latin women. They make great dates but really shitty wives."

"You screwed up and married one of 'em," laughed Jose. "But I married a *gringa*, and the result was the same! She wasn't even that great a date. It's not where they come from, man . . . It's *women*. They don't know what they want."

"Ah, women!" interjected Carl. "Sooner or later it always gets back to them."

"Hey, Boss . . . you got a new woman yet?" asked Billy Joe, speaking for the others, no doubt.

"Time for me to leave!" said Carl, laughing. "See you guys in the morning. If you want to do *Isla Grande* tomorrow, count me in. Next week we'll be swimming oxygen, and I could use a day at the beach."

Carl was out the door. He got in his rental car and drove across the canal, headed toward the Pacific side of the isthmus. He had not really lied to Gabriele. He was in Panama—and he was working on the FID manual. But he had lied to himself, and he knew it. He could not have Gabriele Bach *and* his men. It would have to be one or the other.

Carl sat in Brigadier General Stewart's living room at Howard Air Force Base. The general's wife was out for the evening. Reginald Stewart was the Army's first black Special Forces general officer, and he was quite proud of it. He commanded the special operations command in Panama. In addition to some unlikely direct action missions, he was responsible for the training of indigenous units in the art of drug interdiction. He sent Army, Navy, and Air Force personnel all over Central and South America, providing their counterparts with tactics, techniques, procedures, and equipment. Stewart had sent the helicopter that plucked Carl's team from the Bolivian jungle. He took a long pull on his Corona and studied his *protégé* seriously.

"It's great to see you alive and in one piece, Carl." Stewart leaned forward and lowered his voice. "I wish I could have been on that bird . . . but it would have been hard to explain to my boss." Everyone in the military had a boss, and Stewart's stateside boss hadn't known anything about Carl's mission. No one did; not even Stewart had known the details.

"I only know that our guys picked up five men from the banks of the Mamoré . . . OPSEC seemed really tight," Stewart continued. He could guess what the mission was, but he didn't know the identity of the fifth man. He was too professional to ask; Carl was too professional to tell him.

"I can say that we were sure glad to see that Pave Low coming out of the morning sky," said Carl. "As much as I like to swim, I didn't want to swim all the way to Riberalta." Carl looked Stewart in the eye. "Speaking for my men, sir, we are grateful for your support." If they had not been military people, Carl would have called him Reggie. The general would have preferred that, but he couldn't ask Carl to do it. The two men were the closest of friends, separated by tradition.

"It was our duty . . . and my pleasure. I know you're working the same problems we are, just in a different way . . . we're on the preventive medicine side. You're doing acute care." The medical analogy fit perfectly. Carl himself was a reflection of the two-sided coin. When he wasn't writing about the how US forces could *prevent* conflict, he was fighting in one.

Stewart softened his voice. "Remember, Carl, the bad guys play jungle rules. Just watch your back . . . I have only limited authority to bail you out of a jam."

"Got it, sir. I'm being as careful as I can." The active duty force had to live under strict rules of engagement that Carl could bypass. He was glad to have the flexibility to fight, more or less, as he pleased. He wished that his former teammates could have it too.

The general was not smiling. In fact, Carl noticed that he hadn't smiled since shaking hands. Stewart was a no-nonsense, caring leader. That was what had gotten him a star. That was also what had earned him Carl's respect. The general was proud of his star, but the respect of men like Carl Malinowski was more important to him.

"How long are you in-country, Carl?"

"Just for another week of training. The boys will go back as soon as we're done, but I love this place so much I'm staying to look for birds in the rainforest." Carl though he'd better tell Stewart he'd be around—in case he ran into him. The US footprint in Panama was like a small town.

"Outstanding!" exclaimed the general. "Panama's a much nicer place since we got rid of Noriega. They have a long way to go, but they're on the right path. I hate to leave, but it's time for us to go."

He left the general's house at 2100 for the hair-raising two-hour drive back across the isthmus. He drove carefully, thinking about the choices he'd made in his life. His first marriage had been a disaster, and much of it had been his fault. Continuous operational commitments had been difficult, but his attitude had made it worse. He had even admitted to his young wife that he liked being with his men more than with her! Carl had always considered being childless a blessing; now that he was in love with Gabriele it would be a curse. Suddenly, he wanted a child. The child she had told him she could never have. Carl knew he would be with Gabriele, and he knew he would never have a son.

Carl glided over red and orange coral heads, headed away from the island. He wore a tank on his back, but he could not feel it. Weightless in the warm water, he felt nothing but joy. Jerry followed him, but there was no need for Carl to look back. His friend would be there if he needed him. The others were somewhere close by, happy to be in the water in daylight, without compasses and heavy loads of demolitions. Tactical swims would come tomorrow; for now, there was nothing to do but float like a god over the beauty of the reef.

The island was only a few hundred yards off the Caribbean coast, two bone-jarring hours from Fort Sherman and past the seventeenth-century fort where Morgan the pirate had come ashore to attack Panama City from the back side (Morgan was Carl's kind of tactician). Like fishing in the lake, this was a tradition. The hard work of the previous week had left them tired and sore. Moving among fish—some of them big, all of them colorful—was the most relaxing thing any of them could imagine doing. It was also a good way to ease into the next phase of their refresher training. They would be in the water almost constantly over the next week. But they wouldn't be having any fun.

Later, on the beach, they cooked hot dogs and drank beer. The rain came a little after noon, and they sat under a *bohio* of palm leaves in the cool interlude of an otherwise scorching day. After the rain, they would sleep in the shade before calling the old fisherman back to give them a ride to the mainland. The local beer tasted really good. That was about the only thing that hadn't changed since the invasion. Panama was on an economic roll, fueled by drug money but also the beginnings of a real economy. The Americans were going home. The canal's operation was already in Panamanian hands. Carl and his men were proud of the role they had played in the transition, as violent as that role had been. But they would never be able to train at Fort Sherman again. If they wanted to dive *Isla Grande* next year they would have to do it as tourists.

While his men dozed, Carl walked along the beach. He needed to think about the position he'd put himself in. He wanted to come clean with Gabriele, but the risk of losing her was more frightening than living a lie. He knew, though, that every lie has a shelf life. It was time to fess up. Carl had never been a good Catholic—even with Polish and Italian blood in his veins. But he was starting to understand the role of the priest. As he walked, he began to realize that the ritual of confession had less to do with God than with man. Everyone needed a confessor. He couldn't talk to his men, and he had no family worthy of the name. Maybe he needed a priest after all. That was silly, he told himself immediately. There were no priests briefed into his business.

Gabriele walked back up the hill after a long day in front of the blackboard. The late afternoon sun was brilliant, the air breathing a hint of fall. She had driven to work for a while after the mugging, but parking in Rosslyn was expensive—if you were lucky enough to find it. It also felt good at the end of the day to get some fresh air and exercise. She had gone back to her aerobics schedule when Carl left, but that was indoors. The air—even city air—helped her to decompress. She needed to think—about what she was doing and where she was going with her life. Her mind brewed a mixture of elation and dread.

The last four weeks had been a roller-coaster ride. Although she knew the ride was far from over, Carl's absence offered her an opportunity to catch her breath. The chance encounter with Carl had come just in time. She had been frustrated with teaching but hadn't known what else to do. The cost of living had driven her to the conclusion that a paycheck was more important than a sense of accomplishment. Freedom was a distant dream. Paralyzed by fear, Gabriele had fended off more men than she could count. Safe at home, she had fallen into an emotional limbo. Carl had fixed that in just one week.

She was amazed at how easy it had been. Years of depression washed away so quickly by a sensitive and caring man. Maybe *too* quickly. She had learned to look for the pitfalls lurking in every situation. Having failed to see them early in life, she had become very good at finding them. Her friends, when she'd still had friends, had called it cynicism. Gabriele, well educated in the liberal arts, called it healthy skepticism. But it was not healthy, and she had developed a disease of the soul. The first day they were together, Carl had begun restoring her self-image. By the time he left for Panama he had given her back her spirit. But now he was gone. Out of habit, she was looking for the lurking pitfalls.

She opened the door to the apartment, and Maritza was there at her feet. The little black cat had always been there to make her smile. Gabriele still had problems, but she gave the cat credit for helping her cope with depression. Domestic cats, she thought as she stroked Maritza, are perfectly balanced creatures. They still have a keen instinct for survival, hiding under couches, running from strangers, and sniffing everything before touching it. But they also have the ability to trust people. Once Maritza had decided that Gabriele would not harm her, the cat had been a devoted friend. That, she thought, was healthy skepticism. Gabriele hoped she was capable of devoting herself to Carl, but she didn't know how to trust a man.

For all the wonderful things they had already done together, Carl was still a mystery to her. As she reflected on their whirlwind romance she realized that she knew very little about him. Carl was good at listening, and that had made her feel more comfortable. She hadn't opened up completely, but she had done most of the talking. Carl had talked a lot about the future but not very much about the past. It had seemed as though he avoided references to his family, and to the Navy. She guessed he wasn't very proud of either one. She felt enormous empathy for his caution, though, because she had been avoiding key pieces of her own past. She walked into the bedroom, recalling the history she had tried so hard to forget.

Gabriele had been just nineteen, a student at the University of Freiburg, when her life was interrupted by an older man. He was a professor, and more than twice her age. She had been idealistic and naive. He'd had half a lifetime of experience, she only a small-town all-girls school. They had started a relationship based upon his worship of her body and her worship of his mind. Gabriele's parents hadn't been there to warn her about men; they had died on the autobahn three years before. The uncle who'd taken her in had been totally ill-equipped to deal with a teenage girl. She had gone to university with vulnerability flashing red. Right into an ambush.

Almost without realizing it, Gabriele had gotten married. Her happiness, fragile to begin with, hadn't lasted long. The man she thought she knew had quickly revealed himself as a drunken brute. She had tried to understand him, but the more he beat her, the harder it became. Inevitably, she'd become pregnant. She hadn't known what to do, so she'd just taken his punishment as long as she could stand it. Then she had cracked completely, taking the baby from her womb and running to a women's shelter. From there she had gone to the American consulate in Stuttgart. Two months later—after hiding in the house of a friend—Gabriele Bach had arrived in Washington, DC, as a transfer student and part-time language instructor. But her new life had not erased the nightmare.

Standing naked in front of her dressing mirror, Gabriele felt vulnerable again. She realized she would have to tell Carl about her marriage. She had lied about her past so often it had been easy to lie to him. At least in the beginning. But once a lie was out there it was tough to get it back. You had to keep on lying to cover it up. She didn't want to do that anymore. She couldn't afford to play games with Carl—the stakes were too high. If there were ever a man to trust, Carl would be that man. Without trust, she had learned, there could be no love. Without love, there could be no happiness. This was her last chance to be happy. She knew that he hadn't told her everything either, but she had seen all she needed to see. Whatever his demons turned out to be, Gabriele knew she could handle them.

When their training was over, Carl's men left for the States—along with their weapons, diving rigs, and personal gear—on a military flight from Howard. He hadn't really lied to them by saying he'd take a later flight out of Torrijos. He knew they had assumed he was doing more interviews. He hadn't told them about Gabriele. Nor *would* he tell them until it was absolutely unavoidable. Had they known what he was thinking, they would have been worried. As he replaced his polo shirt with a white *guayabera*, he sifted his mixed emotions once again. He needed to make the mental transformation from Carlos to Carl. While in the field, he had been preoccupied with honing his team to perfection; when alone, he had thought of nothing but Gabriele. After one last look at the empty barracks, he got in his car and drove back across the isthmus.

He was too sleepy to drive safely, especially on the jungle road. But he pushed on, playing Latin music on the radio and singing badly. He visualized the scene of their reunion. It had been only two weeks, but it felt like a year. He feared for an instant that Gabriele had been just a wonderful dream. No, she was real, he reassured himself—and she would be flying into Torrijos in two hours. Carl knew that first eye contact would tell him all he needed to know. If she still wanted him, he would quit soldiering and settle down. He didn't know what he'd do after that, but it didn't matter. He would have to find a way to tell his men. They would have to find another leader (perhaps Jerry could take his place). Carl's whole adult life had been dedicated to his country; he wanted to focus the rest on his own happiness. In the darkness of the jungle road, he began to believe he deserved it.

The road led him into sprawling Panama City, with its gridlock traffic and leaded gasoline pollution. He remembered when these streets had been patrolled by American Humvees instead of buses. When all commerce, legal and illegal, had come to an abrupt halt. Panama was still a money launderer's paradise, but legal businesses were sprouting up everywhere. Carl didn't know where Panama was headed, and neither did the Panamanians. The United States would hand them the canal in less than two years, and they would finally have their long-sought sovereignty. The future, for the first time, would be up to them. As he drove over the old transisthmian railroad track, he noticed that it was still there: a rusty freight car with a tree growing through the roof. He smiled as he read the faded print on the side of the car: *"Commercio Mundial en Marcha."* World commerce hadn't moved on this railroad in a long time.

He saw the American Airlines plane on final approach as he rounded the last curve in front of the airport. He would not be late. Customs would take at least thirty minutes. He parked close to the terminal and walked into the outer corridor. Dozens of Americans stood in a cluster, waiting for other Americans coming in from Miami. Mostly out of habit, Carl stood behind the crowd and away from the Americans. Breaking another habit, he stopped scanning the terminal and stared at the double doors that separated the arriving passengers from their hosts. She would be easy to spot.

And suddenly, there she was. More beautiful than in his dreams. She scanned the corridor and quickly found his smile in the back. Every single man in the crowd watched her as she glided through. *So much for a low profile!* Abandoning the last of his caution, Carl ran up and gathered her in his arms.

"Welcome to Panama, Gabriele Bach . . . You *are* a sight for sore eyes!"

The Panama Canal had taken decades to build, but it could be appreciated in one long minute at Contractor's Hill. Right at the point where the Americans had finally conquered the Continental Divide. Carl and Gabriele sat on a cliff, looking up and down the most famous waterway in the world. A mere five hundred feet across, the ribbon of navigable water below them disappeared into the jungle—on their left to the north, and on their right to the south. Carl had always loved coming up here. It was evidence, which he often needed, that man could do anything. As he focused his camera on Gabriele, Carl felt his confidence peak. He decided this would be a good time to tell her some more of his story.

He sat down next to her on the bench, turned to speak; then he hesitated. She found herself swallowing hard and bracing for the impact of something frightening. In an instant, the ghosts welled up within her. She started to perspire, suddenly afraid to look at him. Still looking at the canal, Gabriele felt his hands on her shoulders. Then she was facing him, and she saw what she had felt. Carl was sweating too.

"Gaby . . . I need to tell you more about my career in the Navy." His face was a strange mixture of love and fear. It begged her to say something reassuring. But she needed reassurance even more than he did. She said nothing, just wanting him to finish.

"Gabriele . . . everything I told you is true . . . but I didn't tell you everything. I did more than just ride ships." He hesitated again, holding her shoulders more tightly. "I love you . . . I want you to know everything about me . . . about the life I led before we met."

He was beginning to relax. He wanted to get this over with. He took a deep breath and continued.

"I didn't get my shoulder wound as an innocent bystander. I was shooting at those Cubans. They were surrounding our position, trying to kill me and my men. If it hadn't been for the Air Force gunships laying down cover for us, I wouldn't be here telling you this." He tried to read her face. It was unreadable. "I didn't tell you before because I thought you wouldn't want anything to do with me."

She frowned. "Is that all, Carl? You killed in combat?" She let out an audible sigh of relief.

"I did it more than once."

"If it was for your country," she replied carefully, "then it was your duty . . . Do you want to tell me about the other times?" She took his hand, squeezing it every few seconds.

"During the invasion of Panama . . . right down there." He pointed toward the Pacific side. "We swam under two Panamanian patrol boats and blew them up at the pier."

"So you were a SEAL." She said it like she knew what it was.

"I prefer the term 'frogman,' Gaby."

"You said you like frogs . . .," she replied. Then, to his great relief, she smiled. "I love you, Carl. I don't look down on you because you killed for your country. I come from a nation where millions of young men killed for their country—even though the place was ruled by a madman. Germany *still* suffers from a collective guilt. There is nothing more destructive than guilt." *I ought to know!*

Carl decided not to go further. Gabriele had surprised him again, and he felt small for doubting her ability to handle the truth. But he hadn't known her well enough—until now—and there was still truth to tell.

She took his hands and started to get up. "Carl . . .," she began, "there is something I haven't told *you*." His fear returned as he recognized hers. Gabriele was perfect, he told himself. What could she possibly have to hide from him? He sat down again and waited for the axe to fall.

"I was married . . . to a German man. I was very young . . . and stupid." She stopped to let it sink in; then continued. "He drank . . .

He beat me. He would have killed me! I left him and ran as fast as I could. I came to Washington, ostensibly to study, but I was really in hiding. I was scared and embarrassed. It was the end of my life. I buried myself in studies, and in building a career. I didn't start to live again until I met you, Carl. I hope you can forgive me for not telling you." She was crying, and Carl suddenly realized why she cried so easily.

"Is that all, Gaby? You were married?"

"But I told you I wasn't . . . I lied to you, Carl."

"Only because of your fear, honey . . . Remember what you said to me about guilt. It will destroy you too if you let it. I'd say you made the right decision under the circumstances . . . lucky for me. You have nothing to be ashamed of."

Gabriele's fear turned to joy.

Carl had only one more thing to say. "Let's not let the past bury the future. Let's have the future bury the past."

"That sounds very good to me," said Gabriele softly.

As she spoke, he brushed away her tears with the backs of his fingers. She hugged him as hard as she could, and there, in the tropical sun, their souls began to heal. For the first time in their new lives, they had run out of things to talk about. They sat for a long time, listening to the Pacific trade wind funnel through what had been the Continental Divide.

Chapter 5

Bogotá

H. Robert Harding strutted into the embassy conference room ten minutes late. He didn't need to apologize. He was in charge. He was the ambassador. Being late was a prerogative and a privilege reserved for him, and him alone. He was late because he wanted to be late. Especially this time. The military people, about to brief him on the results of their security survey, were not welcome here. He had tried to disapprove the visit request. Only a strongly worded cable from the assistant secretary had made him change his position. But Harding had made his point—as he always did. He was a senior diplomat with more time in Latin America than any of his colleagues, and he was a master at sending signals.

"Ambassador Harding," announced the deputy chief of Mission. Everyone stood. Harding looked around the room as if surveying a battlefield, then sat down. Around the table were eight members of Harding's embassy staff and two members of the US Army. In addition to the DCM, who managed the staff for the ambassador, the meeting was attended by the CIA station chief, the defense attaché, the regional security officer (RSO), the Narcotics Affairs Section chief, the administrative officer, the US Information Service officer, and the Drug Enforcement Administration (DEA) attaché. The Army personnel had taken a position opposite the ambassador and next to the RSO, Laura Jensen, with whom they had worked all week.

"Mr. Ambassador," Laura began. "May I introduce Army Captain Ron Dozier and Master Sergeant Pete Eggers. I have had the pleasure to work with them over the last week in drafting a revision to the noncombatant evacuation section of our Emergency Action Plan. They will brief you on the details of their survey." As she sat back in her chair, the ambassador nodded in her direction. He did not smile.

The captain stood up and turned on the overhead projector. "Good morning, sir . . . General Stewart sends his compliments." As he reached for the first transparency he received the ambassador's opening salvo.

"Just who in the hell is General Stewart?"

Dozier spun around instinctively. It was like a bullet whizzing by his head! In the split second before he answered, he remembered what Stewart had told him about Harding. *Don't lose your cool, Ron.* "Sir . . . General Stewart is the commander of special operations forces in Latin America. He is my commander."

"No, he isn't, Captain . . . not while you're in my country! Tell him I said that." Harding spoke with a tone of finality often used by powerful men who didn't have to worry about what subordinates thought of them. Dozier felt like a mouse being tossed in the air by a cat. "Everybody works for somebody, Captain." Harding gave him a cold look. "I work for the president."

"Yes, sir . . . I understand that." Dozier didn't really understand the relationship between an ambassador, the secretary of state, and the president, but he was smart enough to let the ambassador establish the tone for the meeting. He had seen it before. General Stewart called it stump the dummy. *The guy will make you look stupid right off the bat to remind everyone that he's the smartest person in the room.* Dozier knew when to look stupid, and now was that time. He put his first briefing slide on the projector.

"I don't think you do, Captain, but you may proceed," said Harding with a mixture of contempt and glee. Dozier shot a glance at Laura and found her fidgeting with something on her lap.

"Sir . . .," he began again, "I will be briefing you on the results of our annual security survey. We have worked closely with Ms. Jensen all week in revising the military-assisted evacuation section of the EAP. In addition to refining the general plan for noncombatant evacuation, we have listed the vulnerabilities of embassy buildings and personnel to attack by hostile elements within Colombia." He emptied out his inflated lungs.

"Vulnerabilities, did you say . . . Dozier, was it?"

"Yes, sir . . . Captain Ron Dozier."

"Any relation to that idiot who got himself kidnapped in Italy back in the early eighties?"

"No, sir . . . I am not related to General Dozier." He continued without a pause. "The vulnerabilities I'll be talking about are pretty standard. Most of them have been identified before, and there is very little your embassy can do about them that it is not already doing."

"Are these vulnerabilities . . ."—he lingered over the word— "your personal opinion regarding the threat to my post?"

"Partly, sir. We have worked the issue with Ms. Jensen and the station chief. I think I can say that we all agree on what they are."

Harding looked at Jensen and got a nod. He looked at his resident spook and got nothing. Dozier looked at his sergeant and got a furtive show of support. He found himself wishing he'd stayed at home on the farm.

"Go on," commanded Harding.

"Sir . . . in addition to surveying the embassy itself, we have revalidated helicopter landing zones and assembly points within the city. In case the embassy is threatened from outside the city, the plan—if you approve it— would be for potential evacuees to come to the embassy compound. Helicopters will land here, and here, to shuttle people to Panama." Dozier pointed to the drawings and maps he had posted on the wall.

Getting no flak from across the table, Dozier continued. "If the threat is *inside* the city—and potential evacuees can't get to the embassy—the helicopters would come to these LZs here, and here. LZ Alpha is a soccer stadium. Bravo is an open lot on the other side of town. We would need the support of Colombian authorities to make that scenario work."

"And what makes you so sure they will support us?" asked Harding aggressively. "They might be ordered to block our way out. Have you thought of that?"

"Yes, sir . . . we have. If the Colombian government does not cooperate—and your embassy is in danger of being overrun—we will fight our way in to get you out."

"Like hell you will!" Harding almost came out of his seat. "I will be the one to determine when, where, and how you come in." Now he was shouting. "I have already reminded you that I'm in charge here . . . I will not subordinate myself to some crazed general who wants to be a hero." Harding paused and quickly composed himself. "The US is not at war with Colombia and, despite our disagreement over drug policy, I don't see a need to call in the cavalry anytime soon. I have my differences with President Solano, but Colombia is a civilized country, the government of which would not dare attack Americans or their property." He was calm again, but Harding's body language told Dozier to proceed with extreme caution.

"Understood, sir . . . you call the shots. If you get into trouble and you don't need us, just tell the State Department. We don't fly without orders from Washington." Dozier paused, then continued in the same tone. "But if you think you *might* need us, we'll need two days' notice so we can lean forward."

"Very nicely put, Captain. Let me remind you again . . . You don't come down here without my permission . . . but you won't get two days' notice if you do. I don't work that way . . . If I need you, that means I need you now. Got that?" Harding shifted in his seat and looked at Laura again. "I have worked closely with the RSO on this plan for the last six months, and all I need is to make sure you understand *our* plan. I don't need you to force a plan of your own down our throats. Understand?"

"Yes, sir. I understand both your points. We are here to make sure our plan dovetails with your plan. That's especially important if we have to come in without two days' notice." Dozier had to force himself not to grin. He wanted to say that he—Captain Ron Dozier, the ever-diplomatic killing machine—would be there to personally escort the son of a bitch out of harm's way. He'd kept his cool so far, but he had a long way to go.

An hour later, Dozier and Eggers staggered out of the briefing room. Eggers had watched as his team leader was shot again and again. If they'd been in the field, Eggers would have dragged the captain out of the kill zone. In the embassy conference room he could do nothing.

"Are you OK, Boss?"

"Yeah, Top," said Dozier wearily. "I'll live, but I'm a little stressed out. That asshole deserves to be put in his place."

"I wish there had been something I could have done, Captain. It was like watching a bad movie."

"Don't worry, Pete. If you hadn't been sitting there I might have done something stupid . . . like shout at him, or wring his neck. You had an effect in there, believe me."

Laura Jensen came out of the room and approached the two Army men. She walked with breathtaking grace, aware she had their full attention. At first glance, the red hair was her most striking feature. It was curly, but pulled into the longest ponytail Dozier had ever seen. The second glance, which no man in the embassy could resist taking, would be at the designer clothes she always wore. Laura Jensen had the lithe body of a twenty-eighty-year-old athlete, and she knew how to show it off.

"Ron, you did great!" she gushed. "I told you he's hard to brief, but you didn't flinch!"

"Thanks, Laura. You helped me prepare, and I'm grateful. I just hope I never have to brief him again!"

"I've never seen anyone stand up to him like that . . . You were forceful but so . . . diplomatic." She had been aloof to Dozier all week, but now she was grinning.

"He wasn't very diplomatic," replied Dozier. "Especially for a diplomat." Laura was still grinning. He couldn't believe she was coming on to him! He asked himself vainly what had taken her so long. He had thought about her all week. Laura Jensen was the kind of woman who lived under the skin of every man she met.

"He doesn't need to be, Ron. He's the ambassador. He saves his diplomacy for the Colombians." She laughed softly and took his free hand in both of hers. "Thank you for making me look good in there."

Dozier wondered—almost aloud—how anyone could possibly make her look better than she already did.

"You really have a good plan, Laura. I hope the ambassador appreciates all your hard work."

"He does . . . Believe me, he does," she replied, withdrawing her hands. She looked up at the former football player like the cheerleader she had once been. "I realize you didn't have any fun today, but this embassy is glad you came down."

"Even though the ambassador isn't."

"Robert Harding doesn't like military people," she said carefully. "He thinks you're all a bunch of cowboys."

"If things go south down here he's gonna need us," said Ron with a big smile.

"You smile like a cowboy," she teased.

"Didn't you know?" he joked. "I *am* a cowboy!"

"Where do we go from here?" interrupted Eggers. Dozier had nearly forgotten that his team sergeant was standing next to them.

Laura took her eyes off Dozier and put her hands on her hips. She addressed the sergeant in a different tone. "We lock up the classified stuff . . . then we go to the cantina for some lunch. After that I'll get the embassy driver to take you to the airport in the Blazer."

"Sounds good to me," said Eggers without a smile. "Lead on, ma'am . . . I can't wait to get out of this place."

Dozier and Eggers followed the bouncing red mane down the corridor and into Jensen's office.

The day after the Army team left, Ambassador Harding went to the defense ministry. He had scheduled the office call some weeks before, but the verbal combat with Captain Dozier had renewed Harding's concern. He had long been fearful—though he would never have admitted it to Dozier—that the Colombian military would support their president. No matter what. Colombia, despite a history of political violence, was not as coup prone as most other Latin countries. Military officers, mostly from the middle class, had demonstrated a tendency to subordinate themselves to civilian authority. The United States, with a lot of help from Harding, had reinforced that tendency. The assumption was that civilians, elected through a democratic political process, would be better at running a country than corrupt generals. Very little thought had been given to the possible consequences of corrupt civilians commanding loyal troops.

Harding strode quickly into the ministry with an air of authority he did not possess—at least not here. Authority was a habit he had developed early on in prep school. It had continued at Yale, and into a brilliant diplomatic career. What gray hair he had left made him look older than his fifty-five years, but it strengthened the image he carried. The image of authority. Even though he was only five feet, eight inches tall, he commanded attention wherever he went. Any stranger on the street would look at him and say to himself, "Now that's a man in charge . . . of something!"

He was not just in charge of implementing his president's policies in Colombia; he formulated the policies and persuaded the president to approve them. Harding was a fervent Latinist, believing that the United States was wasting a lot of diplomatic effort in Europe, in the Far East—and certainly in the Middle East. He had been a young foreign service officer in Santiago when Henry Kissinger had sarcastically referred to Chile as a dagger aimed straight at the heart of Antarctica. Harding had decided then and there to relentlessly demonstrate to the State Department—and to the American people—that Latin America was critical to the interests of the United States.

Harding ascended the marble steps of the grand staircase, handing his trench coat to a bodyguard without slowing down. He surveyed the open corridors and observed young men (and women) from each of Colombia's uniformed services moving purposefully from office to office. This was not Honduras, he thought, where generals were fat and the services all hated each other. Colombia had come a long way toward having a professional military force. Different services even worked together occasionally to achieve common goals. As he approached the minister's office, Harding ruminated over all the good a strong institution could do, and—in the wrong hands—all the bad.

Dr. Pedro Galindo Ford stepped from behind his desk to greet Harding. He was much younger than the ambassador, with a doctorate in math and no experience in military affairs. He had already learned, though, that personal relationships were more important than special expertise. Galindo also had a sense of humor not normally found in mathematicians. He was universally respected and—at a time when relations between the United States and Colombia were foundering—had cultivated a good working relationship with Harding. He had initiated that effort by assuring the US ambassador that, as far as Galindo knew, he was not related to Gerald Ford.

"Robert! How are you?" he said in Spanish.

"Pedro . . . I am well, considering," he responded in Spanish. "I've come to talk to you about sensitive matters." Harding spoke Spanish well enough to converse on any subject. He had learned long ago that if you wanted something to be taken seriously in Latin America you had to say it in Spanish. Galindo spoke English well, but Harding would never have insulted him by speaking English at a meeting.

"Please sit down," said Galindo, gesturing to a sofa. "All matters are sensitive these days, are they not?" They both sat back in comfort.

"I am afraid you are correct," replied Harding. "Our governments are not getting along, but you are a voice of reason for Colombia. I am not well regarded here in Bogotá, but you have had the grace to listen to me. Now I need to tell you something you do not wish to hear . . . about your president." Harding studied the man to whom he was about to lie. It wasn't a difficult thing to do, especially when the lie was so close to the truth.

"Robert." Galindo gave a wry smile, hesitated, and then continued. "I am sure you know that President Solano wants you out of the country. The only reason he has not sent you home is that he has no legal basis for doing so. At this point, he feels he is better off taking abuse from you here than taking abuse from Washington. In fact, the people like him more when he stands up to you. What do you think you know about him that you have not already announced to the world?"

"Pedro," said Harding sternly. "I know that President Solano ordered Espinoza to get Mena out of the way. Mena's disappearance gives Espinoza—with Solano as his silent partner—the most powerful drug cartel in the world." Harding finished his assault by calling Solano a crime boss.

"Su presidente es un jefe del crimen."

Harding's tone was completely calm. He had just said the most offensive and undiplomatic thing imaginable to one of the best men he had ever met. It had sounded like a routine report.

Galindo's dark eyebrows jumped. "And how do you know this, my friend?" The minister's tone suggested that he and Harding had never been friends. Galindo's fiery eyes said more than his rising pitch. He unfolded his hands and sat forward on the couch.

"I cannot tell you that," said Harding firmly. The voice was diplomatic, but the gray eyes cut into the minister's veil of serenity like a knife. He knew he had found the right target when Galindo replied in a louder tone.

"You know my forces will support him, sir. If you think the United States Army can come to get him like they got Noriega you are mistaken. I can assure you that we will defend him with all our military might. You know, sir, that Colombia is not Panama . . . even though Panama was once part of Colombia." Galindo could not keep his growing anger completely under control. The reference to Panama, recalling the 1903 North American theft (there was no other word) of Colombia's northernmost province in order to build the canal, was a substitute for punching Ambassador Harding in the stomach.

The doctor of mathematics rose to his feet and walked back behind the desk. He removed his glasses and leveled his tunnel vision at Harding. "You cannot tell me *how* you know President Solano is a criminal because you cannot *prove* it!" Galindo swallowed again, this time keeping all the venom down. "I am a mathematician, esteemed Ambassador. What is not proven is not true. You have been misinformed. I do not wish to continue listening to your misinformation. If you will excuse me . . . I must go to a meeting."

There was no reason to feign friendship with Harding any longer. Galindo was now where he least wanted to be—torn between loyalty to his country and loyalty to himself. He knew Harding was lying, but (to use his own logic) he could not prove it. He wasn't sure he wanted to know the truth anyway. Anger at Harding was giving way to fear of Solano. He inclined his head toward the door and, with the back of his hand, waved the US ambassador out of his office.

"Have a nice day, Pedro," Harding said in English as he stood and turned without a handshake. He steamed through the door, drawing the waiting bodyguard into his wake. He walked quickly down the corridor as if trying to get away from the bomb he had planted in the minister's office.

Laura Jensen walked into the high-rise apartment building just after dinner the following night. It was cool, as usual, in the altitude of Bogotá. She wore a long camel coat; her hair was pinned tightly under a matching knit beret. Brown leather boots met her newest Saks skirt at the knee. Laura was only five feet, six inches, but with high heels she looked statuesque. Her nine-millimeter Berreta, fitted with a heavy silencer, was tucked into the left inside pocket of the coat. She carried a leather briefcase in her left hand. The embassy had recently relocated the ambassador's residence to a relatively secure neighborhood, but she still felt safer inside the walls of the concrete structure than on the street.

The Colombian guards who greeted her at the door were embassy employees. They, in fact, worked for her. She tried to remember, as she rode the elevator to the penthouse, which of the Marines would be on duty tonight. One of the best parts of her job was that, as RSO, she was in charge of the Marine guard force. Laura Jensen loved attention. The Marines gave her even more than most men, especially in the embassy gym, where she worked the weight machines right alongside them. In the sultry atmosphere, sweating into her spandex, she could actually *feel* their desire. She had disciplined herself just enough to avoid giving in to her own.

The elevator opened. She walked down a short corridor to a door with a cipher lock. The embassy had leased the entire top floor of the building after street bombings and popular protests threatened Harding's house. Her principal responsibility was to protect H. Robert Harding from harassment and harm. She punched in the numbers, opened the heavy door, and walked the length of a longer corridor.

"Good evening, Ms. Jensen," said Sergeant First Class Valdez and Lance Corporal Belcher, almost in unison. They stood up behind their desks. There was a thick window of bulletproof glass screening them from the rest of the hallway. The screen was open at both ends.

"Hi, guys!" said Laura breezily. "I have an appointment with the boss. Anything going on?"

"No, ma'am," said Valdez with a knee-jerk smile. "It's real quiet . . . just the way I like it. I'm giving Belcher here some Spanish lessons. He's actually learning it. That's how quiet it is."

"Good!" she responded. "Let's keep it that way . . . I'll be in there about an hour. We're working on the evacuation plan those Army guys briefed yesterday. Don't let anyone in without calling me first, OK?" She took a cellular phone from the desk and slipped it into her coat. Love that Valdez, she thought. *What shoulders!*

"Yes, ma'am! Got it!" said the sergeant.

Laura opened the soundproof door and stepped inside Harding's living quarters. Looking around, she noticed nothing unusual. Other than her galloping heart, there was absolutely no sound in the penthouse. She put down the briefcase and the beret, unpinned her hair, and slipped off the coat. Taking the gun in her right hand, she ran straight for the ambassador's bedroom!

She stopped just inside the open door—standing tall, with the Beretta at her side. Laura quickly scanned the room, then narrowed her focus to the bathroom door. Perfectly motionless, she stopped breathing and waited. Poised for action. Sensing something, Laura sank into a combat stance. With both hands, she leveled the silenced pistol at the door.

The door did not open. Breathing again, she relaxed her stance and lowered the weapon, still clutched in both hands in front of her hips. Still facing the bathroom, she threw her head back and slowly shook the long curls away from her face.

He came from behind her, lunging past the bedroom door. He gripped her right arm just above the elbow and spun her around to face him. The gun dropped to the floor as the US ambassador to Colombia, panting like a racehorse, lifted Laura's skirt and took her standing up.

"I love it . . . when you come . . . to me like this . . . you sexy woman!" She wore nothing under the skirt, having learned too often that Harding's lust could not wait. "I've thought all day about doing this to you . . . Tell me . . . how much . . . you want me . . . my beautiful . . . Laura!" His body, cloaked in a thick Turkish bathrobe, was already shuddering out of control.

"You're the best, Robert," she said with feigned passion. "I want to be your sex slave. I love the danger!" She was whispering in his ear and biting his neck.

When he was finished, she sat him down on an overstuffed chair and walked into the bathroom. Bringing back a warm, wet towel, she knelt in front of him and began cleaning him up. He ran his hands through her soft hair as he tried to catch his breath.

"You . . . with your gun . . . you drive me crazy, Laura! *I'm* the slave . . . I can't look at you . . . without wanting to be *in* you!"

He was taking a huge risk to be with her. His reputation—and his finances—were on the line. Having more of Laura Jensen was all he cared about.

"You love watching me, don't you?" She looked up into his worshipping face as she worked.

"Yes!" he gasped. "You're *magnificent* . . . Do me again!"

She put down the towel and coaxed him back to madness while he watched.

"Lie on the bed," she commanded, stripping off her three-hundred-dollar blouse. She dropped her skirt to the floor and stepped out of it. As soon as he was on his back, she walked slowly to the bed and climbed on top of him, rubbing leather boots against his pale legs. Red hair fell in front of her face, obscuring her expression. The face she wore in the gym. A suppressed smile.

Harding was living a fantasy but, in a way, so was she. For Laura Jensen, being adored was the ultimate high. To her delight, she was being adored (right now) by one of the most powerful men in the country. And, for this moment, she was more powerful than he. Their affair had a certain logic: his wife was living in Washington; she wanted to make a career move. He was thinking how clever he was; she was thinking about Paris.

With only a few minutes left in her appointment, Laura sat combing out her hair. She was already dressed. Harding, savoring his exhaustion, was still on the bed. It was payback time, she decided.

"Robert, dear . . . when are you going to tell your wife about us?" It was a question totally without emotion. A question, the potential for which all unfaithful men either dreaded or denied.

Harding sat up quickly. "Laura . . . well . . . honey . . . I'm not sure she's ready to hear about us just yet." He was suddenly without diplomatic skill. "I think it will take some more time. You know I love you, Laura. I have to be married to Norma for a while longer . . . but I want to marry you. You know that."

Laura looked at him for the first time since getting off the bed. She wasn't smiling. "Either you tell your wife about us—right now—or I will. I can't wait any longer, dear." She cast her eyes toward the door and said matter-of-factly, "You could also send me to the embassy in Paris . . . I hear they're looking for a new RSO."

She let that thought hang in the air as she glided out of the apartment. She wore the underwear she had brought in her briefcase. The beret sat on her hair exactly as it had an hour before. The pistol, which she also carried for protection, was tucked in her coat, this time with a bullet in the chamber. Radiant with satisfaction, she paraded past the two Marines and continued to the end of the corridor. When she was gone, Valdez and Belcher looked at each other. Two sets of eyebrows were raised as high as they could go.

"D'ya think the old man is bangin' the RSO?" wondered Valdez aloud. "They've been working on that plan a *lot* the last three months."

"I *hope* so," said Belcher in a heavy Southern drawl. "Any woman looks like that oughta be banged by *somebody* . . . I'm jus' sorry it's not me!"

They both laughed, imagining what she must be like in bed and thinking that Ambassador Harding wasn't such a bad guy after all.

The bombings continued. Who was bombing whom was not entirely clear because the victims included more ordinary citizens than known criminals. The randomness of the terror made Bogotá—even by Colombian standards—a very difficult place to live. Two days after Harding shook him up, Pedro Galindo Ford went to see the president of the republic. Even as he ascended the marble steps of the palace, he was not sure what he would say. Harding had given him a message to deliver, but Galindo could not just walk in and deliver it as he received it. *The US ambassador says you are a crime boss!* But Galindo couldn't think of any other way to phrase it.

He arrived early, having adjusted his departure time from the defense ministry after mentally calculating the probabilities of traffic, street bombings, public demonstrations, and other such delays. He had waited in the anteroom, rehearsing for only a few minutes, when the door opened. Ernesto Solano had the very un-Latin habit of being on time. Galindo strode into the president's office and stood at attention.

"*Buenos dias*, Pedro," said Solano with a gesture toward the window. "A beautiful day, no?"

"Yes, Mr. President. It is lovely today," replied Galindo.

Solano smiled confidently at his defense minister as they shook hands. Galindo tried not to wince as his hand was crushed in the president's legendary grip.

"Please sit down, Pedro, and tell me how the Army is finally beating the FARC guerrillas." Galindo noticed something in the president's eyes. Sarcasm? "Tell me how the Navy is policing our territorial sea in the Caribbean . . . Are they keeping a close eye on the US Navy beyond that? Tell me about the national police and what they are doing about these explosions all over the city." He did not ask about the Marine Corps, whose boat companies had been hitting drug laboratories hard along the southern border.

"Sir," began Galindo. "The Army is not having much effect against the FARC."

"And tell me . . . why is that?" replied the president.

"I am a mathematician, Mr. President. Let me put it in terms I can articulate." Galindo had wanted to give Solano this lecture for months. "The FARC is a flat organization, sir . . . By that I mean it has no structure at all. If it did, you could kill the organization by cutting off its head. The guerrillas have political leaders but decentralized operations. All seventy-three of their *frentes* have a common goal. That goal is to overthrow your government and replace it with a Marxist regime. They are spread throughout the south and east of the country in small bands that have only weak ties to one another." Galindo took a breath and Solano interrupted him.

"So where are you going with this?" The president's intimidating bulk was taking on an air of impatience that made Galindo wish he'd kept his mouth shut.

"I only wish to tell you, sir, that you cannot beat a flat organization without physically occupying the territory on which they live. We are forced to use almost half your combat troops to guard industrial facilities from attack by the guerrillas. I need more soldiers to go after them in their strongholds. But even a bigger Army will not beat the FARC if we go after them one piece at a time. We must hit them all at once . . . The mathematics tells us so." Galindo wanted to add that the FARC was also swimming in drug money. They provided protection for the cartels in order to raise funds for their operations against the Army.

"Very interesting, Pedro. I will consider what you have said when we talk to the generals next week. Let us see what they think about reorganizing . . . Anything else?"

Galindo sat carefully on the edge of the soft couch and placed his hands on his knees. "Mr. President, the US ambassador says you are a crime boss." He blurted it out and just sat there, waiting for a reaction.

Solano remained standing. "He is a liar and a fool, Pedro. I am the president of the republic founded by Simon Bolivar! I am a statesman . . . and a warrior. I am not a criminal!" Solano was shouting now. In a calmer voice, he continued. "And just when did the American imperialist tell you this?"

"Two days ago . . . in my office," said Galindo cautiously. "He is lying, of course, but I thought you should know that he came to me. I am sure he wanted me to come here and tell you this."

"He is also a coward!" Solano thundered. "Is he afraid of me?" A head taller than both Galindo and Harding, the president was an imposing figure. He had been an Olympic boxer in his youth and still looked like one. He and Harding had never liked each other, and one of the many reasons was that Harding considered Solano a roughneck. Harding was right about that; the president—criminal or not—wore the survivor face of someone who'd grown up on the wrong side of Bogotá.

The same side as Juan Espinoza.

"Ambassador Harding is apparently comfortable with me, sir . . . and yes, I think he is afraid of you." Galindo fought to keep himself absolutely still in the chair. In truth, he was also afraid of Solano. He went out of his way to hide it, but he worried that the president saw through him. "But he made me very angry," Galindo went on. "I wanted to make sure that he knew—and that *you* know—I am just as outraged as you are."

"This is bigger than both of us, Pedro. Harding has insulted Colombia!" Solano was now on his feet, pacing up and down the oriental carpet. "What do you recommend I do with him?"

Galindo worried about the president's tone. The question had come across as a loyalty test. A test he would have to pass. "Sir, I told him that, although you have grounds for expelling him, you were not going to send him home. I said that you have benefitted from his criticism. The people are behind you, and he knows that. You are fighting crime all over Colombia."

"But what do you *recommend*, Mr. Defense Minister?"

"There are three possible courses of action, Mr. President," the mathematics professor began in his best academic voice. "You can send him home, you can have him killed, or you can just ignore him. The first course of action would put you in a position of having to explain to the North Americans that the expulsion had nothing to do with Harding's criticism of you. If you throw him out now, it will be hard to make that argument. The second course of action is obviously a throwaway option. I only mention it in order to make the other options appear reasonable. You could never convince Washington that Harding's accidental death had nothing to do with your war of words . . . If I were you, I would make Robert Harding's health a priority of your administration." Galindo actually smiled as he said this, then added, "I would simply ignore him."

"You are a sensible man, Pedro," beamed the president. "I appreciate your coming to me with *Señor* Harding's message, and I will think about what you have said." Solano paused just long enough to signal he had not yet made up his mind. Smiling, he slapped Galindo on the back as they walked to the door. Hiding the pain, Galindo turned to the president and tried one more time to influence the outcome.

"The cruelest thing you can do to a man like Harding is to ignore him. That is by far your best option." Galindo turned, and with an almost audible sigh of relief, walked out of Solano's office.

Chapter 6

Payback

C arl and Gabriele decided, at least for the time being, not to live together. The fantasy of Panama had given them a clearer vision of the life they both wanted, but the reality of Washington had made them cautious. Although he had decided on what he needed to do, Carl did not know how to make the transition from warrior to husband. He knew he couldn't do it unless he buried his growing guilt—or told her everything. He had tentatively decided to just bury the guilt—but he felt guilty about *that*. He realized he would have to come clean. Perhaps she would understand his real contracting business. But what if she didn't? How would he begin the conversation anyway? *Good morning, dear. I'm off to capture a deadly drug baron from his jungle hideout in the middle of the night . . . Please don't wait up.*

To make things even worse, Carl wasn't sure what he would do for a living after making the break. Beyond killing and writing, he didn't have a marketable skill. He couldn't see himself writing tactics, techniques, and procedures after deciding never to employ them in the field again. His writing would lack authenticity (at least to him), and it sounded like a boring way to live. He had to admit it—he was hooked on adrenaline. But he knew that he wouldn't be able to make Gabriele happy without making at least some money. His father's debts were still out there, hanging over his head. A meager Navy pension would not go far enough. Every day brought Carl a bit closer to determining how to do what he wanted to do. But not *that* much closer. Adrenaline, it seemed, would not be involved.

Gabriele had gone back to her teaching with the apathy of someone who has already moved on to something else. But she wasn't absolutely sure what that something else was. Her problem was that she was not quite ready to marry anybody—not even Carl. She knew he loved her, but she was also aware that they had known each other barely more than a month. Gabriele fretted, in her moments of despair, that it might be too late. She had been damaged by her brief marriage far more than she had confessed to Carl. The fear of making another mistake was still strong enough to compete with the fear of being alone. She needed more time, and she needed some space—as long as she could see him every day.

He woke up alone, made some coffee, and dragged a razor across his face. He had never longed for a woman before. Carl Malinowski—veteran of Grenada, Panama, and a classified list of heart-stopping intelligence operations—was worried about security: his own. He finished in the bathroom and got the paper from the hall. In his depression, he had slept through the alarm instead of running. He was in no mood to hear bad news, but that was exactly what he got when he opened the *Washington Post*.

Paul Henning
Where is Mena?

Drug baron Jorge Mena Velasquez is still missing. Most have probably forgotten about the crime boss, taken from his jungle hideout six weeks ago by a secretive commando force rumored to be agents of the Colombian president, Ernesto Solano Vierra. Someone is holding Mena, but no ransom has been offered. We are left to conclude that whoever has him is extracting everything in his brain related to the cocaine business. Who wins? Juan Espinoza Rojas, the boss of Mena's rival cartel, is a big winner. An even bigger winner may be President Solano himself. Why would the president of a country condone kidnapping and, perhaps, murder? Besides being a personal friend of Juan Espinoza, Ernesto Solano is just greedy. He got himself elected with Espinoza's money; now he wants his own fortune.

What should the United States do about this? Without charging the Colombian president with being a drug kingpin, our courageous ambassador, H. Robert Harding, has called for Solano to explain publicly his ties to the illegal narcotics trade. Harding has also pressured the Solano government to put an end to the bombing campaign that has come in the wake of Mena's disappearance. Back home, President Ferguson's administration has been basking in the glow of favorable statistics on crime in the United States. While crime overall may be down, drug-related violence in urban areas is way up. We are becoming a country not unlike Colombia itself. In Bogotá, some neighborhoods are thriving; in others, bullets are flying. Here in the nation's capital, citizens who live on the right side of town are supposed to care what happens to those who live on the wrong side. The question is: do we?

Carl slammed the paper down and got up to wash his reddened face. He felt like a chump for getting himself involved in a war— that's what it was—between the United States and one of its kin countries. A big reason he was still alive was his devotion to situational awareness; the Henning editorial reminded him that he'd been used. He had focused his superhuman discipline on meeting the tactical challenge; he had not thought enough about the strategy. All of a sudden, that strategy was loud and clear. Mena had also been used. And now Mena was probably dead. No big loss, thought Carl, but that wasn't the way bad men were supposed to die. In the jungle, Carl wouldn't have thought twice about killing Mena. On American soil, everyone rated a fair trial. Even bad men.

He finished the paper and went to the office, too angry to eat breakfast. He worked on the FID manual until almost noon and then went to the gym to work out some of his frustration. He didn't want to talk to Gabriele until he cooled off. She was by far the most important thing to him now, and he resolved to protect her at all costs. He would protect her from the knowledge he and his men had been killing for hire. He would also protect her from any blowback that might follow in the wake of his fieldwork. Carl Malinowski had a lot of dangerous baggage. Whatever happened between them, he had to make sure Gabriele Bach would be OK.

Back in the office, Carl picked up the phone to call Gabriele. Instead, he found himself dialing the number he always used to call Jeff. He left a message and waited for the return call he knew would come. He wrote for the next two hours. Now that he had decided to discontinue his fieldwork, he would have to take his pen more seriously. Whoever had claimed that the pen was mightier than the sword, thought Carl, had never been in a firefight. Late in the afternoon the phone finally rang.

"Malinowski Technical Writing."

"Jeff here. Do you want to meet?"

"Vietnam Memorial . . . one hour . . . be there, dickhead."

It made Carl feel good to mouth the word that so perfectly described Jeff. He changed back into his gym clothes and was out the door in one motion. He ran along the path toward the Pentagon and the Memorial Bridge. The Virginia heat was kinder now, making it easier to think. Turning onto the bridge, he fixed his running stare on the temple built to worship Lincoln. *Where have all the statesmen gone?*

As he ran, the anger subsided again. By the time he jogged up to the black marble wall, he felt better. He was early enough to walk around and survey the site. Seeing nothing unusual, he sat down at some distance from the wall and waited for Jeff under a tree. It was late in September, and the leaves were starting to turn. Looking at the scene, Carl realized he had not yet brought Gabriele to the memorial.

He made a mental note to do that soon. There were lots of tourists there today; he and Jeff would have a good crowd to blend into.

Jeff came down the path from the direction of the White House. Carl spotted his confident swagger a long way off and watched his approach to the wall. *How can a guy so young be so cocky? He hasn't done shit in his life.*

Carl got up and maneuvered himself into a rear approach. Jeff was standing still, facing the wall. When Carl placed a hand on the CIA man's shoulder, Jeff jumped a foot.

"Don't you know how to execute a personal meeting, you jerk?" Carl was smiling at the man in the dark suit. "I could have shot you in the back, dickhead."

Jeff, now facing him, was more nervous than Carl had ever seen him. "Let's walk," commanded Carl, leading him by the elbow. *His cockiness is just an act. He's just a scared little brat.* And Carl hated him even more.

"What the fuck do you want, Carl? I don't have time to be out here listening to your complaints, you know," said Jeff, composing himself as he spoke. "Make it quick!"

Carl did not answer until they had walked to where the wall glistened in the sun. "You see this wall, Jeff? Neither of us had the opportunity to get our names on it, but there is something we can learn here." Carl gestured at the wall as he spoke. Jeff stood motionless, listening, but avoiding the cold eyes that stared at him.

"See how the names are displayed?" Carl continued, reading from the wall. "On the left, the wall is low, and there are only a few . . . the Smiths and Browns mixed with Kowalski and Hernandez. No ranks. No hometowns. As you move to the right, the wall rises and there are more names. The number peaks and then falls off until, at the right edge, there are once again just a few. But it takes a long time for the names to go away." Jeff was now staring at the wall. Carl raised his voice and got his attention again.

"That's how we get into a war, Jeff. Just a few names . . . then a few more . . . and a few more. And pretty soon you idiots here in Washington are trying to figure out how we got into such a mess!" Carl took a breath, and continued in a loud voice. "But by then it's too late. War sneaks up on you because you're so focused on tactics, you forget about strategy." *And I learned that lesson the hard way.*

"So what does that mean to us, Jeff?" He led them away from the crowd, then shouted, "Look at me!"

Jeff turned and saw a different man than the one he'd briefed for the last five years. He could almost feel the heat from Carl's growing anger.

"And your point is?"

"My point," said Carl in a hushed voice, leading Jeff further away from the crowd, "is that you and your friends across the river are bringing us to the brink of war with a friendly nation that spends more money and blood fighting drugs than we do. Colombia's only real sin was to try democracy. You think every country should be just like the United States." It was a statement, but with a rising pitch. "Well, I'll tell you . . . It's just not that easy. We are—in case you forgot—a *moral* example . . . not a set of administrative blueprints. Now you go and frame a democratically elected president. Frame! What do you think you're accomplishing with that?" He stopped to take a breath and Jeff jumped in.

"We killed three birds with one stone, Carl. We captured the terrorist Mena—and we thank you for that. We made it look like it was done by a rival cartel. *And* we implicated Solano in the crime." Jeff's voice was steady now, and some of the cockiness was back. Carl decided to hear him out.

"It was a brilliant plan, you see. Mena's gone, the cartels are destroying each other, and the president will be forced out. I agree that it's not something Mr. Lincoln here would have done . . . but he lived in a different time."

"Yeah," said Carl bitterly. "The *Civil War*! There was never a greater challenge to the moral foundation of this country. Lincoln had the courage to stand up for real equality despite the consequences. He held the country together. You and your friends are going to tear it apart. When the public finds out what you've done—and they *will* find out—they're going to come down on President Ferguson a lot harder than the Colombians will come down on Solano. It's going to blow up in your face, Jeff."

"Is that a *threat?*" Jeff pointed at him. "Let me tell you something, Mr. Holier-Than-Thou . . . you're right in the middle of this, so don't go preaching to me . . . OK?"

"I'm out of it now, Jeff. You can take the CIA—and whoever else is briefed into this plan—and shove 'em all up your ass!"

"What makes you think you can just walk away from this, Carl?" said Jeff ominously.

"Only a few people know about my role," asserted Carl confidently. "I doubt any of you can afford to incriminate me."

"How do *you* know who knows, Carl?" Jeff smiled for the first time. "If we can frame a president, you dumb shit, don't you think we can expose *you?*"

Carl's heart and lungs stopped while he found the proper insult. "You wouldn't do that to me, you bastard!"

"Oh, yes, we would, Carl. Ambassador Harding in Bogotá is prepared to say that he knew nothing about your little escapade in Brazil. He will be properly outraged over the multiple violations of sovereignty and human rights. That testimony will also allow him to stick up for the Colombian government for a change. He will say it was the Pentagon's idea."

"So . . . whose idea *was* it?"

"Harding's, of course . . . and your name is on his lips, Carl."

For the first time in his life, Carl felt seasick. He had just explained to Jeff how the government gets into such a mess; now he would have to explain it to himself. Instead of vomiting, he needed to show some bravado.

"What's next for the Washington cartel—or do you call yourselves something with a nicer ring to it?"

"Don't know," said the now-beaming Jeff. "You'll just have to stay tuned." He turned to walk away. "See ya, Carl."

Carl grabbed him by the shoulder and spun him around. "Do you really think you can get away with this?"

Jeff put his finger in Carl's chest. "Don't even think about going to the press . . . or to your buddies in the Pentagon. If you do, your name will be on a cartel hit list so fast, you won't have time to kiss that beautiful blonde woman of yours goodbye."

Jeff swaggered off in the direction of the White House. A shaken Carl went back to his tree and sat down to think. He wasn't looking forward to the run home.

H. Robert Harding took a scotch and soda from the tray and cradled it in his smooth hands. He surveyed the crowded room with a diplomat's eye for social detail. On hand in the residence of the Japanese ambassador were the usual members of the party roster, holding territory with their ladies on the oriental rugs. Harding had brought a small team. Next to him was the new RSO, a bland and boring man virtually invisible to the others. Laura Jensen had been gone for just a week; Harding thought, with some amusement, that this man was part of his penance. Across the room stood the defense attaché an Army colonel who, wearing a dark suit, still looked like an Army colonel. That was it. To Harding, parties were business meetings, complete with agendas and products. The agenda for this evening—briefed beforehand—was to find out whether or not the armed forces of Colombia were solidly behind President Solano. The product of the party would be a cable to Washington, laying out the lines of loyalty within Solano's security establishment.

Harding was speaking to the ambassador from Venezuela when he saw her with the corner of his eye. She was an impression like a painting, standing out in glorious profile from the crowd. Harding had been trying to get an assessment of the situation on the border before his attention span came to a complete stop. Turning her head toward Harding, the woman walked into an adjoining room as he quickly finished the conversation. He had learned that Venezuela, with its powerful national guard and without active guerrillas, had an even bigger rivalry between its law enforcement and military institutions than did Colombia. Ironically, the coup Harding secretly wished for in Colombia was always just around the corner in Venezuela. He got to the bottom line, thanked the gentleman from Caracas, and came about like a sailboat in a stiff breeze. Harding simply had to get a better look at that woman! Who was she? More importantly, who was she with?

He moved a few steps and placed his hand on the RSO's shoulder. "I'll be in the other room, Mr. Wilkinson . . . no need to follow." He had forgotten the man's first name.

"Yes, sir," came the reply with a nod of the head, and the ambassador powered through the crowd, looking for the mysterious woman.

Pedro Galindo intercepted him. "Ambassador Harding . . . I must speak with you."

"Yes, Dr. Galindo," he managed with a noticeable frown. "What do you want now?" *Especially now!*

"I wanted to tell you that I have passed your message to the president," stated a cheerful Galindo. "He appreciates your concern for his reputation, but he will continue to do whatever is necessary to safeguard Colombia's citizens. He is more concerned about violence in our streets than about our relations with the United States. He is a patriot, Mr. Ambassador."

"He is also a liar, *señor*," snapped Harding, more interested in finding the woman than placating the minister. "A patriot does not cavort with criminals. And criminals do not cavort with a president. If you will excuse me, I am very busy. Good evening." The ambassador, whose own president had a bad habit of cavorting with suspected criminals, left Galindo fuming again.

He found her in the library. She was already watching him when their eyes met, as if she had been waiting for him. Harding stopped in his tracks and gave her a long admiring look. To his delight, he was rewarded with a nod of her perfect head. He nodded his powerful head in return and stood there admiring her some more. A bit taller (and a lot younger) than Harding, she wore a low-cut cocktail dress that revealed—and revealed was the right word—a body to weaken the knees. Better even than Laura's, he thought. Not as athletic, but sexier and more natural. She looked like something out of a James Bond movie; he wondered how she would look holding a gun. Jet-black hair hung to the middle of her back in huge curls, and Harding imagined what they would feel like hanging in his face. But it was the eyes that got him. Large dark almond-shaped jewels, set in olive skin. They beckoned him to come to her.

He walked across the room without taking his eyes off her. He *couldn't* take them off! She was clearly enjoying his gaze and seemed to be posing for him. Harding managed to make it to her side without stumbling over the furniture. As she took his free hand in hers, he almost recoiled from the spark.

"How wonderful to finally meet you, Mr. Ambassador," she purred in perfect English. "I am Julia . . . Julia Mendoza."

Harding was still reeling from the shock of her beauty, but he had no difficulty smiling. "I am Robert Harding . . . and I must say that you are the loveliest woman here tonight." He took a much-needed breath. "It is my pleasure to meet you, Señorita Mendoza. Your English . . . it is extremely good. Have you lived in the United States?"

"Yes, Mr. Ambassador, I have. My father was a businessman, and we lived in Miami for a few years. I went to college in Florida before coming back here. I *loved* the States!" Her smile did not belong to Bogotá; it belonged to the beach.

"That's music to my ears, Julia." Now recovered from the shock, he was simply flirting. "And I love Colombia." She looked nineteen, but Harding knew from long experience that a lot of Latin women were capable of looking that age.

She lifted her head and opened her mouth. It was not a smile; it was an invitation. Then she turned slightly, showing him her bare back. "I am flattered that a man as well-known as you takes the time to even speak with a young girl like me, sir."

"Please call me Robert." Harding was trying to walk a fine line between harmless banter and dragging her into one of the spare bedrooms. "How did you come to be here tonight?"

"I know people," she responded.

"What kind of people do you know?" asked Harding, raising his eyebrows in mock surprise.

"Powerful men," said Julia evenly. "I like powerful men . . . and Bogotá is full of them." Her intensity—as powerful as any man's—shot right through him.

Harding looked around the room again. "Many of those men are here tonight, Julia . . . Which one are you with?"

"You." She grinned with a hint of mischief that sent Harding's groin into overload.

"Then I am at your service, Julia. A woman as beautiful as you should never be alone."

"Thank you," said Julia, closing her eyes momentarily for effect. "I was hoping to meet you here, but I could not have imagined how wonderful it would feel . . . You are a charming man, Robert."

"I like it when you call me that," said Harding. "I don't have any real friends here. I'm afraid that, along with great power, comes great loneliness. I have no wife and no personal life. I treasure the time away from all my duties, but I have no one to share it with."

"And where do you spend your alone time, Robert?"

"Mostly in my quarters . . . walled off and locked away." He looked straight into her eyes. "Private conversations are difficult to find out here in the real world."

"But you are talking to me *now*," she offered. "It is as if we are alone . . . in your quarters . . . is it not?"

Wow! "Not quite, Julia . . . not quite." Harding's mind was now racing. "But I can arrange for you to see me up there . . . if you'd like. We could share a glass of wine and talk freely."

"I have a coat and a car," said Julia, putting her glass on the bookshelf.

All he could do was nod up and down like a schoolboy.

She turned to leave the room, hesitating long enough for Harding to get another look at her profile. He followed her into the vestibule, watching her walk. He noticed that she wore leather boots with spiked heels. He hoped, in his madness, that she would wear them in bed. Mesmerized, he almost bumped into her as she stopped for the coat. She handed him the heavy mink and quickly slipped into it.

Julia took her purse and floated through the door. Harding didn't even think about Wilkinson until he was on the elevator. He briefly considered telling her he needed to go back and let the RSO know he was leaving. At that moment, she took his hand and placed it on her hip. *No problem! Wilkinson and the bodyguard will know where I am as soon as we get by the Marine guard.*

Harding had more important things to think about.

Julia led him by the hand as they got off the elevator and left the high-rise building. Security officers were everywhere, and there was enough confusion in the crowd to convince Harding that he would not be recognized. Not that he had anything to hide. Many beautiful women in Colombia were accompanied by men old enough to be their fathers. Here, even more than in most places, physical beauty was a ticket to wealth, power, or both. He was powerful; she was beautiful. End of story.

The valet drove up to them in a new Mercedes. He got out and opened the driver's door for Julia. Harding, taking his cue from her, got in the passenger seat. As soon as he closed the door she was off like a shot through the evening traffic of Bogotá.

"Where do you live, Robert?" she asked, glancing at him long enough to penetrate the sudden rush of caution he felt. The caution, there only by habit, evaporated again. He was in her spell, and they both knew what was coming.

"Go straight until you get to the next light . . . then turn left. It's the third building on the right." He found her hand on his leg and held it there.

He did not notice the car behind them.

Harding fought for control. He had long ago thrown caution to the wind, but he understood deep down how out of control he was. He would have to appear professional—ambassadorial—to the gatekeepers they were about to encounter. With a noticeable lump in his trousers, he didn't feel very ambassadorial at the moment. Now, as they approached the building, he was on the verge of panic. He searched desperately for some remnant of his senses. The first thing he found was his voice.

"Julia . . . we are going to my quarters, but I will have to make up a story for the guards in order to get you in." To hide his nervousness, he simply winked at her. H. Robert Harding, dour professional that he was, had never winked at anyone.

"*El amor prohibido*," she chuckled with delight. "I like that!"

So did Harding.

Julia parked on the street. Hurrying down the sidewalk, he held her hand as he silently rehearsed his lines. Just before entering the lobby, Harding withdrew his hand and moved slightly away from her. He approached the Colombian guards with characteristic severity.

"Good evening," he said in Spanish. "This is *Señorita* Mendoza. She is the daughter of a good friend of mine. She will be staying with me for a few days . . . until her father finds suitable quarters in Venezuela." The normal procedure would have been to search the visitor, but she was with the ambassador. The search was waived.

Julia stroked his leg all the way to the penthouse. When the elevator let them out, she placed her arm around him as they walked to the cipher-lock door. He leaned against the door as she ran her hand under his jacket. She massaged his shoulder as she watched him punch in the numbers. Once inside the corridor, they moved away from each other and prepared to explain their cover story to the Marines.

Suddenly—and without warning—Julia slipped and fell to the floor.

"Oh!" she shouted as she went down with a thud. She put her head down and mumbled something into her fur collar. Something Harding, looking apprehensively down the hallway, did not notice and could not hear. She took his outstretched hand and got up.

"Thank you, Mr. Ambassador," she said loudly enough for the Marines to hear. "These boots are dangerous!"

They walked up to a desk behind the bulletproof glass.

"Sergeant," began Harding, "this is *Señorita* Mendoza. She is the daughter of a good friend of mine. She'll be staying with me for a few days until her father finds suitable quarters in Venezuela." He couldn't have explained why the girl had no luggage, but the Marines had the good sense not to ask.

"Yes, sir," replied Valdez without a trace of mirth. "We'll be here for another hour . . . I'll pass it down to the next shift."

"Tell the RSO where I am . . . and that he doesn't need to come over. Good night," said Harding.

"Good night, sir," said Valdez and Belcher in unison, both wanting to add something like . . . *and good luck.*

Harding opened the door to his sanctuary and led Julia inside.

Outside the door, the Marines were enjoying the ambassador's story, deciding what to do with it. "How does he do it, man?" asked Belcher after a slow whistle. "I mean . . . this one makes Ms. Jensen look like a boy!"

"More power *to* him," replied Valdez. "I'm just sorry I didn't get to pat her down!"

Julia slipped out of the mink and laid it on the couch where Laura had always laid hers. Harding watched her movements with exploding excitement as the eyes came back to meet his.

"Now we are alone, Robert. You can say anything you want . . . and you can *do* anything you want." She dropped the right shoulder strap of her dress. "Do you want to please me?"

"Yes . . . Julia. I want to please you . . . you beautiful creature!" His chest heaved as he lurched forward and kissed her violently. She was already taking off his jacket.

"I have always dreamed of making love to a powerful man like you, Robert," she whispered when he let her breathe. He started to lift up her dress, forgetting that she was not Laura. Julia took his hands and brought them to her face. "We have time, Robert . . . We have time to do it right. Take me to the bedroom."

They came to the overstuffed chair and she set him down gently. "Close your eyes, Robert, and I will make you want me even more." Julia breathed electricity into his ear. Sitting perfectly still, he was shaking with anticipation and closed his eyes, making it easier to imagine what would come next.

Julia undid Harding's belt, slipping the ambassador's pants under his buttocks and over his knees. She reached down and unbuckled her boot with one hand while stroking him with the other.

In a lightning move she'd practiced a hundred times, Julia withdrew a straight razor from inside the boot and spun herself like a cat directly behind him. Before Harding knew what was happening, her arm was around his neck and the razor at his throat!

"One move and I will gladly cut your *garganta* . . . *Señor Embajador!*" She shouted it into his ear, holding the razor just high enough that he could see it. Harding's eyes bulged as she applied a perfect sleeper choke. He couldn't speak or breathe. Spit drained out of his mouth and dripped off his chin. He felt himself passing out and kicked his feet as if he thought that would help.

"I told you not to move!" Harding groaned with pain as Julia almost crushed his windpipe. Then she let in a little air, just to keep him conscious.

Valdez had called the RSO right after Harding entered the apartment, so he assumed the two men coming through the cipher-lock door were Wilkinson and the ambassador's bodyguard. But as he watched them advance toward the desk he realized the men—both wearing overcoats and wide-brimmed hats—were moving too fast. He reached frantically for the shotgun behind the desk as the intruders broke into a run and tossed metal objects ahead of them.

Belcher cocked his pistol and brought it to eye level, stepping from behind the glass to shoot. Before either of them could fire, the flash-crash grenades exploded, knocking them down. As the Marines tried to get to their feet, the attackers closed in and shot both of them in the head.

Harding was startled by the explosions, and he jumped reflexively in the chair. Julia, unfazed by the blast, clamped down on his neck even harder.

"My friends are here, right on time," she announced with venom in her voice. Harding, with eyes as big as dinner plates, did something he hadn't done in years: he prayed. He prayed that the Marines had repulsed the attack and were about to burst in to rescue him. When he saw the men in overcoats come through the door, he stopped praying and started screaming.

One of the men leveled a machine pistol at Harding's face. "Don't kill me!" he managed to plead. Surrendering to the horror of being kidnapped, Harding said it more politely. "Please don't kill me." He was now whimpering.

Julia released her grip and pushed him to the floor. Harding crumbled into a sobbing heap. "Don't worry, Robert . . . you are too valuable to us alive."

She put the razor back in her boot and walked around to where Harding lay. "Now get up and get dressed . . . We are leaving."

Julia's men pulled Harding to his feet. They pointed their weapons at him while he adjusted his pants and put on the shirt. One of them took off his own coat and hat, putting them on the prisoner.

"One more thing," said Julia, still breathing hard. "I want you to open that safe!" She pointed to the heavy gray container next to the bed.

"Not that!" erupted the ambassador. "There's nothing in there but personal correspondence!" His face was panic-stricken.

"I do not believe you, Robert," she said calmly. The calm before the storm. "Now open it . . . or these men will blow you apart!"

Harding opened the safe.

Julia went through the metal container with manicured fingers. There were notebooks and stacks of loose papers lying on the single shelf. She extracted them all and closed the safe. One of the men produced an expanding leather file into which Julia stuffed the documents. The other man stuffed a sock in Harding's mouth and pushed him along behind the boss. As they hurried past the bodies of Valdez and Belcher, Robert Harding almost slipped on the blood streaming across the floor. Marine blood. He forced the vomit to stay in his stomach and found himself wishing the Colombians had killed him too.

Walking quickly, Julia lowered her head and spoke clearly into the microphone buried in her fur collar.

"*Lo tenemos. Dos minutos.*"

The man in the parked car pulled to the curb in front of the lobby. Exactly two minutes later, the three assailants dragged Harding past the twisted bodies of the Colombian guards and onto the sidewalk. Julia looked up and down the quiet street, then signaled to the others. The men hustled their prisoner into the back seat of the Mercedes and got in on either side of him. Julia walked calmly to the right front door and got in. She turned around and looked at her prey.

"You wanted to please me, Robert?" She quickly answered her own question. "You have."

A smiling Julia Mendoza uncoiled her softening torso and settled into the seat.

"Diego!" she commanded the driver. "*Vamenos!*"

Chapter 7

Washington

G abriele sat in Carl's truck as they drove slowly along a dirt road
looking for bald eagles. It was late afternoon, a Sunday, and the
stress of the previous week had long since left her. The emotional
paralysis behind her, she felt more and more secure with each passing
day. Soon, she was certain, Carl would ask her to marry him. And
she would accept.

"Carl . . . there he is!" Gabriele pointed to the sky on her right.
"Pass me the binoculars!" He thrust the lenses into her left hand like
a relay racer passing the baton. "He's huge . . . I've never seen anything so impressive! He's coming lower . . . Stop the truck!"

Carl slowed gradually enough so that the dust wouldn't engulf
them, turned off the engine, and leaned over to her side. He could
see the magnificent bird just over Gabriele's left ear. "That's him . . .
Behold our nation's symbol, Gaby . . . and be glad that Benjamin
Franklin didn't get his way."

"What did Franklin have to do with it?" she asked without taking her eyes off the sky.

"He wanted the national bird to be the wild turkey."

She laughed so hard, she lost her fix on the eagle. "America,
saved again by the grace of God. As I recall, that was about the same
time your forebears narrowly missed the opportunity to designate
German as the official language. You people don't know how lucky
you really are."

"We are lucky to count Gabriele Bach as one of us," said Carl with a smile she could feel.

The eagle landed on a bare branch not far ahead. Carl pulled the truck as close as he could. The vehicle was a blind from which to observe, allowing them to talk without disturbing the bird.

"Carl . . . I've never asked you how you got interested in birds." Gabriele rested the binoculars in her lap. "I mean, a macho warrior like you . . ." It was a legitimate question, and she got a legitimate answer.

"It was in the field, Gaby, in Panama. It must have been ten years ago. I sat all night in a jungle ambush site—during an exercise—listening to the howler monkeys. At first light, the forest came alive with birds. They were not aware of my presence because I'd been there so long without moving. I found out later how hard it is to get close to most birds, but that morning they were all around me. Toucans, trogons, manakins . . . everything. Back then, I didn't even know what they were called."

"It sounds like a mystical experience."

"It was . . . but it was more than that," said Carl thoughtfully. "From that day on, I studied birds . . . both in the field and in books. When you're in the jungle, you need all the friends you can get. Birds help me find food and avoid predators. They tell me when someone's coming down the trail. Most importantly, birds show me the way to the beach. Without them, the jungle is a hostile place. With them, it's manageable."

"Now it all makes sense," she responded. "And I have to thank you for opening my eyes, too. I used to look at the world without really *seeing* it . . . and not just birds." She was tearing up again. "Now I can focus on the things that give me pleasure."

"I hope I can be one of those things," said Carl a little self-consciously. *She'd better never find out what I've been doing for the last five years.*

"Carl, dear," she began. "You are the most fascinating and complicated man I have ever met . . . a man of action *and* a thinker . . . a fierce warrior *and* a gentle lover. Do you know how many men out there can be all of those things at once?"

"I never think of other men, Gaby."

"You should! You're so far ahead of the pack, they can't even *see* you, Carl." She sighed. "I am the lucky one in this relationship, believe me."

He drew a deep breath. "Gaby . . . let's go home." He was about to change his life for good, but he couldn't propose to Gabriele in his truck. "I'm taking you to dinner."

He should not have turned on the radio, but listening to the news was a difficult habit to break. They had been rolling along the highway back to Rosslyn, both with visions of how the evening would unfold. He was composing a speech; she was composing a response. Neither had said a word for a long time. As soon as the report came on, Carl realized that all his plans lay in ruins.

"This is ABC News . . . Robert Harding, the US ambassador to Colombia, has been kidnapped from his residence in Bogotá. Two United States Marines and two Colombian guards were killed in the violent attack. As of yet, there are no indications regarding who might be responsible for the abduction, or where the attackers might have taken the ambassador. Harding was last seen at a cocktail party, given at the residence of the Japanese ambassador. The American envoy has spoken out repeatedly against Colombia's drug cartels and the government's ineffective efforts to deal with them. An investigation into the details of the kidnapping has been initiated by both governments. More on this story as it unfolds."

Carl tried not to be shocked. He felt like someone had just kicked him in the stomach. He tried not to look at Gabriele. He wished he was dead. He wanted to stop the car, get out, and shout at the top of his lungs, *You idiot!* Instead, he said, "Damn State Department! How could they let *that* happen?"

"Wow!" said Gabriele. "*Someone* let their guard down."

Carl tried to compose himself. "I need some time to get ready for dinner, Gaby. Can I drop you off at your place and pick you up in an hour?"

He knew there would be a message from Jeff on his answering machine.

"Sure, Carl . . . What should I wear?"

"Something black . . . and a jacket. We'll be outside." He managed a fake smile.

He let her out at the curb and drove to his high-rise. The message was there—lurking in his study like a snake.

"Carl, Jeff . . . I need to see you. I think you know what it's about. Tomorrow. 2 p.m. My place. Bye."

He *needed* to be outside. It was October, but Washington was having a nice Indian summer. The air would allow him to breathe more easily and avoid sweating. He wished he could be more optimistic about the outcome. His whole future now depended on this one dinner.

Carl ushered Gabriele to her seat and took his own. He ordered two glasses of red wine and held her hand under the table. She had indeed worn something black—a long dress that fell from her mother's pearls to a pair of patent leather pumps, cloaked with a black cashmere jacket open at the front. He knew what she expected him to say. He feared she would be wounded twice: once for the disappointment and again for the truth he had withheld. *She'll either understand what I do—and what I* must *do—or never speak to me again.*

They sipped their wine and lingered over the French menus until Carl couldn't stand the suspense any longer. He drew a deep breath and plunged into the conversation he had always known they would eventually have. He'd rather have plunged into the winter surf in northern Europe. He took her hand.

"Gabriele . . . dearest Gabriele," he began. "I want to marry you . . . to spend the rest of my life with you." She was smiling jubilantly, waiting for him to finish. "But . . . there is something I must tell you first."

Her smile vanished. "What is it, Carl?" She sat straight up with her hands folded, fighting the urge to place them over her ears. Bracing for a bad surprise.

Carl braced for the reaction he now expected. "Gaby . . . I didn't stop killing for my country when I got out of the Navy." He rushed through the lines he had rehearsed. "I have operational contracts as well as writing contracts."

"What does *that* mean?"

"It means that I still go in the field when necessary . . . that is, I *used* to go in the field . . . before I met you."

"So you're a *mercenary*?" It was the first time she had ever shouted at him. Another reason to be outside.

"Not exactly, honey," said Carl carefully. "I have never worked for a foreign government. The missions I have taken on for the US government are similar to the ones I would have done in uniform."

"Why didn't you tell me this before?" It was her turn. "Do you realize how this *sounds*?" Gabriele was still shouting. "Why are you telling me this *now*? Why not just keep it to yourself . . . forever?"

The waiter came toward the table and made an abrupt about-face. Gabriele didn't see him. She was too focused on the nightmare unfolding before her eyes.

". . . Unless you plan to *keep* doing this stuff?" she added. "Are you asking me for *permission* to continue killing for money?"

"I'm asking you to marry me, Gabriele . . . but there's one more mission out there . . . I can't get out of it."

"Oh, sure . . . one last round! You can quit anytime. Have you ever lived with a hard-core alcoholic?"

"I'm not addicted to killing, Gaby." He could see that his defense was not going to work. His tone had lost its authority. He was dead.

"Then why on *earth* would you go back in the field, Carl?"

"Because they have the ambassador . . . and the ambassador knows my name, Gaby. If I don't get him out, he'll tell his kidnappers everything . . . and then they'll come after me!"

Gabriele Bach, humanist and borderline pacifist, leaned over the small table and grabbed him by the upper arm, shaking it. "And what about *me,* Carl? Have you put me in danger too?"

He swallowed hard, still in her grip. "As far as I can tell, Gaby, they don't know anything about you."

"And just who are *they*?"

"Probably one of the cartels . . . but it could also be the Colombian government."

"And can you tell me why drug cartels would have anything against *you*?"

Instinctively, Carl glanced behind his back and lowered his voice.

"Because I kidnapped one of their leaders."

"You *what*?"

"I took the biggest monster they have out of the jungle and brought him back here, Gaby. He's responsible for killing hundreds of Americans. Sending me down there was the only way our government could get him. I'm not ashamed of that . . . just sorry I didn't think harder about the consequences."

A step at a time, the waiter came back to take their orders. Gabriele looked up at him and snapped, "Please bring us the check for the wine." When the waiter had gone, Gabriele raised her wine glass.

"A toast, Carl . . . to the *idiot* I almost married." She drained the glass and stood up. "I'll be in the parking lot, looking for a ride home."

Carl left a twenty-dollar bill on the table and followed her out the door. He almost had to run to keep up.

It didn't get any better in the parking lot. Gabriele, now dizzy from chugging her wine, marched around the parked cars, shouting at Carl behind her. She turned around, and he made one more attempt to explain.

"I love you, Gabriele. I hope you can forgive me. We sometimes let the truth out in pieces to protect the people we love. I tried to protect you by withholding the last piece. I held it too long."

Carl liked the way it sounded, but he could see that Gabriele wasn't buying it. "I promise you that whatever happens to your feelings for me, your life will not be in danger." He tried to stroke her hair, but she pushed his hand away.

"I'm taking you home now, Gaby. Please know that I want nothing more from life than to be your husband."

"You're scared to *death* to be my husband!" she shot back.

"No! It's what I *want* . . . I need you, Gaby!"

"You're afraid, Carl . . . but you're not afraid of losing me." Her wild eyes cut right through the façade he had worn for years.

"Of what, then? What else could I be afraid of?"

"An ordinary life!"

It was as if someone had kicked him in the stomach again. She had stripped away all the bullshit and exposed the real Carl Malinowski. His emotions the last two months had been a struggle between the life he *had* and the life he wanted. But he still wasn't sure—after living on the edge for so long—that the life he wanted would be enough. He hadn't even admitted the contradiction to himself. But Gabriele had known intuitively. Instinctively. Carl had known he couldn't have it both ways forever, but now circumstances had taken the decision out of his hands.

Just when he had made it.

"Touché," was all he could manage to say.

He followed her to his truck. This was the end, he knew. She would never talk to him again.

The ten-minute drive to Rosslyn, conducted in complete silence, was the longest of his extraordinary life.

Carl watched her walk away from the curb. He did not take his eyes off her until she disappeared inside. Then he did something he hadn't done in a long time. He cried. It was a man's cry. Like the incoming tide, tears filled his eyes and then ran down his cheeks. As he sat grieving, there was absolutely no sound. He grieved for the ordinary life she had hoped to have with him. He stayed at the curb for a long time. At some point, he put his head down on the steering wheel. Emotionally drained, he went to sleep almost immediately.

A passing car jolted him awake. Disoriented and wounded, he put the truck in gear and drove slowly to the underground garage. He waited there until he had gathered the strength to go upstairs to his lonely bedroom. To the old life he didn't want. Having destroyed the life he wanted, he now tried to focus on what it would take to stay alive. It was probably too late already, but Carl had to do everything he could to prevent Harding's captors from coming after him—and possibly Gabriele.

He raced upstairs and burst into his study. Walking quickly to the desk, he swept it clean with one powerful backhand stroke. As the papers exploded against the wall and drifted to the floor, he realized the significance of what he had just done. In anger, he had wiped the slate clean. He wouldn't need his notes for the FID manual, and after this operation he would not need his old life. He didn't know what his new life would look like, but he knew it would have nothing to do with national security.

But there was work to do. What he needed now was his field experience, his wits, and his men. He picked up the phone and dialed the number for Jerry Tomkins in Virginia Beach.

"Yeah," said the big man.

"Jerry . . . this is Carl. I'm going to need you and the boys up here tomorrow for a two o'clock meeting. I think you know why."

"I think I do, Boss. We've all seen the news. I'll get them rounded up, and we'll be there by noon. Where do you want us to stay?"

"I'll make your reservations at the Key Bridge Marriott . . . adjoining rooms. Check in and then come to my place. I'll be alone. We have a lot of planning to do, and I need all of you here from the beginning this time. Don't bring your gear . . . I want you guys to stage out of Tidewater. Right now, I just need your brains . . . all three of them."

"You got it, Boss. See ya tomorrow." Jerry started to hang up.

"One more thing, Jerry. I need another pair of hands on this one. Not to go with us, but to stay here from now until we come back. I want Forshay, but I can't find his number. Find him and bring him with you . . . you and him in one car, Jose and Billy Joe in another. Don't say anything to Forshay about what you think is going on . . . and don't encourage the others to guess what we'll be doing. Shit . . . I don't even know yet. Got all that?"

"Yeah . . . I'll get Forshay. He's doing corporate security work over in Norfolk. I know where to find him. We'll be there."

He hung up the phone and took a deep breath. Then he dialed another number.

"Jeff, this is Carl," he said into the machine. "I got your message." That, he remembered, had been before dinner. Back when he had control of his life. He hesitated before continuing. "I'll be coming to the meeting tomorrow . . . with three friends. If you don't like that, call me soon." He put down the phone, poured himself two fingers of bourbon, and waited.

The phone rang before he could drain the glass. "Malinowski here," was all he said.

"Carl . . . I can't let you bring anyone else to the meeting," said Jeff without any preliminaries. "You know the rules."

"*Fuck* the rules!" shouted Carl. "If you want me to do something, you grease the skids and make it happen . . . I won't go unless you do."

"Oh, yes, you will, Carl." Jeff spoke without a trace of anger. "When you get over here, you'll see just how much you'll want to go." His voice was almost sweet. "By the way, did you and Gabriele have a nice dinner tonight?"

The CIA has me under surveillance!

"OK, Jeff. You win. I'll come alone." Carl didn't know what Harding had told his captors—he didn't even know who Harding's captors *were*. Seething over his own entrapment, Carl resolved either to rescue the ambassador, or to kill him. He almost didn't care which.

"See you at two, Carl. Bye."

Have they wiretapped my phone too? I really don't care.

The next call was to General Stewart in Panama. Carl needed some useful information, and he could not afford to wait. Stewart would understand. He got called in the middle of the night all the time.

"Stewart," was all he said.

"General . . . this is Carl Malinowski. Sorry to get you up at this hour, but I'm on the hook for something big again." Carl paused in order to give the general a chance to focus. "I need a small favor."

Stewart sat up in bed as if coming to attention. His wife, who was used to her husband's midnight phone calls, rolled over and went back to sleep.

"Anything you need, Carl. Just say the word."

"Sir, I need to talk to the guy who did the NEO survey in Bogotá this year. I've lost track of who you've got doing that stuff. I have a meeting tomorrow after lunch, and I need a morning source . . . if you know what I mean."

Stewart glanced at his wife and spoke in a low tone. "Yes, I know what you mean. The guy you want to talk to is Ron Dozier. As luck would have it, I just sent him up to the Pentagon. He should be at the Joint Staff tomorrow morning . . . early. You can get him in the office of the J3, Special Operations Division. You got that number?"

"Yes, sir . . . I do. What rank is Dozier?"

"He's an Army captain, Carl . . . and the best officer I've seen since you took off your uniform. He briefed the man you're interested in just a month ago. Call Ron and tell him you talked to me."

"Thanks, General. I might call you back on this one . . . back channel, of course."

"Watch your ass, Carl . . . and I don't mean down south."

"Got it, sir. I'll see Captain Dozier in the morning. Out here."

Carl was on the phone to the Pentagon at 0730. He indeed had not slept well, but he was full of energy that had come from somewhere deep inside him. There was a lot to do before the meeting with Jeff. The good thing about the pressure was that it took his mind off Gabriele. Dozier came to the phone less than a minute after the secretary went looking for him.

"Captain Dozier, sir."

"Captain Dozier . . . my name is Carl Malinowski. I used to work for General Stewart . . . He suggested I call you this morning for some information I need. I need it right away, but I can't take it over the phone. I'd like to meet with you."

Dozier did exactly what Carl would have done in response to a mysterious call from a stranger, urging a meeting about something that could not be discussed on the phone. He asked questions. "When do you want to meet?"

"Right now."

"How do I know you talked to my boss, mister . . . did you say your name was . . . Malinowski?"

"That's right . . . and you have every reason to be cautious. I got the general out of bed last night to ask him who briefed in Bogotá

110

last time. He gave me your name and told me to catch you at J3 (SOD) this morning."

"What service are you in?"

"I used to be in the Navy. Call Stewart and ask him about my background . . . but do it quick, man. I don't have a lot of time!"

"He's already in the field by now . . . I can't." Dozier waited for his brain to catch up. "Just give me one good *bona fide*."

Carl paused. "I'm one of the guys who was picked up by your Air Force folks a few months ago in Bolivia. That enough?"

"Yes, sir. That's enough! Where do you want to meet?"

"At the POAC . . . Have you had your run yet?"

"No, but I have my gear with me."

"See you in thirty minutes . . . at the top of the stairs, ready to run."

Carl put down the phone and drove to the huge north parking lot at the Pentagon. The Pentagon Officer's Athletic Club was the only part of the building in which he had ever felt comfortable. It was a perfect day for a run, but Carl wasn't thinking about exercise. This was to be—as they say in the intelligence business—a personal meeting. He walked quickly to the POAC entrance and saw a large man with young legs warming up at the top of the stairs.

"Dozier?"

"Malinowski?"

"Yeah," they said in unison, nodding without smiling. They shook hands warmly, the way military people do, with the implicit recognition of shared sacrifice passing between them. Carl had experienced it so often, he had come to expect it. Perfect strangers became instant brothers. He felt a pang of nostalgia for his uniform and silently cursed the CIA.

"Give me a second to stretch my old legs," joked the retiree. "Was it Ron? My name is Carl, by the way." He sat down on the cold concrete walkway in the pose of a hurdler.

"Yes, I'm Ron . . . and it's your nickel, Carl. I hope I can give you what you need."

Carl looked up at him. "Even if you can't . . . I want you to give General Stewart a message from me . . . OK?"

111

"Absolutely. I'm going back to Panama the day after tomorrow."

"Let's go," said Carl. "We'll do a slow one down to the Lincoln Memorial and back." He turned and ran off without another word. Dozier followed.

In Carl's world there was no such thing as a slow run. Nevertheless, he adjusted the pace so he could talk. He was glad he didn't have to *race* Dozier; the guy was one of those big men who could also run like a deer. Not as big as Butkus, but a good twenty pounds heavier than Carl. A guy who could carry a heavy load in jungle terrain.

"Tell me about your last visit to Bogotá." Carl was pushing the limit of operational security again, but he didn't care. Although he had never confided to Reginald Stewart, the general understood what Carl was doing. Dozier would figure it out in the next ten minutes or so. Neither Stewart nor Dozier would compromise Carl; of that he was sure. They might even be in a position to save his neck.

"I went down with one of my NCOs to do the evacuation survey," Dozier began. "We spent a week with the RSO and then briefed Ambassador Harding. It was pretty routine."

"Did they have major problems with security?"

"Not really . . . I mean, nothing serious. The evacuation plan was pretty good. The ambassador had obviously taken a lot of personal time to refine it." Dozier smiled. "He didn't like my briefing, though."

"How's that?"

"Harding's a real hard-ass. He loves to make military people squirm. I think he has a grudge against us. The guy reminded me at every opportunity how smart and how powerful he is. He insulted General Stewart and lectured me about how he works only for President Ferguson."

"Sounds like a tough cookie," said Carl. "Not the sort of person who would let his guard down."

"Roger that . . . He even pimped me about my name. He asked me if I was related to General Dozier . . . quote, 'that idiot who got himself kidnapped,' unquote!"

"Well, I guess he's eating those words now . . . assuming he's still alive . . . What else can you tell me about Harding?"

"Not much." The captain loped effortlessly along the path. Carl was thinking faster than he was running. "He has a lot of experience in Latin America," Dozier continued. "Very influential here in Washington . . . extremely bright . . . except that he got himself kidnapped, of course."

"There's not a lot of detail out there yet," said Carl. "Anything heard down in Panama?"

"I had a secure PHONECON with one of our guys last night after I heard the news. He told me Harding was seen leaving a party with a young Colombian woman right before he disappeared. Believe it or not, he didn't tell *anyone* before he walked out!"

"State must be covering that up. It'll come out eventually, though. Who's the RSO down there?"

"When I was there, it was a young woman named Laura Jensen. She left about a week ago."

"What's she like, Ron?"

"A hammer . . . a real knockout. Wears expensive clothes and walks like a model. Works out with the Marines. Red hair, long and curly. Likes to be looked at."

"Was she a good RSO?"

"Not bad. I've seen worse. It's just that it's hard to concentrate when you're around her . . . if ya know what I mean."

"I know the type," said Carl. "You said the ambassador worked on the plan himself. That must have put him in close contact with Jensen. Any idea what he thought of her performance?"

Dozier looked at Carl as they ran onto the Memorial Bridge. "I think they were spending a lot of time together, but I don't think it was all about the plan."

"You mean they were having an affair?"

"Yeah, I think so. The way they related to each other in the briefing was strange. She ignored him, and he ignored her. No man can ignore Laura Jensen unless he has a reason to . . . and there was one other thing."

"What's that, Ron?"

"The way she came on to me after I stood up to Harding. I mean . . . she was cool to me all week, but when I went in the ring with the ambassador and didn't get knocked out she suddenly started flirting with me. It had to be something to do with Harding. Nothing else changed."

"I think we know why she left," said Carl. "The question is . . . where did she go? I need to talk to her."

"I heard she got orders to Paris," said Dozier. "If that's true—and she didn't already speak French—then she's probably here in town at the Foreign Service Institute. You could find her with a phone call."

"That would be a lucky break. I'll try and find her today. Now, about that message I want you to take General Stewart . . . and this stays between the three of us, OK?"

"OK. Anything I can do to help . . . you got it."

"Please tell the general that I'll be going south to look for someone, and that I might need a secondary means of extraction. Last time I was in the region, your Pave Low got me out . . . but that was part of the plan from the beginning. This time, my guess is that the US military will be prohibited from supporting us at all. If we get into a jam down there—especially this time—we might not get out. I can't ask him to risk his career, but I *can* ask him to keep track of what's going on. That way, he could be ready to come in quickly if things turn to shit and you guys get the call."

"You want us to make a plan without being tasked," replied Dozier. "We do that every day, Carl. General Stewart will need to know what you're planning so it all dovetails if you need us. I'd say we need a back channel between your organization and mine . . . starting as soon as you find out what they want you to do."

"Exactly. Just tell your boss that's what I need . . . a back channel. We'll work out the details when I get smarter on what they want me to do. By the way, Ron, my organization is just four guys."

"Sounds like you need a liaison officer," said Dozier, grinning.

"Got anyone in mind?" Carl did.

"That'll be up to General Stewart, but I would do it in a heartbeat."

"Ask Stewart if he's willing to break the rules. If he is, tell him I want you for an LNO."

"Thanks . . . I won't let you down."

"I know," said Carl with a smile. "If I had poor judgment I'd have been dead a long time ago. In the meantime, I need to find Laura Jensen."

Dozier gave him a knowing look. "Good luck . . . and be careful!"

Carl looked ahead to the big ugly building now in front of them. He surged ahead of his new friend and tried to recover some of his ego. He sprinted into the parking lot with Dozier still behind him. But Carl had made his move too soon. By the time they got to the POAC stairs, the younger man was waiting for him. As he stumbled by, he noticed that Dozier was bent over, hands on his knees, gasping for air. As he walked off the pain, Carl felt better about his ego. He was also starting to feel better about the mission.

Carl drove back to Rosslyn. He was in a hurry. He hated to be in a hurry. Mistakes were made by people in a hurry. Before getting into the shower, he called the information number at FSI and got the extension for the French Department. Laura Jensen, they informed him, was indeed a student there. They also informed him that he couldn't talk to her until the lunch break.

"It's a family emergency," said Carl. "I must talk to her now. Please do this for me, and I'll have her back in class in just a few minutes." There was unfeigned urgency in his voice.

"OK," came the reply. "I'll get her."

"*Merci,*" said Carl. "I'll wait on the line. It's important that I not miss her."

Carl waited for three minutes. It seemed a lot longer than that. He glanced at the kitchen clock. It was already after ten.

"Hello . . . this is Laura Jensen," said a husky voice.

"Ms. Jensen . . . my name is Carl Malinowski. I'm sorry to bother you in the middle of class, but it's very important that I speak with you . . . and what I have to say cannot be discussed over the phone."

There was a long pause at the other end of the line. "They said it was a family emergency. My parents are both dead, and I don't have any brothers and sisters. I came to the phone because I was curious . . . so let me know what you really want." Even in annoyance, her voice was melodic and soothing.

". . . And I appreciate your coming to the phone," offered Carl. "That saved me a trip to FSI, Laura. I'm a friend of Captain Ron Dozier . . . You worked with him in Bogotá right before you left. I'm working in the same business you are, and I need some information only you can give me."

"I worked with Captain Dozier on the NEO plan for the American embassy in Bogotá . . . Are you in diplomatic security?"

"No, but my goals are the same as yours. I only need a few minutes of your time, Laura. I'd like you to meet me at the Marine Corps Memorial as soon as you break for lunch."

"Why should I meet with you? I don't even know you."

"I'm looking for Ambassador Harding."

There was another long pause, and Carl could tell she was trying to figure out a way to avoid the encounter.

"I can come up there and pick you up," said Carl. "I know FSI pretty well."

"No!" she responded a little too forcefully. "I'll be at the memorial at noon." Laura sighed. "I'm sure Ron told you I have red hair . . . I'll be easy to spot. Where will you be standing?"

"I'll be at the front end of the statue . . . wearing a red necktie and sunglasses. Thank you for making this easy for me." *And for yourself!*

After a shower and a quick breakfast, Carl made another call.

"Key Bridge Marriott," said a pleasant female voice.

"Has Mr. Tompkins checked in yet?" asked Carl.

The receptionist put him on hold and then came back on the line. "Yes, sir . . . Would you like me to connect you?"

"Please."

"Tompkins," said the big man.

116

"Jerry, Carl . . . I need Forshay over at my place right now. You got him?"

"Yeah, Boss. He's here. You wanna talk to him?"

"No. Just bring him over . . . with all his stuff . . . and hurry," instructed Carl. "After that, you and the boys can get some rest . . . You'll need it. I tried to get you into the meeting today, but they refused. I'll brief you guys at the hotel as soon as I get back."

"Got it," said Jerry. "He'll be there in five minutes . . . Out here."

Carl put down the phone and sat on the couch. He had five minutes to think. He knew what he wanted Forshay to do; he just needed to figure out how to tell him. From here on, he knew, each one of his decisions would be critical. Chess had taught him a lot about making decisions—always leave yourself with more options, and never play defense. But he had never played chess with multiple opponents.

And he would have to play defense for someone else.

There was a knock on the door. Carl opened it and had to look to the left to find his old friend, standing to the side out of habit. "Thanks for coming . . . We don't have much time."

Slator J. Forshay stepped into Carl's living room and looked around. "Well, sir . . . this is better digs than last time I saw you!"

"These are your digs now, Forshay . . . until the rest of us get back," said Carl in his lieutenant commander's voice. Everybody called Forshay by his last name. None of his friends had ever known anyone named Slator. "Tell me you can work this out with your other employer."

Forshay owed Carl for saving his life. He agreed without hesitation.

"OK, Carlos . . . give me the mission and then don't worry about it."

"You can start by calling me Carl," said Carlos with a quick smile. "Beer's in the fridge. I'll be right back."

Carl disappeared into the bedroom to look for his red tie. Slator Forshay got himself a Coors and stood in front of the picture window. He realized immediately what an easy target he was and took a

PAUL SHEMELLA

couple of steps back. He was still looking out the window when Carl came out of the bedroom looking like a bureaucrat.

"Nice view of the government you got here," said Forshay.

"Yes, I do," said Carl. "And that government has put me in a box." He paused to consider exactly how to say what he needed. "I'm trying to get out of that box, and you're going to help me." Intrigued, Slator Forshay sat down to learn how.

"The only thing Jerry told me, Boss, was that I wouldn't be going with you guys." Forshay didn't even try to hide his disappointment.

"That's right. I want you to stay here and watch someone for me. The job starts when I walk out of here in a few minutes. You're the best countersurveillance man I know. The details of our mission are still not clear, but I'm sure we'll be leaving soon . . . probably for a couple of weeks. We're going against one of the drug cartels. The bad guys have known my name for some time. Now they know my girlfriend's name. I can take care of myself, but I can't take care of her at the same time. That's now your responsibility."

"What *is* her name, Carl?"

"Gabriele Bach. Born and raised in Germany. Slight accent but very American. You make sure she's safe and sound when I get back."

Forshay was a rather small man without distinguishing characteristics. That's what made him so good at following people. He could simply disappear in a crowd, but he could reappear with the fury of a wildcat. Under his boring exterior he carried the soul of a warrior. During training, Carl had often gone into the bear pit with Forshay and come out bleeding more than once. Like Carl, his friend was a former wrestler. Hand-to-hand combat was fine, but both of them had always fallen back on old habits: get behind your opponent and take him down.

Then go for the throat.

"What does she look like, and where does she live, Boss?"

Carl produced several pictures of Gabriele and handed them to Forshay. "These are all I have. She lives on the other side of Rosslyn in a second-floor apartment and works just a few blocks away at the Foreign Service Institute . . . Here are the addresses."

118

Forshay glanced at the pictures. "Very nice, Carl . . . She'll be easy to track."

"She doesn't leave the city much, but she might go walking in the woods on weekends. You can have my truck as soon as I get back from this meeting."

"When can I meet with her?"

"You can't," said Carl emphatically. "She must not know she's being watched."

"That makes it a lot harder . . . especially in the city. She doesn't even know she's a target, does she?"

"No . . . and hopefully she never will." Carl stopped pacing for a second. "One more thing, Forshay . . . in case you haven't figured it out. I'm a much bigger target than Gabriele Bach. They'll probably come after you, thinking you're me."

"I figured it out." Forshay looked Carl in the eye. "That's not a problem."

"You get half of my share for this. That's twenty-five grand. If she's dead when I get back, you get nothing."

"OK . . . and if I'm dead but she's alive," Forshay added, "take some of my half and pay for the wake . . . on the beach . . . all night . . . just like the old days."

"You got it," pledged Carl. "And . . . Slator," he added. "Thanks."

"Let's *all* survive," said Forshay. "Then let's have that party on the beach anyway. That's the only chance I'll have to meet your girlfriend!"

Carl looked at his watch. "Gotta go. I'll be with Jerry and the guys at the hotel if you need me." Carl left Forshay to work out his tactics. He had no doubt the man would make it to the party on the beach. Even though Gabriele wouldn't be there, at least she'd be alive.

It was the least he could do.

Chapter 8

Rosslyn

C arl walked to the Marine Corps Memorial, only a quarter mile from his condo. He wanted to get there before Laura arrived—if she came. If she didn't, he had just enough time to go to FSI and find her. But that wouldn't be a very good place to talk. And he didn't want to run into Gabriele. Not under those circumstances. He forced himself to avoid thinking about her. His brain had enough to do, preparing for meetings with Laura and Jeff, then planning the mission he expected to receive.

He went to the front of the huge bronze statue and sat down on the low wall that defined the perimeter of the sacred ground. He looked up at the Marines planting the American flag. Only one of the faces was exposed to him—a helmeted hero, looking at the future he suddenly realized he would have after all. There was no smile. No visible sign of triumph. The man was exhausted. Then there were the hands, five pairs, all grasping the flagpole. *What happened to teamwork?* Beneath the rocks and boots were the places and dates of battles and wars fought by other Marines. Carl stared straight into the stone and read, "Mexico 1846–1848." *From the halls of Montezuma . . .* Another difficult American neighbor, he thought. *Will Colombia find its way onto this wall?* He looked over his shoulder and checked to see if the Washington Monument was still there.

Carl looked at his watch. Almost noon. He peered around the left side of the statue, and there she was. He walked all the way around marble base, watching her from behind. Despite his anxiety, he enjoyed it. *Nicole Kidman's sister, but with better shoulders.* The earth-tone sweater gave her hair the same color as the brightest red leaf on the fall trees. Laura was not as tall as Gabriele, but she looked taller than she was. It wasn't just the boots. She reminded him of a cheetah on the African plain, raising her head above the grass, hunting. Looking for *him.* She backtracked and almost bumped into him.

"Thank you for coming, Laura." Carl had to force himself not to smile.

"Carl!" Laura Jensen was not used to being surprised. "I didn't see you," she said with the same husky voice he'd listened to on the phone.

His eyes darted quickly from the flaming hair to the face. An interesting face. No . . . a fascinating face. Scandinavian features softened by a hint of freckles. A surgeon had pouted her lips, but Carl could see that Laura had sculpted the body all by herself. Standing erect, with a slight arch of the back, she seemed to be offering him her small breasts, perfectly outlined in fine wool. Six months ago, he would have reacted differently. Now, he had a job to do.

"Care for a walk, Laura?" Carl gestured toward the Netherlands Carillon, and she fell in beside him. "We don't have much time, so I'll get right to the point." He stopped walking and looked right at her. "I will be involved in getting Ambassador Harding back, and I need any information you might have on his personality, habits, idiosyncrasies . . . that type of thing. When I go after someone, it's the little things that count."

"Why don't you talk to his wife?" The red lips were pursed, and he realized she had not yet smiled. Carl was surprised at how nervous she was.

"Good question." They were walking again. "First of all, I didn't want to shake her up any more than she already is. Secondly, you have a higher clearance than Mrs. Harding. Finally, my interest is not so much what kind of husband he is, but what he might do in captivity, how he might react when the shooting starts." Carl glanced at Laura again. "I understand his wife wasn't with him in Bogotá. I don't even know where she is."

"She's here in Washington. Her name is Norma."

"I'd rather talk to you, Laura." He studied her as they walked, trying to keep his eyes on her face.

"I don't have much to tell you," said Laura, not quite convincingly.

"What you know might be more significant than you think. For instance, I need to know what kind of shape the ambassador is in . . . If he's in good condition, then I can take him out on foot. If he's not, I might need to carry him. Did he work out, or run . . . or anything?"

"He's in terrible shape. I never saw him use the gym, and I would not have allowed him to run on the streets of Bogotá." She spoke carefully, but Carl sensed momentum and pressed.

"Would he have listened to you? Dozier tells me Harding doesn't like to listen to anyone."

"The ambassador is a very important man . . . He's used to giving orders. But he would listen to me as the RSO. I kept him out of trouble . . . That's more than I can say about my replacement." Laura avoided Carl's eyes by looking down at the asphalt path.

"How do you think he'll react when we take down his captors?" Carl still had no idea who Harding's kidnappers were . . . or *where* they were.

"He's a coward," said Laura without hesitation. "He'll probably start babbling." She looked at Carl, smiled ironically, and continued. "Powerful men, when deprived of their power, are nothing. I suspect the ambassador has been reduced to nothing." Laura's smile dissolved in the acid of her tone.

"So you don't think he'll be of any use to us on the way out?"

"Not at all . . . I don't envy you, Carl." She stopped, leaned in, and looked at him. "Who *are* you, anyway?"

"I said I was a friend of Ron Dozier. That's all you need to know, Laura."

"I think I already know more than you want me to."

Carl felt a pit in his stomach and braced for heavy rolls.

"What could you possibly know about me, Laura?"

"I know that you went to Brazil and kidnapped the drug lord Mena."

He was stunned! *How could she have known that? If* she *knows, who else knows?* Carl caught his breath on its way out of his throat and said calmly, "Really?"

"Really!" All of a sudden, she was beaming. "I was in on the planning of that operation, and . . . I have to say . . . it was hard for me to imagine anyone daring enough to challenge the cartel on its own turf . . . yet here you are!"

Laura was still smiling like a schoolgirl, but Carl was on the verge of panic. Jeff had told him his name was on Harding's lips; now it was on Laura's.

"Was it normal to bring the RSO into an operation as sensitive as that one?" asked Carl carefully. "There were only a few people in Washington who knew."

"The whole thing was Harding's idea from the beginning," said Laura with a certain pride. "He brought me into it because he needed someone to bounce his ideas off."

"Did he bounce those ideas off you in the office . . . or in bed?"

Laura hesitated just long enough to confirm what they both knew. "What makes you think I would sleep with a creep like Harding? He was too old, too fat, and too married."

"He was the ambassador . . . and he was in a position to help you get whatever you wanted, Laura." Carl put both his hands in his pockets as he became more agitated. "Don't tell me you got to be the RSO in Paris at age twenty-eight because of your distinguished record! Just don't try to bullshit me, OK?" He was almost shouting, but Laura didn't seem intimidated.

"OK, Carl . . . no bullshit." Stoic again, she continued. "I had an affair with him. We worked closely on a lot of issues . . . not just your Brazil escapade. He needed someone to talk to. He was lonely. You know, it isn't easy being a powerful man in a small organization. Everyone was afraid of him . . . except me. He needed *me* . . . not the other way around. I felt like I was doing the country a service by letting him share his thoughts with me." Laura's speech should have sounded defensive, but it didn't.

"What other thoughts did he share with you? Anything I might find interesting before I go save his miserable skin?" Carl's panic had given way to a slow-burning anger. If Harding had given Carl's name to Laura, it was just a matter of time before he told his captors. Maybe he already had.

"He told me that CIA wanted to make sure you didn't go public with the Mena thing. He said you would stay quiet if you felt threatened."

"That just proves he doesn't understand military people . . . We consider keeping secrets a solemn obligation."

"There's one more thing you need to worry about, Carl." Now she looked sincere and sympathetic. She was actually wincing.

"What could be worse than telling the cartel my name and where I live?"

"Telling them about Gabriele Bach."

If Laura had kicked him in the groin at that moment he wouldn't have felt a thing. He had known intuitively that Gabriele might be in danger; he forced himself to believe that Forshay could protect her.

But the rules had changed again.

Carl swallowed hard. "Thank you," was all he managed to say. Laura took his hand in both of hers.

"I'm sorry, Carl. Is there anything I can do to help you?"

"No, Laura. You've already helped me enough. Now I need to get that bastard out of the jungle before he gets us all killed. Good luck in Paris. I've got work to do."

Carl withdrew his hand from hers and turned to go. Then he stopped and looked at her again. "Why did you tell me all this, Laura? I mean . . . you don't even know me. Do you still have feelings for Harding?"

"I don't have any feelings for Harding, Carl. He used me as much as I used him. I want you to get him back because of what the kidnappers did to Valdez and Belcher. They were my guys, and they were murdered." Laura paused, suppressing emotions she had not revealed. "I'm also afraid for your girlfriend. I knew when I heard the news that you were both in danger."

"So you just waited until I contacted *you?*"

"The news broke only yesterday . . . and you're not exactly easy to find. Even though I knew that Gabriele works at FSI, I couldn't just walk up to her and start this conversation. And when we met just now . . . I wanted to listen to you first. Forgive me for being cautious."

Carl made a quick decision to forgive her. "I appreciate your concern. Now I need to run . . . literally."

"Take this," said Laura, handing him a business card. "If you need any more help, call me." All the traces of hardness had left her face, revealing a wholesome beauty he hadn't seen before.

"OK, Laura." Carl smiled imperceptibly as he put the card in his pocket. "What should I do with Harding when I bring him back?"

"Make him live with his wife, Carl. That'll do it for me!"

They laughed loudly. Laughter helped vent the pressure that was building inside his chest. The pressure of fear he could never reveal. Merciless fear—and the weakness it brought—would come back to torment him. And he knew he wouldn't have a woman to laugh with anymore. He turned away from her again, started walking fast, and then broke into a slow run.

Jeff sat next to him at the large round table. Two others, face-less men he did not know, sat ninety degrees to either side. A third nondescript man was at the whiteboard in front of them. The room was too cold and too bright. Carl had only a blank notebook and a couple of pens. He knew he was being filmed. He shifted in the chair and rubbed his hands together in his lap. He was nervous, sad, and angry . . . all at the same time. He was on defense. He hated to be on defense. He was looking for someone to attack. Anyone.

"Welcome, Carl," Jeff began. "This is Robert. He will brief you on the situation, giving you as much information as we have. Admittedly, that is not much." He gestured to his left and continued. "Then George here will explain the mission and the concept of the operation." Jeff shifted his gesture to the right. "Then Walter will go over the logistics plan, as well as Command and Signal." Carl nod-ded without expression to all three men. Jeff looked at Robert again. "Let's begin, shall we?"

"As you know from the news," said Robert, "Ambassador Robert Harding has been kidnapped from his residence in Bogotá,

Colombia. The kidnappers killed two Colombian guards and two American Marines in the action and got away clean. We know that one of the kidnappers is a woman, and we know she entered the residence with two male accomplices. We do not know the gender of the person who drove them away. Neither do we know who any of these people are." Robert paused long enough to take a breath and Carl jumped on him.

"Are you telling me that CIA has no idea who did this?"

"That's right," responded Robert in the same monotone that gave Carl the impression the man wanted to be somewhere else. "We have no hard evidence. The ambassador left a party at the Japanese ambassador's residence in the company of a young Latina. Everyone who saw her accomplices up close is dead."

"Does anyone know if the woman speaks English?" Carl was not going to make this easy for any of them. He was annoyed that he had to ask such a basic question.

"Yes. One of the people interviewed said she heard them speaking English just before they left."

"What were they saying?" asked Carl. "Did this person hear anything at all?"

"No, sir. Nothing . . . but the source did say that the woman was dressed provocatively and that she was obviously flirting with the ambassador."

"Why am I not surprised?" Carl asked himself out loud.

"Carl. Let Robert get to the end of his pitch. Then we can all discuss what we know and what we don't know," Jeff interjected. "Go ahead, Robert."

"There is speculation, of course," Robert continued, "that the government of Colombia is behind the abduction. Specifically, the ambassador had been putting President Solano under a lot of pressure regarding his alleged criminal ties. He had avoided accusing Solano of cooperating with the Espinoza Cartel, but Harding's criticism had fueled much public speculation and media interest."

"In this country too," interrupted Carl.

"Yes. The columnist Paul Henning has been particularly scathing in his editorials on that line of reasoning. This agency feels that

Solano got tired of hearing such speculation and may have asked Espinoza to take Harding out of the picture."

"Only if Solano was actually being hurt by the accusations," challenged Carl.

"There is some evidence that he was, and is, being hurt—at least within the international financial institutions that keep his economy afloat. It is true, on the other hand, that the Colombian people have rallied around Solano the last several months. We expected that. They are quite nationalistic and, having elected Solano, they almost don't have a choice."

"I know the Colombians well," said Carl. "They will side with their own leaders every time. I don't understand why Ambassador Harding didn't understand that."

Jeff glared at Carl. "Go on, Robert."

Carl spoke up again. "Where have they taken the ambassador?"

"We don't know for sure, but there are reports that they put him on a plane and flew him out right after the abduction."

"What *kind* of plane, Robert?"

"We have one sighting of a small propeller plane . . . We're checking the airports within range of such a plane now. Some of us think Harding is still in Bogotá. We're working all our sources to pinpoint his location."

"Yeah . . . both of them! Look . . . if they wanted to hide him in the jungle, it would make sense to fly him away in a Cessna. Clandestine airstrips in the south are not exactly designed for Learjets. Does Southern Command have the AWACS up?"

"Yes, they do . . . but there is no track that corresponds to the time frame during which they would have flown Harding out of the capital."

"Assuming it was Espinoza's men, they probably flew low-level, stopping to refuel a couple of times along the way. The government doesn't own much of the territory between Bogotá and Peru." Carl sat forward even more. "What else did they steal besides the ambassador . . . any papers, that sort of thing?"

Robert looked at him sheepishly. "Actually, it looks like they got everything in Harding's personal safe." With well-concealed alarm, Carl let that disclosure sink in. "We don't know what he had in there," continued Robert. "I don't suspect the ambassador would have kept classified documents at his residence."

"You didn't suspect he would leave with the party with a complete stranger and not tell any of his staff!" Carl's Italian side had finally kicked in; he was now talking with his hands. "Just a comment."

"Your comment is accurate, sir. Ambassador Harding took an astonishing risk for a seasoned professional."

"Can you tell me why the bad guys went home with the ambassador before they kidnapped him? I mean, why didn't they just drive him to the airfield after putting him in the woman's car?" Carl then answered his own question. "They must have known there was something important in that safe, or they wouldn't have risked a forced entry."

"We hadn't thought about that."

"I suggest you do . . . and try to find out what Harding's safe may have contained."

"Good idea, Carl," interjected Jeff. "We'll run that down. Let's move on, Robert."

"That's all we have at this time, Jeff. That being the case, I'll yield the floor to George."

George stood up and walked to the board. He was not quite the geek that Robert was, and Carl suspected that, unlike the others, George had some field experience under his belt.

"Good morning, Mr. Malinowski. Your mission will be to infiltrate southern Colombia and link up with elements of the Colombian Marine Corps. In company with the Marines, you will perform reconnaissance of the border area with Ecuador and Peru. You will report your findings to our office on a predetermined schedule. This is a reconnaissance-only mission. I repeat—recon only. You are not to engage any targets unless you are required to defend yourself and your men. If you locate the ambassador, you are to report his position to us and set up a surveillance regime. Under no circumstances are you authorized to rescue Harding yourselves. We have contacted the leadership of the Marines—but not the civilian authorities—and arranged for you to come into the country through Ecuador. As you probably know, the Colombian Marines are engaged in fighting narcotics traffickers along the Putumayo River and its tributaries. We have notified the Ecuadorans, and you should not be opposed on that side of the border. I believe you know the officer in charge of the Marine riverine force, Major Luis Corvalán Perez."

"I trained him and most of his men," said Carl, looking right at George. "Major Corvalán is the best officer I have ever worked with in Latin America. Both his parents were murdered by the cartel, and he inherited a flower-growing fortune. Corvalán harbors a personal hatred for the traffickers and cannot be bribed. Also, I like him personally."

"Good. I can see we're on the same page here," said George. "Do you know a river outpost called Tipishca?"

"I spent some time there in my previous life. It used to be an Ecuadorean riverine base—until the Ecuadorans were ambushed by the FARC. Tipishca is on the San Miguel River. I remember we drove there from Quito."

"That's the place where Corvalán has been instructed to pick you up. The linkup is scheduled for Friday at midnight."

Carl had to look at his watch. It was Monday. He would have to hustle to get there. He hated to prepare a mission in haste. "That doesn't give us much time. I need to talk to my men . . . but before we get to the log plan, I have just one other question."

"Shoot, Carl."

"How do we get out of there?"

"Corvalán will deliver you back to Tipishca. You'll have a car staged there . . . or you can call the embassy to come and get you."

"That's not what I mean, George. I want to know who gets us out if the situation turns brown . . . if we get compromised and have to fight our way out."

"Your security will be the responsibility of the Colombian Marine Corps . . . You said you have great confidence in Major Corvalán."

"That's not the same thing as having the 82nd Airborne on alert."

George looked at him with empathy that confirmed Carl's suspicion that the man was an operator. "We have to keep the US military out of Colombia on this one, Carl . . . at least until we're sure who has the ambassador and where they have him."

"Yeah . . . I got that, but I don't like it," replied Carl. "I'll take my chances with Corvalán."

"Sorry, Carl, but that's the best we can do."

Walter got up and limped to the board. "We will deliver the weapons you need to the US embassy in Quito via diplomatic pouch on Thursday . . . As you've already heard, there will be no logistics support beyond that." Walter leaned against the board and waited for Carl's tirade. It did not come. He breathed a visible sigh of relief. "What do you want, Mr. Malinowski?"

Carl stood and walked around the table to where Walter was propping himself up. "Here's a list of weapons, ammunition, pyrotechnics, and specialized equipment we'll need. There are also two SATCOM radios on here, with crypto."

Walter looked up from the paper in his hand. "This is a lot of stuff—especially for a simple reconnaissance."

"There's no such thing as a simple reconnaissance."

"I didn't mean to suggest it would be easy, Mr. Malinowski."

"Don't fight me on this," said Carl evenly. "If I don't get everything on that list by Thursday night, we don't go in." He turned around to make sure Jeff was listening. They all nodded.

"What about the communications schedule?" asked Carl. "How often do you want me to check in?"

"In accordance with the execution checklist or every night at midnight, your time."

Carl stroked his chin for effect. "I'll try and make that, gentlemen. If you don't hear from me, you'll know I'm extremely busy doing something else."

After surrendering his truck to Forshay, Carl took a cab to the Marriott. He got out and walked to the front desk. It was an effort not to run. At times like this, when panic waited at the edge of his consciousness, he had to force himself to walk slowly. Like an exhausted running back returning to the huddle, he knew he would carry the ball again soon. But Carl had no blockers, and he was about to run into a dark tunnel to look for an oncoming train. He had a lot of thinking to do; walking slowly helped him concentrate.

"I have a reservation, miss." He didn't even make eye contact with the pretty girl behind the counter.

"Good afternoon, sir! Your name?"

"Carl Malinowski. I should be in the room next to Mr. Tompkins."

The young woman punched the computer and smiled at him. "Yes, sir . . . you're all set. Mr. Tompkins paid me cash for your first night. Here is your key card . . . Have a nice stay!"

Carl thanked the girl but could not muster the goodwill to smile back at her. He dragged a heavy sports duffel to the elevator and went to the top floor. He dropped the bag in his room, looked longingly at the comfortable bed, and went back into the hallway. Jerry's doorknob had a "Do Not Disturb" sign on it. He knocked.

The big man opened the door quickly, as if he'd been standing behind it all day, waiting. He took Carl's hand and practically pulled him inside. Billy Joe and Jose were in the room. Before he shook hands with them, he noted with pleasure that the hotel room had been converted into a planning cell. The bed had been broken down and moved against the far wall. A large table, procured from the hotel staff, had been placed in the center of the room, with chairs and lamps around it. His men had maps and papers all over the table, with cups of coffee at each corner. Jerry handed Carl a steaming cup and a pencil.

"We're ready to put the plan together, Boss," announced Jerry. "Welcome to our hootch away from home!"

Carl sat down and let out the breath it seemed he had been holding since the briefing at Langley. "I wish I had more information for you to plan with, guys . . . Here's the sum total of what the Company gave me." And he proceeded to fill them in.

His men asked him the same questions Carl had asked his briefers. He gave them better answers, using their concerns to build the outline of a plan. He covered their departure from Virginia, the transition to Quito, the drive to Tipishca, the linkup with Corvalán, and the characteristics of the operations area (which they already knew). He also told them they would have to come out the same way they went in. They reacted the same way Carl had—it was a recipe for ambush. For now, however, it was the only option available. What upset them most was the prohibition against actually rescuing Harding . . . but they trusted Carlos to adjust the rules if necessary when the time came.

Carl was not happy with the lack of support, but he was used to it. He had already given himself the option of rescuing Harding. He did not like the order to find the American, and then just hang around to watch. Carl and his men, as always, would do whatever they needed to do. What his briefers did *not* know, because they had never been on a jungle river themselves, was that riding around in boats—even at night—would be like walking into a bar full of drug traffickers and guerrillas to ask for the American ambassador's new address. They would be seen, and word would travel faster than the current.

He got his men started on the plan and went to his room while they worked. It was almost six when he dialed into his home phone to check messages. There were two: one from Ron Dozier and one from Laura Jensen. Carl didn't believe in coincidence; he had wanted to talk to each of them.

"Carl, this is Ron. I talked to General Stewart. He says you need an LNO and I'm it. That's all I can say here. Where do you want me and when?" Carl nodded vigorously and listened to the next voice mail.

"Carl, this is Laura. I was thinking that you might need more information on my old boss. Maybe we could do that over dinner somewhere. Call me if you can make it tonight. The number is 777-1452. I'll be home."

He hung up the phone and sat looking out across the Potomac. He was feeling the pressure. He needed a way to release it, so he dialed another number.

"This is Gabriele Bach. I'm not home right now. Please leave a message so that I may call you back."

He wasn't sure what to say to the machine. She had told him not to call her. Actually, it had been an order. And she had not called *him*. Her outburst at the restaurant had been delivered with thought as well as emotion. It was the finality of her tone that had convinced him it was a clean break. Still, he had wanted to try one more time. Beyond his obligation to protect her from his enemies, Carl realized there was nothing he could do. It wasn't the first relationship he had blown, but he knew it was the last time he would allow himself to fall in love.

So he just hung up. After a few deep breaths, he picked up the phone again and called his LNO. He could see from the number that Ron was already back in Washington.

"Dozier."

"Ron . . . this is Carl. I got your message. Be at the Key Bridge Marriott tomorrow morning at eight. I will leave a note for you at the front desk."

"Got it, Boss . . . See you then."

There was one more call to make. He stared at the phone for a while. He looked out the window a while longer. Then he dialed the number.

"Hello."

"Laura . . . this is Carl."

"Carl! How nice of you to call back! I hope everything is going well at your end." The husky voice soothed his fraying nerves. Instead of the tension he'd anticipated, he felt an immediate sense of calm. He imagined her face at the other end of the line and began to relax.

"Can you meet me at *Casa Tampico* on Glebe Road in one hour?" The restaurant would be crowded, and far enough away from Rosslyn. "That's the noisiest place I can think of."

"Sure," said Laura, "but if you want to talk without anyone hearing us we could do it here . . . As far as I know, this place isn't bugged." He could not see her smiling, but he knew she was.

"I'm very hungry, Laura . . . and I have to work all night."

"How much time do you have?"

"That depends on what you have to tell me."

"I have a lot to tell you, Carl."

133

"I'll be at a corner table in the back of the restaurant. Do you need the address?"

"I can find it . . . See you there."

"Thanks, Laura." He hung up and looked out the window again. The leaves were turning. A seductive interlude before the menace of winter.

Five minutes later, he went to Jerry's room to check on his men. They were making progress on the preliminary plan and would not need him until around midnight. Carl gave them a few more pieces of guidance and dismissed himself. There was no point in looking over their shoulders; he had the best planners in the business. And he had other things to do.

Carl stood in the shower, thinking about all that had transpired. How quickly his life had changed. Yesterday, he had been enjoying the birds of Virginia with Gabriele, dreaming of a suburban house with a white picket fence; today he was a hired gun with a dangerous mission, about to have dinner with a beautiful stranger. The hot water could not lift the depression from his shoulders. He was angry—with himself, with Jeff, and, selfishly, with Gaby. Carl was capable of major mood swings. One minute he could be the animated Italian, shouting and gesturing, just happy to be alive. The next minute he could be the melancholy Pole, just waiting for the next oppressor to overrun his dangerously flat homeland.

He was in a Polish mood.

Carl closed his eyes and stuck his head back under the spray. He visualized himself in the jungle. He saw the river, and the trees, and the birds. Then he saw a muzzle flash. He could actually feel the sting in his shoulder. But it wouldn't be that simple this time. He would die in the vast rainforest of southern Colombia, without honor and without anyone to mourn him. He turned off the water and got out of the shower to towel off. This hired gun, he said to himself, would at least go out in a blaze of glory.

He took a cab to the restaurant and found it suitably crowded. He slipped the young waiter a ten-dollar bill to seat him at a corner table and sat down to wait for her. He was nursing an iced tea when Laura came through the door. She looked around, saw his hand waving, and walked toward the table wearing a big smile. Carl had never seen a sexier walk. Laura was modeling a light gabardine trench coat, curly red hair spilling over her shoulders. She reminded Carl of a glamorous spy right out of Hollywood.

"Hello, Carl. Mind if I join you?"

"You're right on time, Laura . . . please." He was trying not to smile, but he couldn't help it.

He helped her take off the coat and found himself staring at a suede leather miniskirt that seemed to cover only the upper part of her thigh. He folded the coat carefully and sat down across from her. A large emerald glittered just above the top of her blouse. Resting on pure white skin, the stone matched her eyes. *Hush money from the ambassador?*

"I learned it from the Marines . . . to be on time, that is."

"I appreciate that . . . Do you mind if we order right away? I'm on a schedule."

He ordered food and wine while Laura watched him. "I hope you're not in *too* much of a hurry, Carl. This is already the most fun I've had since I got to Washington."

Carl got right down to business. "What else can you tell me about Harding?"

"He kept all the plans for the Mena abduction in his quarters," said Laura evenly. "It occurred to me this afternoon that the safe might have been opened by the kidnappers . . . Why else would they go into the residence? If that is what they did, then everything is in their hands."

"Well, that's what they did, Laura. You should work over at Langley, you know. What *exactly* was in that safe?"

"All the notes from our discussions about your mission in Brazil. Harding had classified cables from Washington detailing the whole thing. There was enough in that safe to get President Ferguson and half his cabinet fired!"

"Or get me killed."

"And Gabriele, Carl . . . By the way, I saw her at the institute this afternoon. She looked terrific . . . Lucky you."

Carl felt his heart being ripped from his body. All at once, he feared for his own life, worried about Gabriele's safety, lamented the loss of her love, and wondered why she looked so good the day after breaking up with him. With so much on his mind, he just let it slip out.

"My luck ran out, Laura. She left me."

Laura reached for his hand across the table. "I didn't know, Carl . . . I'm sorry."

"It's OK. I didn't deserve her anyway. She found out what I really do for a living. She didn't like it."

"Well, *I* like it, Carl . . . I think you're the bravest man I've ever met."

Laura had never been in love before, so it took her a moment to realize why she suddenly felt so good. She guessed she'd been with dozens of men in her ten years of womanhood, but Carl, who had not shown the slightest interest in her, was altogether different. She wanted him badly.

Carl's heart popped off like a red star cluster. He took a furtive deep breath, squeezed her hand and, trying to recover, withdrew his own. "Thanks for the vote of confidence, Laura. Right now I need all the help I can get. What else can you tell me?"

They continued while Carl slowly ate his burrito. He had a lot of questions; she had a lot of answers. In fact, he found that Laura had a keen mind and a very good memory. She picked at her salad and sipped wine. Carl tried to ignore the curve of her shoulder and the tight little muscle that formed in her upper arm every time she bought the glass to her lips. He couldn't. As soon as he finished his meal, he told himself, he would need to break contact and get back to work.

Without warning, Laura changed the subject. "I've been sitting here wondering where you got your Latin features, Carl Malinowski." She placed her elbows on the table and playfully rested her chin on her hands. She looked more like a cuddly house cat than a prowling cheetah. *So much for breaking contact!*

"My mother was Italian," explained Carl.

"My mother was Irish."

They both laughed. The planning cell could wait a few more minutes.

"Have you ever been married, Carl?"

"Once," he replied cautiously. "It didn't work."

"Any children?"

"No," he said rather less cautiously. "Sometimes I regret that . . . and sometimes I'm glad. It's complicated, but as a professional leader, I feel I missed the ultimate leadership challenge—parenting."

"You probably won't believe this," Laura said with conviction that startled both of them, "but I'm starting to feel that settling down and having children would make me happier than anything."

"It happens to most people . . . sooner or later," said Carl thoughtfully. To his surprise, a warm current flooded every inch of his skin. This woman, he realized, was actually serious. It made him think twice about his own situation . . . and that made him uncomfortable again. The mixture of physical beauty and honesty was almost more than he could take.

He shifted gears quickly. "Ah . . . thanks for all the help on Colombia . . . and Harding. Better intelligence will get me closer to bringing this guy back. Then I think I'll be looking for a new line of work . . . I'm getting too old for this stuff."

"Just make sure you come back, Carl. I owe you a dinner . . . in a place less noisy than this."

"Now I *have* to come back!" he said with a sudden burst of humor. He watched her smile disappear momentarily.

"Do you have time to see my etchings before you go?" Laura looked at him seriously to emphasize the invitation, then grinned and fluttered her eyelashes to make him laugh again.

Carl looked into her game green eyes, imagined running his hands all over her toned body . . . and mustered every ounce of will-power he possessed.

"Not now . . . maybe when I get back . . . if I get back." And he began again to close the grim curtain of sorrow Laura had pried open.

"You'll come back, Carl. And I'll be here when you do."

Carl left the restaurant and walked quickly around the corner. He hailed another cab and rode back to the Marriott thinking about Laura. It wasn't until he walked into the lobby that he was able to concentrate on the plan. He got on the elevator as a vulnerable man torn between thoughts of two women; he got off as a warrior ready to fight men he didn't know for ideals he no longer understood. He was more comfortable getting off. He would find Harding and let the chips fall where they may. Jerry opened the door and Carl went to work.

"They know everything," he said to the group. "They got the contents of the safe in Harding's quarters . . . and I just found out that's where he had all the plans, notes, and cables on the Mena snatch. We have to do more than find Harding for the boys at Langley . . . We have to get whoever grabbed him, or we're fucked."

Billy Joe was the first to speak. "You think those assholes are gonna send hit men after us, Boss?"

"*Sicarios*," Jose interrupted. "Yeah, they'll send *sicarios* to take us out when we're not looking. Those guys are just cruel. Young men here work at McDonald's. In Colombia they ride around on motorcycles and shoot people."

"Guess we'll have to get 'em first," said Jerry without expression. "Bring it on."

Carl looked at them one at a time. "Listen to me. The Company says our mission is recon only, but this is a whole new ball game. Fuck CIA. We're going to grab the ambassador . . . then we're going to shoot our way out."

They all nodded. Kill or be killed. It was pretty easy to understand.

"Who told you, Carlos?" asked Billy Joe. "About the files, I mean."

"I just talked to Harding's former RSO. She was in on all the planning."

"A *chick?*"

"That's right," said Carl with a flash of anger. "A *smart* chick who just might have saved our lives!"

Jerry looked at Carl and started to ask him a question, then scratched his head and studied the floor. There was something in the atmosphere of the small room that had not been there when he left. The big man looked at him again, but Carl interrupted him before he could speak.

"What's on your mind, Jerry?" Carl could feel the leadership being sucked out of him.

"Boss . . . the guys and me . . . we were wondering what Forshay is doing up here. Can you tell us anything about that?"

"What you mean to ask is . . . how much is he getting paid . . . and is it coming out of your pocket?" Carl shot back. "Isn't that right?"

"Well . . . yeah. It's not that we don't want him in on this. We just want to know what you've promised him. We trust you, Boss. We just want to know."

"He gets half my share . . . You guys get all of yours. Anything else?"

"No, sir," said Jerry sheepishly. "I just wanted to clear the air before we all go downrange."

"Forshay will be staying here. He'll be protecting a friend of mine whose name was also in the safe." Carl hesitated and then added, "I should have mentioned it sooner . . . I've had a lot on my mind. Thanks for bringing it up."

The others nodded up and down, thankful that Jerry had had the courage to challenge the boss. If there was one way to get Carlos angry, they all knew, it was to give him the impression they didn't trust him. Now they were ready to move on. There was a mission to execute.

They worked far into the night and, when Carl was satisfied with their progress, everybody got a few hours' sleep. Jerry slept on the floor of the planning cell; Jose and Billy Joe used the twin beds. Carl went back to his room on the other side of the wall. At precisely eight o'clock the next morning, Ron Dozier knocked on Carl's door, waking him up. It wasn't that he'd forgotten about Dozier; Carl was simply exhausted. He went to the door and motioned his LNO into the room.

"Looks like you worked late, Boss. Can I make you some of that lousy coffee on the counter?"

"Thanks, Ron." Carl managed a smile. "After I get my heart started we'll go next door and introduce you to the boys. Have a seat while I shower . . . and read this." He tossed the preliminary plan on the bed.

Ron looked happy to be there, and it made Carl feel good to have him. He still wasn't sure how he would use him in the field, but Captain Dozier was a lifeline to General Stewart. The only lifeline they had.

After Carl got cleaned up, they went over the draft, with Dozier asking good questions—for which Carl did not have all the answers. He had arranged with Jerry to resume work at nine. He ate a couple of PowerBars and washed them down with the last of the coffee. They went next door. As they waited for Jerry to let them in, Carl looked up and down the hallway. He saw nothing and heard nothing. He wished he'd given the front desk a false name, but there was nothing he could do about it now. They would be gone tomorrow.

"Good morning, frogs," he announced at the door. His men were seated at the table, drinking their own lousy coffee. They stood when Carl entered the room.

"Please . . . guys . . . what am I, the pope?" Carl looked at them with pride. "This is Captain Ron Dozier from SOCSOUTH. He's Special Forces, with experience in Colombia. The captain will be an attachment to our patrol and a link to General Stewart for this mission—a link that can never be revealed to anyone."

One by one, they shook the Army man's hand. Any doubts Carl had had about the chemistry of the team were put to rest right away. He had prepared them for the newcomer the day before—no military man liked surprises. Not even nice surprises.

There would be many surprises waiting for them in the jungle—none of them nice.

Carl rode a Company car back to Langley to procure airline tickets and visas. He picked up almost no additional information. Harding's captors were still unknown, and the Solano government was not saying anything. He felt like a canary being carried into a coal mine.

He had instructed his men to eat dinner separately and settled for room service by himself. Dozier had gone to shop and pack for the unexpected trip. Jerry and the others would leave for Virginia Beach in the morning. The next time he saw them would be in Quito, each having arrived separately on commercial airlines. They would all sleep well tonight, knowing it would be the last time for at least a week.

But Carl would not sleep well. His demons were back. The phone teased him from across the room. He sat down on the bed and dialed her number.

"This is Gabriele Bach. I'm not home right now. Please leave a message so that I may call you back."

Carl slammed down the receiver. "Damn it!" he shouted out loud. There were three possibilities: first, she was home and not answering *any* calls; second, she was home and monitoring *all* calls to make sure she didn't talk to him accidentally; or third, she just wasn't home. He didn't know which was worst. Just thinking about it took him to the brink of madness. He considered calling Forshay for a status report but decided he didn't really want to know. There were probably men lined up to see her. Besides, he couldn't call Forshay in the middle of a surveillance operation.

He did some deep breathing to get his heart rate down. Then he picked up the phone again. He was surprised he remembered the number.

"Hello."

"Laura, this is Carl."

"Oh! What a nice surprise! I thought you'd be on your way by now. Is there anything I can do?"

"You can show me your etchings."

There was no hesitation. "With pleasure, Carl. Please come. I'll give you a show you won't forget."

"I'll be there in forty-five minutes."

He took a combat shower and put on his only pair of clean jeans. He threw on a cotton rugby shirt and looked in the mirror to comb his hair. The unfamiliar face had fear written all over it. Fear he could not define. He needed someone to comfort him. Someone to tell him everything was going to be all right.

He walked quickly to the Metro station and took the Orange line two stops to Clarendon. The apartment was a short walk from there, and a shorter elevator ride. He stood at her door with a strange mixture of feelings. Anxiety and anticipation. No, he thought, fear and excitement. He rang the buzzer.

Laura opened the door almost immediately. She wore a terry cloth robe and nothing else. He sensed the humidity coming from the shower.

"Hi, Laura . . . did I come too quickly? Looks like you might still be wet."

She loosened the waistband of the robe and parted her lips before speaking. "The only part of me that's wet, Carl, has been wet since you called."

Without a word, he swept Laura into his arms, kicked the door shut behind him, and carried her across the apartment into the bedroom. She lifted her head and kissed him hungrily until he laid her on the bed and stood up to unbuckle his belt. Wriggling out of the terry cloth, she admired him as he pulled the bulky shirt over his head.

"So this is what a warrior looks like."

"Yes, Laura . . . but this warrior is too weak to fight."

"I know how to fix that."

Reaching up with both hands, she gently pulled him down next to her. He buried his face in her bosom and forgot about everything that troubled him.

Later—much later—she cradled him in her arms like a baby and, for the first time in three nights, he slept like one.

Chapter 9

San Miguel

R obert Harding lay on the mud floor of a medium-sized canvas
tent. It was steaming hot, and the mosquitos swarmed around
his bloody face. The chains that bound him had made deep gouges
in his ankles and wrists during the last seventy-two hours. The sores
were already infected. The flies had come to feast, drawn by the smell
of rotting flesh and the stench of the ambassador's diarrhea. He was
alone again . . . and he was grateful. The beatings had been brutal. At
first, he had been afraid they might kill him. After one day of torture
he had been terrified they might not. They had taken him, quite
obviously, for a political purpose; he knew they needed him alive. He
didn't know for how long.

A very large man came crouching into the tent. He had blood on
his hands—Harding's blood. The ambassador looked up at him and
cringed reflexively. Instead of striking him again, the man reached
down and unlocked his leg shackles.

"Now you must clean yourself . . . It is time to see *La Jefa.*"

Harding got up, fell in behind the brute, and stumbled down
to the river. With the guard at arm's length, he fell into the water
and, for a brief moment, felt pleasure. When he came to his senses,
he thought about submerging and just swimming away. He looked
at the chains still linking his wrists. Then he remembered—he didn't
even know how to swim. In between beatings, he had actively considered suicide, but he hadn't found a method for doing it. Drowning

was certainly better than disease or bleeding to death. He took a silent deep breath and leaned toward the current in the middle of the narrow stream. His heart was racing but, for the first time since his capture, he felt no pain. This was it, he thought, as he started to go under.

A huge hand grabbed the back of Harding's tattered shirt and lifted him halfway out of the water. "No swimming allowed . . . you have two minutes to use this!" Without letting go of the shirt, he handed the ambassador a bar of coarse soap. Harding got the blood and most of the dirt off his face before the guard yanked the soap away from him.

"*Vamos,*" commanded the giant after he had washed the blood off his own hands. "I have dry clothes for you to wear when you go to see the boss."

"*Gracias,*" was all Harding could manage to say. Having been denied the easy way out, he steeled himself for the reality that lay ahead. He had no idea what that reality would be. He would soon find out. Terror had given way to resignation. Prevented from taking his own life, Harding now had a strange sense of curiosity. He didn't think his situation could get any worse.

He found clothes and sandals in his tent. The guard unlocked his wrists, and Harding stripped off his pants. The shirt was so torn, he just ripped it off his body. He fell upon the clean clothes and slowly put them on. When he was ready, the giant produced a pistol and pointed it at his face.

"Walk in front of me and do not try to run away. I will shoot you, but you will not die. I will make *sure* you do not die . . . pig! Now move!"

Harding walked along a forest trail with the gun to his back. As they got away from the river, the jungle became thicker and the light diminished to almost nothing. He didn't know the time, but the sun had been up for many hours. Though dehydrated, he was sweating in the relentless heat. After about two hundred yards, they came to a small compound carved from the rainforest.

There were several buildings with thatched roofs, suggesting a common purpose. Harding had never actually seen one, but he knew this was a drug laboratory. The open building ahead to the right had rows of tables with vats of various liquids on and under them. The guard led him to a smaller hut on the far side of the cleared area.

"Go in and get on your knees," commanded the brute as he pounded softly on the plywood door. "I will be waiting here if you try to escape."

Harding opened the door, stepped inside, and sank to the leafy floor. Julia Mendoza walked out from behind a cloth curtain and sat down on the padded bench in front of him. It was the first time he had seen her since the kidnapping.

"*Buenas tardes*, lover boy," she said sarcastically. Harding stared at her with the same bewildered look he had worn while being dragged out of his residence. He was still confused . . . and stunned. Julia crossed her legs and leaned back on the delicate hands that had proven so powerful. Even in his wretched state, Harding noticed that jungle fatigues did not hide her beauty. Looking up at her now, he began to forgive himself. No man, he was sure, could have refused this woman.

"The last time we saw each other, Robert, I was the one on my knees. The tables have turned, no?"

Harding swallowed hard. He spoke in a voice weakened by dryness and fear. "Why have you done this to me?"

"A good question, Mr. Ambassador . . . and one that I would like to answer." She was actually smiling at him. It was a private smile, as if she was pleased with herself. "That is, in fact, why you are kneeling before me." The smile vanished.

"So you want to know why we took you away and beat you half to death?" With a sharply rising pitch, she was suddenly shouting at him. "I'll tell you why . . . you worthless North American pig!"

Julia uncrossed her legs and sat forward, waving a manicured finger at him. Harding flinched, thinking she might spring from the bench and kick him in the head with her boot.

"Please don't hurt me anymore," he pleaded. "I'm no good to you dead."

"That is correct . . . Your government will move heaven and earth to get you back. We are suggesting a simple trade."

"What do you want from Washington?" Harding felt a diplomatic role engulfing him. It was like a blast of cool air. He pressed on. "Whom do you represent?"

"I do not represent anyone, you pompous ass!" she hissed. "Thanks to you, I am now *running* this organization!"

"Which organization is that?"

"A commercial enterprise . . . we make a product that sells very well in the United States." Without taking her eyes off Harding, Julia withdrew a cigarette from her breast pocket.

"Cocaine."

"Very good, Robert!" said Julia as if to a youngster. She lit the cigarette and blew smoke at the ceiling.

"What are your political objectives?" asked Harding, having finally found his ambassador's tone.

"It is very complicated, so you will have to listen carefully," she began, slowly rising from the bench. "I am quite proud of what we are doing. You—of all people—know how it feels to put a good plan into action, right?" She stood up and glared down at him. Harding's mind raced, as Julia paced back and forth.

"We have two main goals, then . . . and you are going to help us reach them. The first—and these are not in order of importance—is to increase our market share. You know, this is a very competitive business we are in." Her face took on a crazed look, erupting into an almost maniacal spasm of laughter. What frightened Harding was how quickly she turned it off. Without a trace of amusement, she continued.

"The second goal is to force your government to give back to Colombia all its citizens now incarcerated in the United States." She let that sink in, then delivered the punch line. "Starting with Jorge Mena Velasquez."

"What's your interest in Mena?" responded Harding. "With him out of the way, you should be able to corner the cocaine market."

"You *idiot!*" Julia stopped and turned to him again with the scolding finger. "You still have not figured it out!" She paused to let him catch up. "Latin Americans all have at least three names, do we not?" Harding found himself nodding like an attentive student.

"What is your full name?" he asked meekly.

"My name is Julia Mendoza de Mena."

Harding gasped. "I . . . I didn't know he was married again."

"There are a lot of things you did not know, Mr. Ambassador. For instance, you did not know that business competitors talk to each other in Colombia, just like they do in the United States. Did you really think you could kidnap my husband and blame it on the president?" Without waiting for an answer, Julia continued. "We knew almost right away that it could not be Solano or Espinoza. It *had* to be the Americans—and that meant you! Nothing happens without the ambassador's approval. You work directly for your president, do you not?" She stopped and glared at him again.

Harding was still reeling. "How did you know I kept the plans at my residence?"

"A lucky guess . . . but we also found other papers that will help us track down the murderers who took Jorge from my side."

"You were *with* him?"

"I was sleeping peacefully in his arms when your *sicarios* came for him." Julia hesitated momentarily for effect. "But we have our own *sicarios* . . . and they will even the score."

"You can kill all the Americans you want," said Harding firmly. "But you won't get your husband back."

"Then I will kill you last!" Looking into her fiery eyes, Harding realized that Julia Mendoza de Mena was capable of using her own delicate hands to kill him.

Julia continued her lecture as Harding's remaining energy flagged. "Your plan had its good aspects, though . . . I must thank you for giving me the opportunity to get rid of both Solano and Espinoza. Yes, we talk to each other . . . but we also kill each other. It is only business."

"What do you plan to do with President Solano?" Harding suddenly felt protective of the man he had tried to topple politically.

"You are afraid we will kill him?" she spat. "Do not worry . . . Espinoza will kill him for us."

"But they're childhood friends!"

"They are also business partners."

"What happens next?" asked Harding, still on his knees.

"You made Espinoza the prime suspect in the kidnapping of Jorge Mena. He is now the prime suspect in *your* kidnapping!" Julia bent forward to within a few inches of Harding's face. "I think Solano's days as the president of this country are . . . how do you say... numbered."

"What then?"

"We are going to hold you in silence until Solano is gone. Then I will use you to get my husband back. Brilliant, no?"

Harding had to admit that it was. With the false information he had been planting for months, Julia could anonymously credit Espinoza with kidnapping him, then sit back and watch Solano squirm. The president would try to prove his innocence—to the United States and the rest of the world—by coming down hard on his close friend. Espinoza's men would then come down even harder on the president; Solano would fall one way or another. After that, Julia would be able to go public and deal with American authorities for Mena's release. Harding didn't know where that would leave him, but at least he had some time.

"Diego! Come and take this pig away!" Julia Mendoza de Mena threw her cigarette at Harding's feet and turned to leave. As he watched her walk into the back room, the front door opened behind him. Julia's faithful servant escorted the ambassador back to his tent, inflicting as much pain as possible in the process.

Carl was the first to arrive in Quito. He took a cab from the airport to the hotel he had preselected for the team. It was outside the Amazonas shopping district where most Americans stayed but far enough from the slums and higher street crime. It was Thursday afternoon. They would only be there one night. He locked his single bag in the closet of the small room and took another cab to the embassy. Carl had not shaven in two days, and he didn't plan to do so until they got back from the field. He had instructed his men to do the same. He wore European-style casual clothes and, when he could not avoid speaking, spoke Italian mixed with broken Spanish. This is the easy part, he thought.

He instructed the driver to drop him off around the corner from the embassy and walked the rest of the way. The Marine at the guard post looked at his passport and called a number. Moments later, an officer from the embassy political section came to the checkpoint and escorted Carl into the building.

"My name is Simmons," said the man without shaking hands.

He was a short, plump man, roughly Carl's age, who would never have stood out in a crowd. Or even at a party. They went directly to the ambassador's office and waited in awkward silence in front of his administrative assistant.

The door opened and Ambassador Samuel Sporkin swept them quickly into the room. He closed the door behind them before offering his hand. Sporkin was as tall as Simmons was short. He was youthful for an ambassador and, by reputation, very confident. In secret conference with a stranger who could ruin his reputation and his career, Ambassador Sporkin was anything but confident. He looked at Carl like a used car salesman who had just discovered a body in the trunk and didn't know what to do about it.

"Welcome to Ecuador, Mr. Malinowski." Carl was surprised the ambassador knew him by name. He wondered what else Sporkin knew about him. "Are you getting everything you need?" He spoke to Carl but glanced at Simmons, the CIA station chief.

"That's what I came here to find out, sir," said Carl, also glancing at Simmons. "Mr. Simmons and I have not had time to check the diplomatic pouches I requested. We were told to come straight here to see you."

"Yes . . . well, very good," said Sporkin. "I understand you'll be leaving in the morning."

"That's right," replied Carl. "You're supposed to provide my team with two armored Blazers."

Simmons nodded slowly without speaking while his eyes scanned from Carl to the ambassador and back to Carl.

"Good, then," said Sporkin. "I trust that everything will be in order when you open the crates. I don't even want to know what's in them . . . I just want all of us to do everything we can to help

Washington get Robert Harding back. When one ambassador is harmed, you know, we are all harmed. Good luck, Mr. Malinowski."

He shook Carl's hand quickly and practically shoved him out the door. Carl had the impression that Sporkin, a political appointee, didn't have the slightest idea what he and his men were about to do. It was better that way. There wasn't anything they needed on this side of the border except the vehicles and the contents of the crates.

"Let's go downstairs," said Simmons. "You can go through everything and let me know if there are any discrepancies."

The crates had come in the night before on a cargo flight from Miami. Simmons had picked them up and transported the stuff to the embassy. If he was curious about what was in the crates he didn't show it. Carl followed him to the basement and watched him unlock the equipment cage. There were five crates in all. Carl opened them one by one and inspected the contents. There were Lowe mountaineering backpacks, equipment harnesses, GPS receivers, MP5 submachine guns, Sig Sauer pistols with silencers, night vision goggles, squad radios, SATCOM radios, batteries, small charges of plastic explosive, signal flares, boxes of ammunition, dehydrated rations, canteens, and medical kits. He also found Colombian camouflage uniforms, life jackets, K-bar knives, swim fins, and binoculars, as well as large nonmilitary kit bags in which to carry everything.

It was all there.

He turned to Simmons. "I'd like to bring my men here to jock up at 0600. We'll need about an hour . . . That OK?"

The station chief nodded. Then he locked the cage and the outer door.

"Can you show me the Blazers now?" Carl looked at his watch and saw that it was already 1900.

"Sure," said the CIA man, pleasant but all business. "Let's go out to the motor pool."

Simmons bounded up the stairs, surprising Carl with his quickness. He reminded Carl of his friend Forshay—a Volkswagen with a Porsche engine. They went outside in back of the building to find two beige-colored four-wheel-drive vehicles parked in the open. They looked like off-road vehicles should look, thought Carl—liberally dented, with some rust. He got into each one, started them up, and sat for a few minutes. The cars were armored, they had enough storage space, and they had radios.

"What's the range on these?" asked Carl, pointing to the handset.

"Only about thirty miles, line of sight. You won't be able to talk to us from the *Oriente* except by SATCOM . . . or telephone. The telephones here are actually quite good."

"Except for the execution checklist transmissions, we shouldn't have to talk to you at all until we come off the river. Can I leave the Blazers in Tipishca?"

"We have an asset near there who can watch them," replied Simmons. "I'll contact him tomorrow night. You should be able to drive back here after you come out of the field."

"If we come back that way."

"There's no other way that I know of . . . except continuing down the Putumayo to the main Amazon. That's a very long trip . . . and there's no one to pick you up in Leticia or Manaus, assuming you make it that far."

"We don't have a lot of options," responded Carl grimly. He hated not having options. "It's a good thing we're not going to actually rescue the guy."

"Why all the gear, then?"

"Just in case," said Carl firmly.

And Simmons finally smiled.

Carl left the embassy, walked a few blocks, and took a cab to the hotel. Jerry had just come in on the Houston flight, seated apart from Dozier, and was waiting in his own room when Carl got back.

"The captain will be along in a few minutes, Boss. He wanted to give me a head start."

"Did Billy Joe and Jose get off OK?"

"They're coming in from Miami tonight."

Carl nodded. "We got all the stuff I ordered. It's at the embassy."

"Great! I'm getting pumped for this one. How long is the drive to the border?"

"About nine hours in good weather," estimated Carl. "But you know all about the weather down here."

"Yeah . . . we need to leave early in the morning. We'll have a lot to do before the linkup with Corvalán." Jerry motioned Carl to sit down on a flimsy chair. "Have you decided what to do with Dozier yet?"

"I need to think about that one some more," said Carl evasively. "Captain Dozier is an active duty soldier. If he gets killed or wounded, it will cause a political firestorm."

Jerry raised his eyebrows. "Yeah . . . and if one of *us* gets killed nobody says anything! Is this a great country or what?"

Ron Dozier was coming into the country on false orders to see the commander of the Military Group in the US embassy for a planning meeting. The colonel whose name appeared on the orders had not been made aware of Dozier's arrival, and Carl had not mentioned it to the ambassador. Dozier's boss knew where he was, but even Reginald Stewart did not know what his star junior officer was going to be doing. Carl knew . . . but he wasn't going to tell anyone just yet. The general trusted Carl, and Dozier had no choice.

Carl and Jerry were discussing changes to the plan when the knock came. *"Quien está?"* asked Carl, keeping his hand on the doorknob.

"Yo, Carl. It's me, Ron."

Carl opened the door and shook Dozier's hand. "Have a seat . . . Jerry and I will fill you in."

After thirty minutes without speaking, Dozier had a question.

"Are you going to put me in the boat, Carl? That's where I can do you the most good. If you leave me in Tipishca with a Colombian battle buddy I'll be out of the loop." The voice was steady and professional, not pleading.

"I don't know yet. I need to talk to Corvalán before I decide."

"I understand," replied the Army man. "I'm just glad to be here."

"Can you swim, Captain?" asked Jerry seriously.

"West Point swim team . . . Eastern Champion . . . four-hundred-meter freestyle . . . 1989."

"You should have been a frogman!" joked the man known as Butkus. "We ordered you a pair of fins, just in case." Carl was glad to see Jerry loosening up.

"What's your field name?" asked Carl.

"Leroy," answered Dozier. "My A team was known as Leroy's Boys."

"Works for me," said Carl, grinning calmly at Jerry. Pre-mission euphoria would soon give way to unrelenting tension. They tried to enjoy it for as long as possible.

Carl went down the street and bought Chinese takeout at an inconspicuous hole-in-the-wall where he'd eaten on his last visit. They shared a large meal in the privacy of Carl's room, telling war stories.

Billy Joe and Jose came in late. Carl briefed them and directed the pair to get as much sleep as they could. He knew they would be up most of the night, just like him. It was always that way the night before a mission. Carl also knew, from long experience, just lying still in the dark was almost as refreshing as sleep. He went to bed and relaxed by running images of Ecuador through his mind. In sharp contrast to Colombia, Ecuador was a country he remembered fondly.

At dawn they took separate cabs to the embassy. One by one, they went through the Marine guard post where Simmons was standing. He took each of them downstairs to the staging area until they had all assembled. Then the station chief quietly disappeared. One hour later, Carl picked up the phone in the basement and dialed a number. Simmons came down immediately to escort them, with all their gear, to the motor pool. The parking lot had been placed off-limits, and those few employees present at 7:00 a.m. did not consider the restriction unusual. Simmons had posted the word that the area was being sprayed for rats. It took three trips apiece for Carl and his men to load the Blazers and cover the equipment.

Fifteen minutes later, the Americans were driving through the streets of the old colonial city. They wore brand-new khaki and green tourist clothing, with well-worn jungle boots. Jerry drove Carl and Ron in the lead vehicle, with Billy Joe and Jose following. There was a loaded pistol in each glove compartment, just in case they were stopped by the wrong authorities. They followed the main road east until it became the only road. Descending from high in the Andes, they drove around the north face of the snowcapped Antisana volcano. Farther down, they went through the town of Baeza and headed north along a narrow river tumbling toward the rainforest.

The grandeur of the landscape contrasted sharply with the reality of the road. Stricken faces of Inca people walking back and forth between towns of mud dwellings, carrying heavy loads. Before he had seen too much of the Third World, Carl had wondered how anyone could ever work his way out of such a place. He knew now, of course, that there was no way out. They were stuck. Stoic men and tired women walking along a road to nowhere, sliding in the mud or choking in the dust. The only entertainment they seemed to have was making babies. New souls condemned to the same cycle of misery.

Slipping and sliding along serpentine tracks without guardrails, they followed the swelling river gradually northeast until the foothills flattened into farmland. They passed through Lago Agrio at 1600. A frontier town that reminded Carl of the American Wild West. But this was Ecuador's Wild *East*. Lago was the last real town they would see until after the mission, but they could not risk stopping. There were Colombians all over the *Oriente*, many dealing with the oil industry for chemicals needed to make cocaine. Such men would not mistake Carl and his men for tourists.

The road was straighter now but still made of dirt. To keep down the dust, someone had sprayed it with a thin coating of crude oil, making it more slippery than mountain mud. Driving toward his linkup with Corvalán reminded Carl of the way his country conducted its foreign policy. As long as you drove in a straight line you could stay on track. But when you came to a curve you had to slow down and think about how to get through it without sliding into a ditch. His government had slid into a ditch. That was why Carl and his men were on this road: to get the president and *his* men out of the ditch.

For money. For personal survival. But not for country.

They pulled over for a pit stop about an hour past Lago. Well off the main track, beyond the vision of road peasants, they took the time to finish getting ready for what lay ahead. Test-firing weapons, even at the edge of the jungle, was a tricky business. There is nothing that attracts the attention of people faster than the sound of automatic gunfire. Ordinary people are conditioned to ignore a loud noise (unless it is accompanied by a rising cloud of dust); they tend to *run* from the sound of machine guns. And report it to the authorities. The team assembled all their weapons and fired them into the jungle single-shot. Then they cleaned the guns and reloaded.

Then they ate dinner. The afternoon shower had come and gone.

"It just doesn't get any better than this, man," cracked Jose, holding a spoonful of brown goop in front of his face. "Humid tropical air, green grass, the sweet smell of petroleum, and Meals, Ready to Eat!"

"Tactical Constipation!" joked Billy Joe. "I had better chow in the Everglades with just a rifle, a frying pan, and a bottle of steak sauce!"

"You forgot the mud," added Jerry, smiling at Jose. "I can't wait to get on the river."

"Once you do, you'll wish you were back here," said Carl without humor. "The hard part starts tonight . . . the needle in the haystack."

"Do we have any real idea where they took Harding?" asked Dozier. They all looked at Carl as he replied.

"We think they have him in the south of the country. As you know, FARC owns everything south and east of the Andes . . . They have effectively cut the country in half. That means protection for the cartels . . . as long as they pay for it. Assuming one of the cartels took Harding, somewhere along the Putumayo River would be the logical place to hold him."

"Why wouldn't they hide him further into the rainforest, away from the river?" asked Dozier. "It seems to me they would feel safer there."

"Maybe," ventured Carl, "but if they keep him on the border and the Colombian authorities find them, they can scoot across the river into Peru or Ecuador." He hesitated for effect. "Remember when your Air Force guys picked us up on the Bolivian side of the Mamoré in the middle of the night?"

Dozier's eyes lit up. "Yeah . . . but I still don't know who the fifth man was."

"You didn't need to know before . . . but you do now." Carl looked around, purely out of habit, before finishing the thought. "That man was Jorge Mena Velasquez . . . He'd been hiding just over the border in Brazil."

Dozier let out a long whistle. "And Mena wanted to be able to escape from Brazilian authorities by running across the river . . . very clever."

"Not clever enough!" bragged Billy Joe. "We took him to Bolivia and arranged for a free ride to the United States!"

Dozier nodded up and down. "I'm just happy to be out here with you guys. I'll do whatever I can to help you find Harding."

"Glad to have you aboard, Captain," said Billy Joe, extending his gravy-smeared hand.

"The captain's field name is Leroy," announced Carl.

"That has a nice ring to it," said Jose. "Better than Bosco . . . But once you're named in this outfit you're stuck."

"We should've named ya Bozo . . . That was my vote," laughed Billy Joe.

"So," said Dozier carefully, "I hope I'm on this patrol for the duration."

Carl had finished weighing the risks and benefits. "I'm gonna tell Corvalán he has to make room for all five of us."

"Thanks, Carlos," said the man now called Leroy. "I won't let you guys down."

They all nodded approval, then got back on the road.

They pulled into Tipishca just after dark and parked the vehicles in the elephant grass downstream of the barracks. The last time he'd been there, Carl had trained Ecuadoran soldiers to patrol the border in fast boats. But they hadn't been fast enough to outrun an ambush by the Colombian FARC. That disaster had cost Ecuador eleven lives and a river patrol program. Carl shuddered at the memory, illuminated in his night vision goggles by the deserted barracks.

As the San Miguel River slowly drained into the Putumayo, they waited with the mosquitos for the linkup. There was no sign of Simmons's agent.

Gabriele bent down and gently picked up Maritza. The little black cat seemed to sense the woman needed comfort and buried its head in her neck. With no one else to talk to, Gaby often asked Maritza for advice.

"I don't know what to do, *liebchen*," she began. "I still love him, but everything is different now. He lied to me." She sighed as the cat purred. "I trusted him, baby . . . and he let me down . . . like all the other men. I just can't seem to find someone I can love *and* trust." She started crying again, wondering aloud if she could ever forgive him.

She had withheld from Carl the ugly secret of her former life. Full disclosure would have obliged her to explain that the pregnancy had lasted only six months, and that she had ended it herself. Gabriele had been so traumatized by the beatings that she hadn't wanted to bring the baby into life. A scarlet letter, hanging from her neck like an albatross. She would carry the guilt for the rest of her days. But why should she have to tell anyone about it? Even Carl. He didn't need to know. If he *had* known, she rationalized, he would have left her anyway. Besides, she thought, not telling him the full story was different than the deliberate deception he'd used on her. *Wasn't it?* She was forty years old. Carl had been her last chance for real happiness. Now she had nothing. Then Maritza purred again, giving Gabriele the strength to face the day.

Gabriele put Maritza down and slipped into her wool coat. It was Friday, and the week had taken a severe toll on her. She could not maintain the veneer of cheerfulness another day. Picking up the phone, Gabriele dialed her supervisor and described the symptoms but not the cause. A sick day, to be sure. Then she left the apartment to see if the late October air could help her cope with the sadness.

That's what it is—sadness.

Getting into the Jetta, Gabriele noticed a pair of binoculars on the back seat. Carl had given them to her so she could go birding when he wasn't with her. The gift had allowed her to live the romantic dream of sharing her life with the man she loved *all* the time. Now the binoculars only made her think of what she'd lost. The dream had turned into a nightmare. She stood up and took off her coat, then laid it on top of the binoculars.

Gabriele backed out of the parking space and drove past the Metro station where hundreds of commuters hurried to work. She was glad she didn't have to do that today, but the feeling of despair was overwhelming. It was the same feeling she had experienced coming out of the hospital in Stuttgart to start her life all over again. Memories, thought Gabriele, are either the most constructive or the most damaging things one can own. She merged into light congestion on 66 and headed west toward Manassas with no particular destination in mind. Between the traffic and the tears, she didn't notice the gray Subaru directly behind her.

Nor did she notice the motorcycle behind the Subaru.

Slator Forshay had eyes in the back of his head. He knew something was there before he saw it in the mirror. It wasn't the sound; it was a feeling. When he saw the powerful bike, he wasn't sure whether it was following him or Gabriele. He needed to find out before deciding on a course of action. He changed lanes and slowed the Subaru, allowing the motorcycle to pass him on the left. He glanced through dark glasses as the machine glided by, noting that the rider was a small man with long black hair. Everything else was covered up by black leathers and a high-tech helmet. But Forshay smelled an assassin underneath. Another feeling. The man's jacket, partially open to the cold wind, was a couple of sizes too big. He let the rider get far enough ahead to observe him in the motorcycle's mirror. Without taking his eyes off the quarry, Forshay initiated a right turn signal and held it for almost a mile.

The motorcycle did not slow down.

Instead of turning right, Forshay moved the Subaru left and closed to just behind the bike. He had taken the precaution of leaving Carl's truck parked in front of the condo and moving to a motel down the street. He had then rented a car just as inconspicuous as himself. That strategy had apparently paid off; the cartel wasn't after him. They were after Gabriele! He looked around for signs of a second gunman. There were none. He knew what he needed to do.

Gabriele took the first battlefield exit and headed north along a country road. The motorcycle followed a few car lengths behind, with Forshay still a few lengths behind the bike. The fall colors were still on display, and he could see Gabriele looking from side to side. He didn't believe she even noticed the bike. There was no one else on the road as far as the eye could see. If I were him, thought Forshay, this is where I would make my move. *He knows I'm here, but he has a job to do.*

As if on cue, the biker started closing the distance between his machine and the Jetta. Forshay touched a button and the driver's window came all the way down. He felt for the pistol between his legs to make sure it hadn't slipped off the seat. A round waited in the chamber of the Sig Sauer automatic. He had trained himself to shoot left-handed, and now he was glad he had. Grasping the gun, he stood on the accelerator and held the wheel with his right hand. Slipping his finger inside the trigger guard, he prepared to remove the slack on the long double-action trigger. He aimed the pistol out the window as the car surged forward.

The Subaru was closing slowly—behind and to the right— when the assassin reached for something inside his jacket. As Forshay calculated the relative motion of the three vehicles, the man extracted a machine pistol and held it at arm's length, pointing down. It was done so professionally that almost anyone following the man would have missed it. Not Forshay. He guessed he had about five seconds until the bike was alongside the Jetta and the weapon came up. The assassin would not fire until he had a sure kill shot.

Gabriele didn't seem to notice anything going on behind her. As the gunman swerved left and closed in for the shot, Forshay realized he wouldn't catch the bike in time. And he wasn't close enough to shoot the biker. Not without the risk of hitting Gabriele. Locking the wheel with both knees, he punched the horn with his right hand . . .

and kept punching. The sound almost knocked the surprised gunman off the bike. The assassin turned his torso to the right and fired
a short burst at the Subaru, shattering the windshield.

Glass flew into Forshay's face, but he managed to keep the
car on the road. The ploy had gained him the precious seconds he
needed as Gabriele suddenly raced the Jetta farther ahead of the bike.
She started screaming so loudly he could hear her twenty yards back.
The gunman, fighting to maintain control of the situation, raised his
weapon and closed the gap by half. Forshay gunned the Subaru again,
wind and blood blurring his vision, and closed faster. The undulating
road curved unpredictably as the three vehicles sped toward certain
death. For someone.

The gunman came left for his firing run. Forshay was beginning
to think he had failed when an oncoming car forced the motorcycle
back into the wake of the Jetta. That was the extra moment he needed
to close with the *sicario* and take him out. Forshay surged another
five yards and raised his pistol. The biker pointed his weapon blindly
behind him as he swerved left again for another run at Gabriele.
Forshay knew that if he didn't take the guy out now, the killer would
get both of them with one arcing burst.

Panic gripped at his throat. These were the very circumstances
he loved. Running along the line between success and failure. Life
and death. This was where Slator Forshay wanted to be. To prove
himself worthy of the ultimate accolade from his peers: to be "good."

But, for now, not good enough!

The motorcycle crept even with the left rear bumper of the
Jetta, closing fast.

Fast enough!

Forshay willed the Subaru's front bumper to a point opposite
the middle of the motorcycle's rear tire and jerked the steering wheel
hard to the left. The bike went down in a sea of sparks, sliding across
the pavement and into a tree. Forshay managed to stay on the road as
he leaned on the horn and signaled through the open windshield for
Gabriele to pull over. Foolishly, it seemed to him, she obeyed. Both
cars came to a stop on the shoulder of the road about one hundred

meters past the crash site. He sprang from the Subaru and raced forward on foot.

"Get down and stay down!" he shouted, temporarily forgetting he still had the Sig Sauer in his left hand. "I need to take care of that guy before we leave here!" Shifting the pistol to his right hand, he ran back to the wreckage and surveyed the damage. The Colombian had been thrown clear of the bike. He lay broken, like an old rag doll, against a fence post. Forshay was glad he didn't have to finish the guy off in front of Gabriele, still on the ground but watching him.

Forshay lowered the pistol and ran back to Gabriele. He stood in front of her, trying to catch his breath. Slowly, she got up off the ground and faced the man who had just saved her life. Or not. Was this a kidnapping? A robbery? Still frozen with fear, she waited for instructions.

"We need to get out of here, Gabriele! Your car . . . I'll drive."

"Who *are* you, and how do you know my name?" Her voice wavered with post-traumatic stress.

"Carl sent me . . . He said you might need another guardian angel while he's gone. My name is Slator Forshay."

Gabriele ran to Slator and threw her arms around him. She sobbed into his shoulder and wouldn't let go for one long minute. He kept looking around as he held her, knowing their anonymity would not last long.

He persuaded her to let go of him and get in the car. They sped away in the same direction as before, leaving the motorcycle a smoking wreck for the cops to figure out. He had rented the Subaru with false identification, so he wasn't worried about the police coming after him. He was *very* worried about other gunmen out there, hunting both of them.

"I know a motel south of here that's hard to find," said Forshay finally. "I'll rent two rooms and get us a car . . . You'll have to ditch the Jetta . . . Got that?"

"OK, Slade," she replied, coming out of her trance.

"Slator," he corrected her. "Most of my friends call me Forshay, but I prefer Slator."

"I'll do whatever you say, Slator," said Gaby tentatively. "But I have a cat to take care of!" She looked at him for the first time since they'd left the crash site. "And what should I do about work?"

"Call a friend to feed the cat . . . and tell your supervisor you can't come in for at least a week . . . Make up some excuse. We have to assume they've been watching you as closely as I have."

"And how closely is that?" She smiled. It was the first time Gabriele had smiled outside of work in a week. She was back among the living. The chase had terrified her, but the terror seemed to have blown away her depression. Gaby was starting to feel an exhilaration she could not explain.

"Close enough," said Slator gently. "If I watched you any closer, Carl would refuse to pay me."

Laura Jensen sat in front of her vanity dresser, thinking about Carl and Gabriele. Carl—her instant hero, midnight lover, and future husband. Gabriele—her State Department colleague and unknowing rival. Ever since her father had walked out on her mother twenty years earlier, Laura had been conflicted about men. She had needed them—lots of them—to fill the emptiness, but she had made them pay dearly for wanting her. She had never taken money, only gifts and dreams. Carl was just the second man Laura had ever met who did not remind her of her father. Now she had a dream of her own. She wanted a son. A son who would grow up to be like Carl. The rarest of men. Strong *and* sensitive. Different than her father.

She felt sorry for Gabriele. Laura had bested many women in the cutthroat competition for strong men. She had figured out what each one wanted and simply given it to him. Beauty, intelligence, humor, and sex. Not necessarily in that order. It had been easy for her. She hadn't thought about all the losers, strewn like flower petals in her wake. This time it was different. Different but not unfair. At least no more unfair than life is apt to be anyway. Laura had not even needed to compete this time. Gabriele's loss would be her gain. If the woman did not already know, she mused, Gabriele would soon find out that Carl had chosen Laura.

It was a dream come true.

Laura put the emerald Robert Harding had given her back in the jewelry box, filled with so many other bad memories. She appraised her new self, smiling serenely in the mirror. Laura Jensen could see the excitement in her moistening eyes as she anticipated Carl's return and their new life together.

Chapter 10

Putumayo

T wo ghoulish green shapes came into Jerry's night vision goggles. From the top of the steep bank he could see the boats moving slowly upstream in the black void. He whispered sharply to Dozier and Billy Joe, now dozing next to him, and continued to monitor the progress of what they hoped were Colombian Marines. Carl raised himself into a crouch and went to the other side of the hasty base camp to take Jose off the road watch. Without sound or light, they rolled their poncho liners, tightened the laces on their boots, donned the heavy rucksacks, and cradled their submachine guns. They were now clustered together on the bank, each aware that this was the moment of maximum danger. Jose kept his eyes on the road. Billy Joe and Ron watched up and down the river. Carl looked over Jerry's shoulder as the big man continued to track the boats with his goggles.

"They're about fifty meters out now . . . almost dead in the water. Three men in each boat . . . all weapons manned . . . M60s bow and stern. Looks like they have enough room for all of us." Jerry's voice trailed off as he concentrated to see more. Then he added something they were all thinking. "If they don't shoot us first."

Jerry ran his finger around the trigger housing of his weapon, now shouldered, to make sure it was on safe. He sensed the team moving out to his left but did not take his eyes off the boats. Carl led the others down the bank directly in front of Jerry, and pulled a red flashlight from his web gear. He pointed it toward the idling engine noise and pressed the button three times in short succession. Then he waited in the shallow water, looking into the black hole of the night jungle. Carl felt reasonably secure as the others covered him with overlapping fields of fire. But all the vigilance wouldn't help much if the Colombian crews opened up on them by mistake.

The response came in the form of two long red flashes from the river. The red light did not destroy their night vision, but it crashed into their consciousness like a starter's pistol. Carl had done this a thousand times, but he was still astonished at how close the boats had gotten to them in the darkness. Someone without night vision would not have known the Colombians were there. He flashed his signal again so Major Corvalán could maneuver right to the spot where they stood. Jerry, having seen the signals, switched his field of fire to the road, their only remaining threat axis. At least for now. They had hidden the Blazers in the tall grass where Simmons's agent would find them. One at a time, they boarded the lead boat. Carl got on last.

The race to find Ambassador Harding was on.

"*Carlos! Qué gusto!*" said Corvalán softly with a smile Carl could barely see in the red light.

"*Lucho! Qué tal?*" whispered Carl. He embraced the friend he hadn't seen in five years.

That was the extent of the reunion between two men who had shared months of their lives on the rivers and tributaries of southern Colombia. There was no time for questions about families, political discussions, or war stories. Each hoped that opportunities for camaraderie would come later. But they knew it would be *much* later. Corvalán backed the lead boat into the current and took both engines out of gear. They drifted in the middle of the San Miguel, fifty meters from the nearest unfriendly eyes and ears. There was only one way out of Tipishca—the same way they'd come in. Having announced their presence on the way in, they had to assume an ambush was waiting for them now.

Carl and Ron stayed in the command boat, with the rest of the team taking positions in the second craft once it had joined up. It was only then that Carl noticed the long wooden canoe tied to the other boat. With hands and paddles, two crew members kept the boats rafted together in the middle of the lazy river while Corvalán discussed the plan with the Americans. The other Colombians manned weapons fore and aft, searching the riverbanks for drug traffickers—or their partners from the FARC.

"We must return to the Putumayo," said Corvalán in rehearsed English. "That is the only way to get down to where most of the *narcotraficantes* are. All of my experience tells me this."

"I agree," said Carl in Spanish. "We have to assume they took the ambassador to one of the clandestine airstrips near the river . . . but which one?"

Many of the airstrips had been carved out of the rainforest along the north bank of the Putumayo, just inside Colombia. Cocaine base was transported there from coca-growing areas in Peru over the vast Amazon riverine network. Laboratories, also carved from the jungle, converted the base into cocaine hydrochloride, using a variety of industrial chemicals. Small planes would then carry most of the product north for ocean shipment to Florida, or to Mexico for ground transit across the southwest border. From there, the drug would find its way into the lungs of American youth and the noses of the well-to-do.

"We will find out," said Luis Corvalán.

They floated for almost an hour, searching for threats while riding a slow current toward the Putumayo—the five-hundred-mile haystack that concealed what they came for. When they felt comfortable, Corvalán gave the order, and they engaged the enormous outboard engines. The twenty-five-foot Piranha Class patrol craft lacked armor but made up for that with speed and firepower. The boats—a gift from the American government—patrolled at moderate speed, towing the canoe alongside the second boat. They made the confluence of the Putumayo by dawn.

They found a small tributary on the south side of the river and camouflaged the boats in the lush foliage along the stream. The main river was still visible as Corvalán and one of his men prepared the canoe. It was time to listen to the heartbeat of the river, but they could not listen from patrol boats bristling with weapons. If they wanted intelligence information they would have to approach the citizens of the river in the craft of the river. That craft was a hollowed-out log about twenty feet long with a lawnmower engine. The engine, called a peki-peki for its sound, was linked to a long shaft. The shaft dragged a shielded propeller well behind the boat and just below the surface. The canoe was a marvel of ingenuity and a testimony to mechanical evolution. It was narrow enough to present minimum resistance to the current, yet wide enough to be stable at ten knots through (and over) the debris of the mighty river. The canoe could transport hundreds of pounds of bananas. Just as often, it carried cocaine or the chemicals to make it.

Carl watched his friend Lucho getting into the canoe. The young major he remembered so well had aged terribly in the last few years, the victim of constant stress and frequent combat. His closely cropped hair, once shiny black like Carl's, was now flecked with gray. The challenges to Colombia were monumental, but Corvalán had made a real difference on the southern front, busting large numbers of laboratories and killing or arresting countless *ladrones*. Drug traffickers and guerrillas—they were all the same to the major. In any other war he would have been called a hero. Here in the jungle he was invisible. His deeds went unheralded. He didn't care. He had a job to do and men to protect. Like his mentor.

Corvalán and his sergeant wore peasant clothing as they motored the canoe into the current and glided downstream. Both sides of the river were now visible to them. They watched other canoes coming upstream, along either bank where the current diminished to almost nothing. The Putumayo was not yet high enough to be dangerous, but it was growing every day with the rains. The Marine canoe idled just fast enough to maintain a straight course. Corvalán hoped the real peasants didn't notice that he and his sergeant were extremely fit and well-fed. With a fake cargo of empty boxes and barrels, he figured they would blend right in. At least long enough to pick up some rumors.

Carl and his men relaxed a bit in the hide site. Jerry monitored the radio for a possible distress call from the canoe. They felt about as safe as North Americans could feel—surrounded by dense forest, drug traffickers, and guerrillas—far removed from the protective umbrella of Uncle Sam. It was a beautiful morning on the river. Carl felt alive with anticipation, too keyed up to sleep. Dozier sat across from him, peering out at the current from behind the green curtain.

"Carlos," he said in a low voice, leaning forward. "Did you ever get a chance to talk to Laura Jensen?"

"I got more from her than I did from our friends at Langley," replied Carl cautiously. "Most of the stuff I gave you in the brief came from Laura. I'd be a lot more anxious about this mission if I hadn't talked to her. I owe you for setting that up."

"What did you think of her?"

Carl hesitated for a second, trying to evaluate exactly what the captain meant. "She's a hammer, all right," he replied with a smile. He continued with the most serious look he could muster. "But she's also very sharp and, I thought, serious. Really a nice girl at heart." He stopped, even though he wanted to go on.

"I'd like to meet her again someday," proclaimed the younger man. "She's hard to forget . . . know what I mean?"

"I know," said Carl, turning his head toward the river and adding quickly, "I think I hear a boat."

The river parade had started. Suddenly, one after another, canoes bearing everything from mangoes to machinery began passing them in both directions. Carl had never ceased to be amazed at the volume and diversity of river traffic this deep in the rainforest. Not very many people lived here, but they all seemed to be on the river at the same time. In a region without roads, the Putumayo was the only way for the inhabitants to move themselves and their commerce. It was Main Street, with an occasional side street. The river didn't just link communities; it *was* the community. That's why Corvalán was out there.

He didn't come back until midafternoon. After the rain shower that had bathed them on schedule every day. The Colombians motored along the bank as far as the hide site, then throttled back until they could see no other boats. When the way was clear, Corvalán merely turned left and coasted into the jungle. He cut the engine and fended off as they drifted into Carlos's Piranha. He and the coxswain climbed in and sat down.

"Carlos, my friend, we have—as the *Nortes* say—good news and bad news." He did not smile. "The good news is that one of the people we talked to, who told us he had come all the way from Brazil, said that he noticed unusual activity near the town of Puerto Maldonado."

The others listened as Carlos and Lucho talked in rapid Spanish. "Our source stayed in Maldonado three nights ago and heard a lot of boats going back and forth all night. This is not, in itself, unusual. There are drug shipments in that area all the time."

"Where is Puerto Maldonado?" interrupted Tinker.

"Far below Puerto Leguizamo, halfway to Brazil," answered the major. "We have not been down that way in quite a while."

What Corvalán did not say was *why* the Colombian Marine Corps had not been down that way in quite a while. Jose, squinting in the shadows, seemed to know why, but he waited for the major to finish.

"So what's different this time?" asked Dozier.

"It is not the amount of boat traffic. It is rather the *type* of boat."

"This *is* good news," interjected Jose.

"Yes," said Corvalán. "The source told us he could tell by the engine noise that these were ocean racing boats . . . the kind you sometimes see on the main Amazon. You call them go-fast boats."

"That's right," said Carl.

"I have not seen these boats on the Putumayo before," said Corvalán.

"That doesn't necessarily mean anything is different," observed Jerry. "They could just be doing drugs, only faster."

"True," said Carl abruptly. He was getting impatient. "What's the bad news, Lucho?"

"The bad news is that the area around Puerto Maldonado is infested with FARC guerrillas."

Had he been in Washington, Carl would have heard the news. The drug lord Juan Espinoza was now sitting in a high-security prison, having been arrested by the Colombian National Police. The most interesting aspect of this story was an unconfirmed report that Espinoza had been arrested while meeting with Colombian president Ernesto Solano at a restaurant on the outskirts of Bogotá. It had been widely reported over the last several days that Solano—in order to demonstrate his innocence in the Harding case—had been pressuring Espinoza to deny publicly the rumored linkages between himself and the president. Solano had also demanded that he deny any role in the kidnapping of Robert Harding. According to the media, Solano had been disappointed in Espinoza's response to this pressure—which had been to say nothing at all. A cloud of uncertainty had settled over Bogotá.

If Carl had not been patrolling the Putumayo that afternoon, he would have wondered where Gabriele and his friend Forshay had gone. She had parked the car in Annandale, and they had taken a cab to the motel Slator knew in Alexandria. He had booked them into rooms across from each other and rented another inconspicuous car. Gaby was spending her days reading magazines she had managed to buy. Slator spent his time watching her room from his own window when he wasn't prowling the neighborhood. They went to the store together—a different store each time—to buy essentials, and they ate fast food on the way back to the motel. Pizza, delivered to Slator's room in the evening, was the only other thing they shared. Even in boredom, Slator remained on watch. For Gabriele, who had never heard a firearm discharge before the *sicario* tried to kill her, the dull routine was just fine. She was glad to sacrifice her trademark independence for security.

If Carl had been home, he would have received a card from Laura every day. She sent the cards even though she knew he wouldn't read them for at least a week, maybe longer. Writing and sending the cards prolonged the afterglow of their time together and focused her dreams. She thought of how foolish she had been in her young life, and how happy she would be from now on. Her feelings for Carl had overwhelmed every other thought. It was more than passion; it was honest, sincere love. She would leave her career at State and begin a new one at home. She had stopped thinking about Paris and now amused herself wondering where Carl wanted to live in retirement.

Carl was fortunate to be somewhere other than Washington. Jeff tapped nervously on his desk, waiting for George to come up. The small office had a window, but that was the only hint that the thirtyish man in the gray suit had an important position in the organization. In fact, he was the special assistant to the deputy director for operations. The DDO had made it clear to Jeff that he was being groomed for the top job, even though it would be years before he qualified. The Harding plan for framing President Solano had been Jeff's only project for the last six months. Now that it had gone horribly wrong, he was in a precarious situation. If Harding survived the ordeal and resurfaced in Washington, he would almost certainly blame the agency for planting the stories that led to his capture. If, on the other hand, Harding were to die in the jungle, Jeff might be able to cover it up. He didn't want to embarrass the CIA, and he definitely didn't want to jeopardize his own career ambitions. The knock came, and he calmly opened the door.

"Nothing from Simmons today, sir."

"So we only know that they're on the river?"

"Yes, sir. That's all we have at this point. I expect another call before the end of the day tomorrow."

The station chief had called George on a secure telephone after receiving a brief status report from Jerry Tompkins. The report was a single code word from the execution checklist indicating the position of the patrol.

"Do you think there's a problem, George?"

"No, sir. They have a long way to go . . . if they find him at all."

"And if they do find him?" Jeff wanted to hear his coconspirator mouth the words.

"Then we can take Harding out . . . but we have to get Malinowski and his team out of there first." George looked at his much younger boss. "Can I ask you why you didn't just let Carl take him out? He certainly seems capable."

"Because he wouldn't do it, George."

171

"What makes you think that, sir? He's just a hired gun."

"Malinowski is carrying too much moral baggage to be just a hired gun," said Jeff evenly. "He's the best field operator there is, but he has . . . limitations."

George offered no comment on Carl's moral baggage. "I'll let you know when we hear from Simmons again, sir."

"Thank you, George."

The older man left the office to the sound of Jeff tapping his fingers on the desk.

The patrol rested the remainder of the afternoon, preparing to move downriver. When darkness fell, they waited for the parade of canoes to stop and then eased out into the current. With each coxswain wearing night vision goggles, they would be able to navigate safely at high speed. They needed the speed because they had over 250 miles to go. The night movement would enable the men to continue their information gathering around Puerto Maldonado the next day. It was difficult to keep secrets on the river—theirs or anybody else's. No one would see them on the transit. Those who heard them would assume they were transporting drugs. That would not alarm the river people.

Carl tried to sleep, but he could not. It was not the engine noise. He had learned long ago to ignore that and sleep sitting up. He was thinking about the rest of his life. An ordinary life. He would not feel the excitement of sitting on ambush, or the rush of killing the enemy. He would never jump out of an airplane again. He would still have his birds, though, and there were even a few rainforests left where he could find them. Rainforests without drug traffickers and guerrillas. Lacking someone to love, he had maintained his sanity by risking his life. Now he wanted more than his sanity. He wanted to *share* his life. For the first time in a long time, Carl Malinowski was ready to be really happy.

But there was one thing left to do.

Corvalán roused Carl from his daydream by grabbing him on the shoulder. "Carlos!" he shouted over the roar of the engines. "We are coming to Puerto Leguizamo." Carl looked at his watch. It was just after 2300.

Puerto Leguizamo was a field headquarters of the Colombian Marine Corps, a riverine base very familiar to Carl. Five years before, he had spent several months there, teaching Major Corvalán and his men everything he knew about riverine warfare. Jerry, Jose, and Billy Joe had been there with him.

"You are not going to stop, are you?" Carl asked Corvalán.

"No . . . I am tempted, but there is no reason . . . and there could be someone on the base who might alert the kidnappers. You never know in this jungle who is who."

"Good, Lucho . . . I agree. It would be best to drift past the base, no? If there is a spy there, the sound of your boats will be enough to tip him off."

"You are right, my friend," said Corvalán with a vigorous head nod. He left Carl's side and leaned over to the coxswain. As if dancing in the dark, both boats slowed to idle speed at the same time. They got out the paddles, turned off the engines, and floated slowly past the base.

Toward Puerto Maldonado.

When they had cleared Leguizamo, Corvalán gave the order to make best possible speed downriver. They ran hard for the rest of the night, encountering no other boats. At dawn they found a new hide site and disappeared into the branches on the south side of the river. Carl changed into peasant clothing and joined Lucho in the canoe. With his unshaven face and longish hair, he blended in better than his military friend. But although Carl's Spanish was as good as anyone on the river, he didn't *sound* Colombian. He had always tried to hide his American accent behind an Italian one, and this made him sound like an Argentinian. Not a bad cover, he thought. Che Guevara was from Argentina.

Carlos and Lucho motored downstream, looking and listening. Puerto Maldonado was about ten miles from where they had hidden the Piranhas. Carl had concealed the radio under a pile of rags, next to his weapon. He hoped he didn't have to use either one. Ten miles was a long way for the patrol boats to come to their rescue, even at

173

forty knots. Ammunition did not last that long. He and Corvalán were hanging it out, he knew, but there was no other way to determine what to do next. Carl had learned a long time ago that if you want the best intelligence you have to generate it yourself. Business on the river was picking up. There were intelligence sources to be questioned.

They spotted a small canoe plodding along the north bank. They could see that the canoe, driven by a middle-aged local man, carried bananas and no other people. They slowed down, made a U-turn and pulled alongside, motioning to the coxswain that they wanted to talk. The river man slowed slightly and finally looked at them with both eyes.

"What do you want?" asked the man warily.

"We are looking for Puerto Maldonado," shouted Corvalán. "How far is it?"

The man did not respond right away. His caution confirmed Lucho's suspicion that he carried contraband. Drug products were by far the most valuable things on the river, and they were stolen regularly. This trafficker would not tell them much.

"I passed it one hour ago," was all the man would say. He refocused on the bow of his canoe and cranked the engine back to full power.

"*Gracias,*" was all Corvalán said as he steered back into the main current and headed downstream.

They passed several other craft without making contact, looking for someone who might tell them something about expensive boats that didn't belong to the river community. They were getting close to the town when they saw a family of six coming at them. The canoe was larger than many of the others. Even though it carried four children, a pile of baskets, and several chickens, there was plenty of room for drugs. Or weapons. Carl held up his hand as Lucho came around behind the craft and pulled alongside.

"We are looking for our friends . . . They have big boats . . . loud boats . . . near here . . . Have you seen or heard them?" Carl wanted to sound like a foreigner. He wanted this family to think that he and Lucho worked for ruthless traffickers. That they were, themselves, ruthless. Intimidation was the most effective tactic they had, as long as they didn't overplay it. They both stared at the nervous man in the canoe.

"I have not seen these boats, *señor.*"

"But you have heard them? They are very loud."

"I heard something last night . . . It sounded like an airplane . . . but I think it was a boat. That is all." The father of four looked away from Corvalán's canoe.

"Where did you hear this?" asked Carl with a tone somewhere between questioning and threatening.

"On the other side of town . . . about an hour downstream from here . . . It was dark . . . I was running behind and had to make Puerto Maldonado before stopping. It was after eight o'clock."

The man looked at his wife and children as if to say *Please!* Carl looked at the man's family and said, "I hope you're telling us the truth," letting that sink in. Then he locked his eyes on the man and said, "We really need to find our friends." He motioned to Corvalán, and they continued downstream toward the river town.

Puerto Maldonado, like many other river settlements in the Amazon Basin, was more a spot on the map than a real town. There were only a dozen structures lining its one mud street. The gas station, a cluster of fifty-five-gallon drums on a raft of logs, was there to service rivercraft on their way to and from who knows where. There were no roads to anywhere, and no airfields. At least no legitimate airfields. There was only the river, the rain, and the mud. And strangers, coming from everywhere and nowhere. Carl and Lucho were simply two more dirty strangers. They pulled into the raft and took their gas cans to the fuel drums. As they topped off, the ragged attendant, one of the only people actually living in the town, told them something they needed to hear.

"Get out of here as soon as you can, my friends . . . This is not a safe place to be."

"What do you mean?" asked Corvalán.

"There are strange things going on down there," said the attendant in a low voice, pointing east.

"What kind of strange things?" asked Corvalán. Lucho looked at Carl with a degree of anxiety worthy of two dirty strangers with legitimate intent.

"Big boats on the river . . . powerful boats . . . airplanes coming and going . . . gunfire, too, I heard . . . some of my customers told me." The man was shaking in the jungle heat.

"FARC?" Lucho had a lot of experience asking this question.

"I do not know . . . but the boats and airplanes are real. I have never seen or heard such machines here before."

"And why do you tell us these things?" This time it was Carl doing the questioning.

"Please . . . you did not hear this from me . . . I only wish for the safety of my customers."

Corvalán gave the man ten times what the gas was worth. He didn't know if the tip would be appreciated; the man was probably getting rich off the traffickers, but his fear was real. It was time to find the source of all the noise.

Carl pushed the canoe away from the log platform, and Lucho steered the craft downstream again. They traveled as slowly as they could in the middle of the river, looking left and right for signs of the strange activities about which they had just learned. It would be unusual, thought Carl as they floated through the thick rainforest, if they saw anything unusual at all this time of day.

"There!" said Lucho without pointing. Carl looked first into his friend's eyes, then followed his focus to the left bank. It was a tributary no more than ten meters across, flowing into the main river from the north. There was nothing else.

"We will not see the go-fast boats on the Putumayo in the daytime, Carlos. But this *tributario* is large enough for them to navigate at night. I think we should check it out."

"Not now," Carl said firmly. "Let's plot this position and continue downriver for a while. There might be other places they can hide boats. We can come back to this one later."

"That is fine with me," agreed the Colombian. "I have seen many laboratories along the Putumayo, and most of them are along this type of *tributario*."

They motored downstream for another hour, searching for small rivers where the ocean racers could penetrate into the rainforest for clandestine activities. They found several such creeks but all were on the Peruvian side of the Putumayo. The Colombian authorities did not venture into Peru along such tributaries without a very good reason. The vast uncharted area was a perfect sanctuary for traffickers and guerrillas. If they ever needed it.

"Lucho . . . which side of the river do you think they are on?"

"The Colombian side. They will run into Peru if we discover them . . . They have done that before."

"What do you do then?" asked Carl.

"We do not follow them unless we know we can catch them quickly. My government and the government of Peru have an understanding, but it only covers what we call hot pursuit. You know how we Latins are about sovereignty, my friend."

"Brother, do I!" replied Carlos. "I've seen it hamper your counterdrug efforts for years. But I understand where it comes from . . . and I respect it. We will try and find them on the Colombian side first. If we cannot find them, I am going to ask you to lend us your canoe, Lucho."

"You would take an unarmed canoe into Peru?"

"Yes, I would," replied Carlos. "Unless you are willing to take the Piranhas in there to look for them."

"*Estás loco, Carlos?*"

"It's important that we find this guy. He has secrets we cannot afford to let him reveal."

"What secrets?"

"Secrets, Lucho . . . I wish I could tell you."

"Then we go together," said Luis Corvalán.

Late in the afternoon, they turned against the current and ran slowly up the north side of the main river. They looked again at the creek they had marked on the chart. With Lucho steering and Carl holding a field of fire ahead, they idled a hundred meters into the jungle void. From every tree came birdsongs Carl knew by heart. There were no signs of human activity, but the geography was perfect. Carl and his men would have to come back after dark and look for trouble.

Jeff had insisted the team only *locate* Ambassador Harding and report the grid coordinates to his employers. But no coordinating instructions for a handover had been given. That should have set off all kinds of alarm bells in Carl's mind, but it had not. Now that he was thinking more clearly (and there was nothing like the bush to enliven brain cells), all he could think about was *recovering* the hostage and getting out of there. He would send the grid coordinates to CIA, but he would take the ambassador out of there before the soldiers arrived. *And just how would the rescue force get in there anyway?* Carl, not Jeff, would decide what to do with Harding after that. Before leaving, however, it was clear that he would have to take care of Harding's captors.

All of them. *No comebacks!*

As they left the tributary in their gentle wake, Lucho turned to his mentor. "I am afraid that by going into the jungle without more information you will be opening the box of Pandora." The Colombian, who knew more about this jungle than anyone, locked eyes with the man he owed so much.

"It's the only way," said Carl in English, as much to himself as to his friend.

Chapter 11

Contact

The brute stood in front of Robert Harding and laughed. He kicked Harding in the groin again and watched with delight as the ambassador writhed in the mud like a fish out of water. Daylight disappeared as the jungle swallowed the sun.

"We are going to see *La Jefa* again. She has good news for you." Harding didn't even look up as the man tossed a wet towel onto his head. "Wash, pig!"

As the pain subsided, he ran the towel over his ragged face and tried to get his composure back. He was hungry, thirsty, and scared to death. He had not seen Julia since their initial encounter the day before, and he dreaded dealing with her again. It was almost easier to face Diego; at least he knew what to expect. Julia Mendoza was enjoying her unexpected power. She was drunk with it. Harding had concluded by now that the vixen that held his life in her hands was mentally unstable. What news could she possibly have to tell him? What was good news for her, he knew, would be bad news for him. He struggled to his feet and handed the towel back Diego. This time the shackles did not come off.

The only man Harding had ever wanted to kill pushed him along a muddy trail. It was dark, and the brute shined a flashlight in front of the prisoner's soggy feet. They stopped outside Julia's private hootch and waited for her to open the door. Harding couldn't tell whether he was shaking from the fever he knew he had, or just plain fright. It must have been both, he thought, because he shivered violently in the dim Coleman lantern light.

The door opened and a clean athletic-looking man about Julia's age walked out. He was dressed in starched khakis and carried a flashlight. A gold chain hung around his neck, and Harding noticed a large diamond in his ear. The young man continued down the trail toward the river as if he were in the city, simply out for an evening stroll. Julia came to the door a few minutes later in a bathrobe.

"Well, Mr. Ambassador . . . come in and sit down!" She motioned for Diego to leave, and Harding looked for something to sit on. Finding nothing, he sat down hard on the canvas floor. At least it wasn't mud, he thought, as he tried to calm himself down.

"I have news that should make you feel very good, Robert . . ." She hesitated just long enough for his imagination to run the gamut of possibilities. Her face was glowing with pleasure as she continued. "Espinoza is in prison . . . Solano's police put him there yesterday. And today . . . we have just heard the news that Solano himself is dead . . . Espinoza's people killed him. I'm so excited!"

Harding had included each of these events on his list of possibilities—but not both! He found himself more impressed than shocked. The plan, after all, was well conceived. Better conceived than *his* plan had been. Then he remembered he was about to become a pawn in the second phase of her operation—getting Mena back. If she still needed the kingpin.

"Now I want my husband, Robert . . . and you will help me bring him home." She was still smiling. It was a smile you'd see in a fashion magazine: beauty without a hint of warmth.

"The president and his secretary of state will never agree to extradite Mena . . . I feel I must point that out." The voice was weak, but it resonated with experience in such matters.

"Yes, they will, Robert. You are too valuable to them . . . Remember, I have the file on your terrible plan. I can make your government look very bad all over the world. They do not want that, do they?"

"The United States wants to stop drugs from coming into the country, corrupting our youth, and feeding crime."

"Is that really the most important thing to your president, my dear Robert?" Baby talk. She was obviously having a great deal of fun with him.

"That's not my call," said Harding. He was getting stronger now, almost ready to accept his fate.

"We will see how important your miserable life is to President Ferguson. I am sure he will be more loyal to you than Solano was to Espinoza! I am counting on that." She stopped for a long second and studied him. "You gringos are not tough enough to sacrifice someone in public."

Harding wanted to tell her that he wasn't valuable enough to save, but he knew that wasn't true. At least he hoped it wasn't. The president would do everything in his power to get one of his ambassadors back. If he did not, then all American ambassadors would become more vulnerable than they already were. Harding had another reason to hope for his own survival, and it was indeed the extradition card. He was willing to bet that Julia wanted to make sure no Colombian citizen was ever imprisoned in the United States again. He was beginning to think this was more important to her than seeing her beloved husband again. No matter how the deck was stacked, Julia had all the cards.

"I will present our demands to your president in the morning, Mr. Ambassador. Your life will then be in his hands." She adjusted her robe and looked past him at the plywood door.

"Diego . . . get this pig out of here!"

They huddled around the console of Corvalán's lead boat, listening to Carl conduct a briefing in two languages. Concealed in the foliage along the bank of a small stream, each man had spent the day preparing himself for the risky business of reconnaissance and surveillance. It was already dark.

"The American government wants us to find Ambassador Harding and wait for reinforcements. Those reinforcements have not been identified—at least not to me. Also, now that we're in the AO, I don't see how anyone else could get in here to do the job. When I was given this mission, the instructions were clear: find Harding, but do not attempt to rescue him yourselves." Carl paused, and Jerry jumped in.

"Like you, Boss, I've assumed all along that coordinating instructions for a rescue force would be forthcoming . . . since we had to launch so quickly. So far, we've heard nothing from Washington. That makes me very nervous."

Carlos looked at everyone he could see before responding. "We *are* the rescue force now. There is no one to coordinate *with*. I have no doubt that the five of us, supported by Major Corvalán and his men, can find Harding and get him back to the United States. We have the tactical skill to do that, as well as the firepower."

"But that's not the whole issue, is it?" said Bosco from the back, a voice from outside the dim red aura around the console. He spoke in English to make sure Jerry, Billy Joe, and Ron Dozier understood.

"That's right, Bosco . . . There is a second act in this play, and it might get a little hairy." Carl took a deep breath. "The traffickers know who we are . . . They have our bios, taken from Harding's personal safe."

"So, maybe we'll just have to kill *all* of 'em," said Billy Joe with an eager, toothy grin.

"That's *exactly* what we're going to do," responded Carl firmly. "We don't want to live the rest of our lives wondering when some guy on a motorcycle is going to take us out . . . We are all targets."

"Then we'll have to go with what we have right here," said Jerry, stroking his MP5 like a pet. "The trick will be to make our basic load last long enough."

Carlos nodded and continued in English. "We have enough 5.56 ammo, and the major has the M60s." He looked at Corvalán.

"We will be there for you," said Lucho. He said it in English, then turned to his crews and explained in Spanish. After less than a minute of discussion, he turned back to the American. "*Estámos de accuerdo, Carlos.*"

It was agreed. They would take no prisoners.

The river was beyond dark. Carl had always been amazed by how quickly and how thoroughly night came to the jungle. It was almost as if the trees beckoned them to become part of the forest. And that was exactly what they were preparing to do. Wearing Colombian camouflage without insignia, the men inspected one another meticulously. Web harnesses, soap dish charges, rucksacks, night vision goggles, leg holsters, silenced pistols, squad radios, ammo pouches, medical kits, canteens, red flashlights, and fins—all carried in the same places on each man—were touched and verified. They jumped up and down, listening for the sound of buckles in need of more tape.

Next came the ritual of applying camouflage makeup. There was something about face paint that had always intrigued Carl. Warriors had applied it since the Stone Age, a cultural inheritance as well as a military one. The greasy colors completed the human bonding needed by teammates facing death together. But the paint gave them more than camouflage and group identity; it gave individuals a feeling of invincibility to counter the unspoken fear. Jungle beauticians, in a sense, helping one another get ready to go onstage.

They stretched and twisted, making sure their loads were balanced and comfortable. It would be a long night of sitting and watching. When they were ready to go, Jerry turned on the satellite radio and transmitted the code word that would indicate to Simmons they were putting men in the bush, but had not yet located the target. Dozier, equipped exactly like the other Americans, sent his own code word to Panama. Corvalán and his men, whose camouflage uniforms bore the insignia and rank of the Colombian Marine Corps, stood by their positions as the boats eased away from the hide site.

Carl was the first one in the canoe. As he floated next to the lead patrol boat (now drifting to the launch point), he tilted the engine forward. Then he reached up, found Jerry's wrist, and gave it a firm squeeze. Carefully, the others followed the big man down and took their positions in the wooden craft. Dozier handed them all paddles from his position in the cover boat. When they were in place, they waited for Corvalán to tap Dozier on the shoulder so he could pass it on to Carl. The four of them received the signal and stroked out together, taking the canoe away from the heavily armed mother craft.

They paddled away from the security of Corvalán's boats to what they hoped was the *in*security of a possible jungle laboratory. Or a guerrilla base camp. Or both. As he dipped his paddle into the river, it occurred to Carl that an ordinary person would find no logic in his actions. A sane man would have stayed in the boats. Or back in the States.

Corvalán let his boats drift in the current as Carl's team paddled to the mouth of the tributary. Carl knew the patrol boats, with their machine guns and 7.62-millimeter rounds, would be waiting not more than five minutes downstream from the confluence. What he did not know was just how far up the tributary his team would have to go. He had seen small streams in flat terrain reach for miles into the jungle, and he hoped this would not be one of them. In the event of a compromise, the firefight would not last much longer than five minutes. Their safety rested, not on blending into the environment, but on becoming *part* of it. With senses properly tuned, they paddled into the tributary and glided under the triple canopy rainforest.

The stream was only a little wider than the length of the canoe and, at some points, the branches closed over the water. Carl, sitting in the stern, kept the canoe moving forward, but only as fast as the vegetation would permit. If someone came down the tributary, there would be nowhere to go. Billy Joe wore night vision goggles, but the lenses could not help him see through the giant leaves hanging in every direction. The leaves cut both ways, blocking *all* vision. The jungle was neutral, not caring who won or lost. In the end, the trees would conceal . . . whomever, or whatever. As Jerry handed him another branch to lift quietly over his head, Carl intensified his focus. He silently willed the target to appear soon.

If it was there at all.

They had picked their way about half a mile into the forest when Billy Joe passed the signal from the bow. Movement! Although the vegetation had thinned out a bit, Carl could not see anything. Nevertheless, he knew they could proceed no further. At least not in the canoe. He held water with his paddle and coaxed the dugout under the branches on the east side of the stream. Billy Joe duck-walked aft to whisper the details to him.

"There's a couple of guys up there on the left side of the stream, Boss . . . 'bout fifty meters. Looks to me like they're coverin' somethin' with branches . . . pro'lly a boat . . . sitting next to a break in the trees."

"Got it," whispered Carl. "This is where Butkus and I get off. You and Bosco can now go around and plug the back door."

Carl found the big man's wrist again and gave it a squeeze. He stepped carefully out of the canoe and squatted on the bank, training his goggles up and down the creek. Jerry knelt next to him, pointing his weapon at the jungle behind them. Carl watched the other half of his team paddle their canoe slowly back toward the main river. Jerry donned his goggles, and they looked for an observation post at which to spend the rest of the night.

As Carl and Jerry settled into their OP, Billy Joe and Jose moved silently along the north bank of the main river. Carl didn't know if there was a camp in front of him, but if there was, he knew it would have two exits. It was Billy Joe and Jose's job to find the alternate trail that would lead the bad guys back to the Putumayo. Carl and Jerry, at some point, would flush them, like pheasants. Billy Joe and Jose would take them out before they got to the river. An hour passed before Carl got the message he needed in order to press on his end.

"Carlos, Bosco . . . we're knocking on the back door." In the dark, they had found what they thought was a trailhead leading into the jungle. And out. "Will investigate and report."

"Bosco, Carlos . . . roger that . . . Keep us posted . . . You there, Leroy?"

"Carlos, Leroy . . . I copy."

The men waited in the blackness, absorbing themselves into the forest. They watched and they listened, visualizing the actions they might have to take with only seconds' notice. The waiting was the hardest part.

Carl watched as the unidentified figures finished dragging branches to the edge of the tributary. Jerry was sitting behind him, training his eyes and his weapon downstream and into the bush. The men were about twenty meters away from them, talking in normal voices. Carl could not hear exactly what they were saying, but the Colombians appeared relaxed. The Americans were not at all relaxed.

Suddenly, one of the men produced a flashlight and shined it into the water directly in front of them! Carl closed one eye and found the trigger housing on his submachine gun. Had they been seen? Had they been heard? Or, was this guy just going through the motions of looking around? Carl quickly assessed the situation. Worst case, he and Jerry would have to shoot their way out. Then swim. Corvalán would not be able to get there in time and neither would Billy Joe. There weren't many rules here, but one of them was to avoid a firefight initiated by the enemy.

Carl started to slowly reach for his secondary weapon, a silenced Sig Sauer. He and Jerry sat tight and tried not to breathe as the white light danced across the narrow creek and all around them. As they averted their eyes, the beam passed over them one more time. When it had passed, Carl quickly slipped off his goggles. He looked up to see the men turn away, and he watched the flashlight disappear into the forest. A path!

Ten minutes later they were in the water, side stroking to where the traffickers (if that is what they were) had vanished into the trees. Both men were out of the water in less than a minute, patrolling very slowly along the jungle path. They had their goggles back on, weapons locked and cocked. The big man kept one hand on Carl's rope belt and trained his weapon behind them with the other. The forest floor was wet, and they made no sound. It took them almost an hour to reach the clearing.

About half a mile away, Billy Joe and Jose froze in horror as two of the loudest powerboats they had ever heard came racing by, pushing large waves rarely felt on the banks of the Putumayo. The intruders began to slow down at the entrance to the tributary. *Carlos has company!* Jose called Corvalán and asked him to move the Piranhas closer, explaining exactly where they had left Carl and Jerry.

Jose called Jerry but could not raise him. Either their teammates were dead, or they were on the move. Since he hadn't heard any gunfire, he chose to believe they were picking their way through the forest. He kept the earphone in his ear and waited for a status report.

The threatening engines slowed, and the racing boats idled into the tributary. Headed directly to the point where they had left Carl and Jerry!

Where are *those guys?*

With tension rising, Billy Joe and Jose held a quick meeting in the jungle.

"We have 'em surrounded, man!" Billy Joe's mangrove-laced accent came through even in a whisper. "We got Carlos to their front, Lucho on the flank, and us on the other side. What more could you want, Bosco?"

"An answer from Butkus," came the reply.

"He'll let us know if he needs us, man . . . I say we stay right here and see how this thing goes. Chances are nothin'll happen till daylight."

"Yeah," said Jose. "I'm not in the mood for a firefight just yet . . . but we have to check out this trail to see if it actually leads to the enemy camp."

"We're gonna have a *doozy* of a fight when the time is right," said Billy Joe. "I jus' wanna take out as many bad guys as I can before we leave!"

"You and me, we're gonna take 'em *all* out, *hermano.*"

Carl and Jerry were standing at the edge of the clearing when they heard the boats behind them. They looked at each other and raised two fingers to the lenses covering their eyes. The hand signal for "enemy" always made Carl's heart pound but, this time, he knew they were in deep trouble. In front of them lay a collection of crude buildings. Lights burned in the two thatched structures on the left side of the open area. Barracks, thought Carl, though the smaller building didn't seem big enough to house more than one individual. There were several structures to the right of the clearing, but they appeared to be unoccupied. The boats would drop off more people, and those people would come down the very path on which he and Jerry now stood!

"Butkus!" Carl cupped the man's ear with this hand. "We'll have to sit this one out in the trees . . . not the safest OP, but it's all we have. Follow me . . . then call Bosco and get the status of their recon."

They sidestepped into the forest and found a layup point about ten meters off the trail. When they were seated back-to-back, Carl had a partial view of the path. Jerry could see into the compound without goggles. A quick call to Jose confirmed that the boats had passed them on the main river, and that Corvalán was moving his boats closer.

Minutes later they saw flashlights coming down the path. As they sat frozen, the lights came directly at them, veering into the clearing at the very last moment. Carl knew that if he and Jerry kept absolutely still they would not be seen. There were six men, all but one carrying a heavy piece of equipment. The man without the equipment, fourth in line, had no flashlight. He shuffled along, head down, with his hands in front of his groin as if chained.

The profile of a prisoner!

As the hunched figure came into the dim light, Jerry could see the details that had eluded Carl.

"Boss," he whispered. "That's Harding!"

Carl shifted his body position enough to see into the compound and stashed his goggles. They watched with fascination and horror as the procession reached the center of the clearing and stopped. Harding's handler threw the ambassador to the ground as the others began putting together what a military person might have called a field-expedient film set. When the men were finished, Carl and Jerry found themselves looking at spotlights driven by a portable generator, a camcorder on a tripod, and two stools. Oprah in the jungle, thought Carl with a smile.

The smile disappeared when he saw a woman clad in military fatigues walk into the clearing.

Jerry sent the coordinates to Dozier, along with the code word for Harding. Dozier passed it on to Simmons in Quito. It was exactly 2230. There were no roving security patrols in evidence. The Americans were still wet but relatively comfortable. Without relaxing their guard *too* much, Carl and Jerry sat back to watch the show.

The National Security Council had met twice since the kidnapping of Robert Harding. The first meeting had been called at once, the second after the assassination of Ernesto Solano. There was no need to meet again until something changed the situation. A situation everyone agreed was close to hopeless. At the first meeting they decided to punish Colombia with economic sanctions. The second meeting had been called to reverse the imposition of sanctions and help the new Colombian president stem the tide of political chaos he had just inherited. The day after the second meeting, President Ferguson took a call from his CIA director on the red phone.

"Mr. President," began the man responsible for all US intelligence activities. "Robert Harding is dead."

Silence from the Oval Office. Then a long sigh. "I was afraid it would come to this, William. Now what do we do?"

"We go after them, sir."

"Do we know who *they* are . . . and where?" asked Ferguson.

William Tyson Randolph, eminent scholar, born politician, and habitual pleaser, answered with the confidence of a man who had forgotten his academic roots. He had stopped asking questions of his subordinates and started nodding up and down to his superiors. The DDO had reported Harding's demise; Randolph had not challenged him. The CIA director would do whatever the president asked him to do. Even if it made no sense.

"Yes, we do, sir," said Randolph, nodding into the phone. "Cartel thugs, sir. Their camp is right on the Peruvian border . . . north bank of the Putumayo River. Here are the coordinates."

The president of the United States got out a pen and wrote down the numbers.

"Are there any more Americans down there?" asked the president.

"No, sir. I have received assurances from my deputy director for operations that all our information is coming from Colombian assets. His special assistant, Jeff Girardin, has been on this case from the beginning. Jeff doesn't make mistakes, sir."

"OK . . . I'll call the SECDEF and get him to turn off the rescue force and lay on the stealth fighters," said the president. "Keep me posted."

"Yes, sir. This thing will be over soon. There will be no political fallout, Mr. President. It will be the tragic case of a brave American ambassador, losing his life for upholding the moral principles of the United States. Colombia will pay, sir . . . but you will not."

Allen Ferguson put down the red phone and picked it up again. He punched four numbers and waited a few seconds. Not long enough to reconsider.

"Secretary of Defense's Office, sir . . . Lieutenant General Miller."

"Good morning, General . . . this is the president."

"I'll put the secretary right on, sir."

Another few seconds passed . . . still not long enough to reconsider.

"Yes, sir!" said a Latin voice. Victor Ozal, descended from Turkish immigrants and former congressional representative of the Tampa area, had grown up in Venezuela before being brought to the United States as a teenager. He was a civilian, but with a warrior soul and the bearing of Kemal Ataturk. When Ozal was given a mission, he did whatever it took to get the job done. The president had total confidence in him.

"Vic," said Ferguson sternly. "I have just learned that Robert Harding is dead. Plan B is in effect. Here are the coordinates. I want the hostage takers to pay."

Ozal copied down the numbers. "We'll have GPS-guided bombs on the target early tomorrow evening, sir."

The president interrupted. "Those bombs are experimental, aren't they?"

"As long as the coordinates are accurate," responded Ozal, "the warheads will detonate within three meters. No one will see the planes come in, and there will be no one left on the ground to see them leave."

"Have a nice day, Victor."

"You too, Mr. President."

Ozal hung up the phone and called the chairman of the Joint Chiefs of Staff. "Harding is dead. Plan B is in effect . . . Time on target is 1900 tomorrow. Here are the coordinates." He waited for a few seconds. "Also, I want you to keep the Rangers on alert . . . just in case. Got that?"

"Yes, sir," came the reply from the chairman.

While Carl and Jerry watched the bizarre videotaping, Billy Joe and Jose advanced on the other side of the objective. They had figured the trail would have to be fairly obvious so the occupants of the camp could find it in the middle of the night. And they would be running. The Americans had found a ledge on the bank of the river with footprints . . . and cigarette butts. A short search had revealed the jungle path they were on. The howler monkeys had gotten used to their presence. Jose was plugged into the radio; Billy Joe was plugged into the night.

"Butkus, Bosco," whispered Jose into the boom microphone resting on his cheek. "We are following what appears to be the backside trail, headed your way."

This time, Jerry came right back. "We are on the other side of the compound, looking across," said the big man. "Give me a shout when you reach the compound."

"Got it," was all Jose said.

Just a few hundred meters away, Carl turned to Jerry and listened to the recap. Then he trained his ears on the compound again, straining to hear. "Butkus, can you pick up any of this?"

"No, I can't, Boss," whispered Jerry, momentarily taking out his earphone. "It looks like they're making two tapes, though. The woman's gesturing a lot, but I can't hear what anybody's saying. Maybe it's an argument?"

"It's either a dispute over what to do with Harding," said Carl, "or it has something to do with the ratio of men to women in the camp."

"I wouldn't want to be the only woman out here . . . and it looks like she's in charge! This chick must be one tough cookie."

"Harding is just sitting there," observed Carl. "I don't think he even knows where he is."

"I bet they kicked the shit outta him," said the big man. "Can't we just take him and run?"

"Not yet . . . not yet. We need to watch and listen until we're out of surprises. I'm not as worried about getting the hostage as I am about taking care of *all* these guys and getting out of here in one piece."

"Roger that, Carlos."

A few minutes later, the taping session was over and the equipment was being dismantled. There were indeed two tapes. The woman took the second cassette from the camera and gave it to one of the men. She slipped the first one in her pocket. *A proof-of-life video?* Carl and Jerry hunkered down to observe the procession back to the racing boats. One by one, the men filed by, with Harding shuffling along in the middle. Had they brought the hostage with them in one of the boats? Or, was there a makeshift prison somewhere between the clearing and the river? They had to find out, and that meant they would have to move quickly.

"Bosco, Butkus . . . the bad guys are going back to the tributary with the hostage. We are following them . . . no one coming your way as far as we can tell." When Jose did not answer right away, Jerry called Dozier in a more urgent tone.

"Leroy, Butkus . . . did you hear my last to Bosco?"

Dozier came on immediately. "Butkus, Leroy . . . that's affirm . . . We are concealed and will not engage unless compromised." Carl and Jerry huddled quickly as they got ready to go. Events were forcing them to take chances they did not want to take.

"Leroy, Butkus . . . if they leave in the boats with Harding, you will have to follow them on the river . . . We are in pursuit and will advise." Jerry was now practically running after Carl. He had to assume there was nobody behind them because he didn't have time to look.

Jose's response finally came as Carl quickened the pace even more. "Butkus, Bosco . . . roger that . . . We are about two hundred meters into the forest . . . They won't see us if they come this way."

What Jose did *not* say was that he hadn't bothered to camouflage the canoe. The craft was tied off and floating in the river. They had decided not to tell the others, thinking it would just worry them. If the go-fasts came back the same way they had come in—and they saw the canoe—Billy Joe and Jose would be trapped between the river and the compound. There was nothing they could do now. If they had to fight it out, thought Jose, he and Billy Joe could hold their own.

But it would be sloppy.

Carl and Jerry caught up with the flashlights about halfway to the water and began walking again. Luckily, the video equipment had slowed the men down. They were also now *dragging* Harding. Jerry picked up his field of fire to the rear, while Carl brought him to within twenty meters of the last man in the parade. All of a sudden, one of the men—the largest one by far—pushed the prisoner into the trees on the left side of the path while the others continued in the direction of the boats. Carl followed the prisoner. Jerry followed Carl, making a call to Dozier on the run.

"The prisoner is *not* on the boats . . . Repeat, *not* on the boats. Let them pass . . . Repeat, let them pass."

"Butkus, Leroy . . . got it. Staying put. Out."

Ten minutes later, Billy Joe and Jose heard the engines fire up in the distance. They froze in their tracks and listened—even more intently than the others—until the boats were out of the tributary, on the main river, and past their free-floating canoe.

"Dodged that bullet," said a relieved Jose. "Guess they're in a hurry."

"They sure missed a good firefight," mused Billy Joe.

"I think we'll see 'em again, Tinker . . . Don't you worry about that." Jose was beginning to miss the Queens neighborhood his mother had given him. Even the mean streets of Medellín, he thought, would be better than this. The man just had a bad feeling that this operation wasn't going to turn out very well. He shook it off and refocused on covering Billy Joe. They crept along the trail as it wound its way through the jungle thickness. It was after midnight by the time they made it to the edge of the clearing. They sent the proper signal to Jerry and sat just off the path, waiting for guidance from the boss. They didn't have to wait long.

"Bosco, Carlos . . . tell me what you see."

Jose described everything he could make out, demonstrating to both of them exactly where he and Billy Joe were sitting. Satisfied that the pair was sitting across the clearing from where he and Jerry had observed the taping, Carl directed them to return to the trail-head on the river. Jose and Billy Joe backtracked quickly to the spot, concealed the canoe properly, and set the watch.

"Carlos, Bosco . . . we are in place at the trailhead on the river."

Dozier chimed in. "Carlos, Leroy . . . we are downstream from the tributary, about three hundred meters. The go-fasts are proceeding upstream, very fast, toward Maldonado."

Carl and Jerry watched from their third OP of the night as the giant pushed Harding into a canvas tent surrounded by three thatched buildings. There were five other Colombians, all standing around laughing. That brought the total number of enemy sighted to twenty.

Nineteen men and one woman.

Carl and Jerry sat like statues. They had the hostage in sight. The code word—with eight-digit coordinates—had been sent to Quito. Though they did not talk, both men were thinking the same thing. Technically, the mission was over—at least as far as CIA was concerned. There was still no word on the rescue force Jeff had insisted would rescue Harding. Carl was still shaking his head about what a rescue plan would look like, where the troops would come from, where they would insert, and how they would get out. *No way!* He felt, literally, like a sitting duck. If they left now, they could be back in Tipishca in two days—assuming they could extract themselves without being detected.

But they could not just leave *now.* Harding had a right to be rescued; Carl and his men had a right to live into old age back home.

Back on the command boat, Dozier was thinking the same thing. If there were to be a rescue force, it would have to be Rangers. They would have to jump in blind to a clandestine airfield no one had yet located. After that, they would have to patrol through impassable jungle to where Carl and the team now sat. Then they would have to get out! If Carl and his team were successful, there would be no hostage to rescue! And Corvalán's boats would be gone. Ron Dozier, sitting in relative comfort and surrounded by medium machine guns, had finally worked out the big picture. He could not allow a rescue force to launch from the States. Protocol dictated that he explain this to Quito. He tried five times before he got someone to talk to him.

"Dilbert is not here." Dilbert was the call sign for Station Chief Simmons.

"Get him!" shouted Dozier, forgetting for a moment where he was. He continued in lower tone. "I have urgent traffic for Gotham. I'll be waiting on this frequency . . . Out." Gotham was the call sign for Jeff's Washington control cell.

Dozier pulled another SATCOM radio out of his rucksack and made a second call—to Panama. He got a much better response from General Stewart.

It was almost one o'clock in the morning. They all heard a sound that did not belong to the jungle. A small airplane took off from somewhere upstream, away from the river, and headed north. Toward Bogotá.

Dozier still hadn't heard back from Simmons.

Chapter 12

End Game

"**G**ood morning . . . White House switchboard . . . how may I help you?"

"Listen carefully," said the heavily accented male voice. "I have information on the whereabouts of Ambassador Robert Harding."

"Who is this?" asked the operator. She had heard her share of prank calls, but this one did not sound like a prank.

"No games, gringo bitch! I will say this only once . . . There is a package at the Miami airport . . . locker number 3801 at the main terminal. Get it, and give it to President Ferguson right away! We have Harding, and we will kill him unless the United States fulfills two conditions. These are *demands* . . . Do you understand?"

"What are your demands?"

"The president must release Jorge Mena Velasquez—we know you have him—within two days. And we must receive assurances that no Colombian citizen will ever be extradited for what the United States thinks are criminal offenses." There was a pause. "You got that?"

"Yes, I understand," said the operator, still writing. "How do you wish the president to communicate his response to you?"

"Tell him to use CNN International. We will be watching." Then the man hung up.

The operator looked at her watch as she dialed the president's chief of staff. It was just past noon.

Ten minutes later, William Randolph got another call from the president.

"William . . . we just got a call from someone claiming to have a package for me regarding Robert Harding. The caller said Harding is alive!"

"I don't see how that could be true, Mr. President. Our sources are right there in the field—with Harding's captors. This call has to be a bluff."

"The package is supposedly in a locker at the Miami airport . . . I'm sending a fighter from Andrews to pick it up now. The caller says they will kill Robert if they don't get what they want."

"And what do they say they want, sir?"

"They want the kingpin Mena back . . . plus assurances that we will never extradite any Colombian citizen for criminal behavior."

Randolph was shocked but did not let his voice waver. "Those animals have already killed Harding, sir. They're trying to make it look like your fault!"

"But, William," continued the president. "It *is* my fault . . . I'm responsible either way."

"Yes, sir . . . but if we stay with the plan, we can blame Harding's death on them. I can assure you, Mr. President, Robert Harding is dead. We will ensure that the public knows there was nothing you could do. Whatever is in that package needs to be destroyed."

"But what if it contains a picture of Harding . . . alive?"

"All the more reason to destroy it, sir. We can't afford misunderstandings. The chief of staff won't say anything about the phone call, and we can make sure the operator forgets all about it." Randolph was suddenly concerned about his own job. More important than that, his reputation. *What if the DDO was wrong? What if Harding really is alive?* It wouldn't matter, he explained to himself without emotion. It was easier this way.

Allen Ferguson retrieved and destroyed the package. William Randolph did nothing. Neither said a word to anyone.

Dawn came as a general awareness of light. Each surveillance team had set watches during the early hours, but now increased vigilance. They passed the bulk of the day like the nocturnal creatures they had become. Each man sat perfectly still, waiting for darkness and the violence it would bring. Rain soaked them until they shivered, even in the warmth of the jungle. It was difficult to separate good thoughts from bad thoughts. In the quiet chaos around them, all thoughts ran together.

Ron Dozier had been awake all night, watching, listening, and worrying. He was just nodding off when the radio came to life. He glanced at his watch; it was already after 1400.

"Leroy, this is Robinson, over." The signal was as clear as a telephone call. Dozier recognized General Stewart's bass voice.

"Robinson, this is Leroy, over."

"Leroy . . . I cannot go into detail here, but listen carefully." There was a slight pause as Stewart took a deep breath. "Get out of there! Do you hear me? *Get out of there!*"

Captain Dozier's knee-jerk response was, "Yes, sir!"

But he needed more.

"Sir . . . I don't know if we can do that . . . What is the problem? Carlos is in the bush . . . I need to tell him."

"Leroy . . . the force you were told would come after you were extracted? That force is ready to come *now*—and they don't know you're there! They have not been briefed on your mission. How copy, over?"

"Robinson, Leroy . . . roger that . . . The rescue force is coming and does not know we are here." Dozier paused, and then added, "How the hell did *that* happen?"

"I'm trying to find that out, son, but I can't get anyone at the Pentagon to tell me what is going on. I told them they have a possible blue-on-blue situation developing, but they think I'm nuts!"

"We don't need any help in getting the hostage out of here." Dozier was jolted by a blinding flash of the obvious. "The CIA chain has the same coordinates I passed to you . . . They must have shared them with the Pentagon. When is TOT?"

"Time on target looks like early this evening, Leroy . . . I will try and turn it off, but you have no choice . . . Get out of there as fast as you can. Do you hear me?"

"Robinson, Leroy . . . I'll tell Carlos . . . and call you back soonest. Out here."

Dozier fumbled for the other radio and picked up the handset. Corvalán hadn't understood all the English, but he knew they were in big trouble. He sat down across from the American as they conferred in the shade of the hide site. In bad Spanish, Dozier filled the major in on the situation. Corvalán then sprang from his seat to ready the boat crews for action.

"Butkus, Leroy . . . I have private traffic for Carlos."

It seemed like a long time before he heard anything. He didn't *have* a long time! He knew Jerry was getting the boss to relax his surveillance of the target and put on the earphone. *What the fuck is taking so long?*

"Leroy, Carlos . . . this better be good."

"Carlos . . . the shit is hitting the fan . . . I just got off the horn with my boss . . . The rescue force is coming . . . and they don't know we're here! Robinson says we gotta leave *now*!"

Dozier couldn't hear it, but he knew Carl was swallowing hard.

"When is TOT?" asked Carl without emotion.

"Robinson didn't know for sure, but he guessed early this evening. He's trying to call it off, but there are only a few officers in the Pentagon who even know what's happening . . . and he hasn't been able to talk to them. He did say the Rangers are getting ready to go . . . somewhere, but he doesn't know if they are the force of choice."

"Leroy, Carlos . . . you know as well as I do that not even the *Rangers* are capable of getting in and out of here."

"You're right, Carlos. I think there's another plan, but I can't imagine what that would be."

"Leroy . . . listen to me. We can't just leave without the hostage . . . You know that."

"Let's just take him and get out!"

"We can't just *take* him . . . You know that too. Let me think this through and call you back . . . When is Robinson getting back to you?"

"He didn't say, but it'll be as soon as he finds out what the hell is going on. Carlos . . . I hate to say this, but it sounds like we got set up."

"I'll call you back. Out here."

Carl sat for a full minute, trying to calm himself before briefing Jerry. He was more angry than afraid. He had not trusted his CIA employers, but he had assumed that Jeff would send the coordinating instructions. He knew the rescue force would not be able to get Harding out alive. *Maybe that was the plan!* And it suddenly made sense . . . not to Carl, but to a man on the low end of the moral spectrum.

A man trying to cover his ass.

It wasn't a rescue force preparing to come in; it was an *attack* force! Hell, thought Carl, the military commanders had probably been briefed that Ambassador Harding was already dead. Carl was now sure they had also been briefed that everyone at his coordinates was a target—justifiable revenge for the kidnapping of an American ambassador.

"Butkus, old friend." He leaned toward his teammate of twenty years. "We are in deep shit." He explained the situation as quickly as he could. Jerry wanted to explode but kept his surveillance discipline. Next, Carl got on the radio to brief Jose, who would pass it on to Billy Joe. Then he called Dozier back.

"Leroy, Carlos . . . this is the new plan."

Carl could not remember ever moving against the enemy before nightfall. He had been trained from the beginning to fight at night. An inferior force, to be successful, had to choose the time of the attack. And the place. But none of that mattered now. They would have to go ahead with what they had, and what they had was late afternoon. At least he would get to choose the location of the battle.

Harding was still in his tent. The guard outside the tent flap was sitting on a stool—the same stool Harding had sat on during the taping—with a submachine gun in his lap. The rain had stopped, and the giant man was reading a magazine. During the surveillance, Carl and Jerry had tried to keep track of where all the targets were. Three of them had walked out of the makeshift prison compound an hour before in the direction of the tributary landing. There would have to be a go-fast at the landing, perhaps fifty meters away, but Carl had not confirmed it. That left two men in the thatched building opposite the tent. Carl waited as long as he could for the three men to return—but he didn't have a lot of time. He hadn't heard an engine, so he guessed the men were doing some kind of repairs. Maybe they were refueling the boat.

It was time to move.

Carl quietly extracted the Sig Sauer from its leg holster. The silencer made the barrel heavier than he liked, but the small difference in balance would not matter at such short range. He slipped the MP5 over one shoulder, got his breathing under control, and nodded to Jerry. They stood up together and, in slow motion, stepped carefully to the edge of the clearing.

The brute saw something moving in his peripheral vision. He looked up from the magazine, expecting to see his comrades returning from the river. Instead, he took a bullet in the very center of his forehead. And another through the cheek as he went down. At the same instant, Jerry burst into the building behind Carl and fired four suppressed rounds. Two more bodies melted into the forest floor.

Carl threw open the tent flap and fell to his knees in front of the ambassador. The man was still in chains.

"I'm taking you out of here, Mr. Ambassador," he announced in low voice, thrusting his hand over Harding's mouth. "Where are the keys?"

"The guard has them," mumbled Harding through Carl's fingers. "Is he . . . dead?"

Carl didn't answer. He ducked under the tent flap and frisked the huge corpse. Jerry was on one knee at the entrance to the compound, training his pistol down the trail toward the tributary. He nodded at Carl to acknowledge that he'd done his job. Carl duck-walked back into the tent and unlocked Harding's shackles.

"Stay here . . . You got that?"

"Where are you going? Please don't leave me!" The ambassador sounded to Carl like a hysterical woman. If they ever made it out of here, thought Carl, it would be a long ride home with this kind of civilian baggage.

"I'll be right back, sir . . . If anyone other than me comes into this tent, shoot 'em!" He gave Harding his MP5 with the stock extended. "This is the safety . . . Just aim, push the lever off safe, and pull the trigger. I'll announce myself before I come back in here."

Carl left the tent, darted past Jerry, and led his teammate down the path to the tributary. They both carried pistols at arm's length with both hands as they strode quickly to where they thought the men would be. Not a good situation, thought Jerry, but it's the best we'll get. *We just have to be fast!*

The men were exactly where Carl had predicted they would be. One was crouching over the port engine, another was standing on the starboard engine hatch, and the third was leaning against the side of the boat, smoking a cigarette. The Americans didn't even stop to consult one another.

Carl turned his head to Jerry as he broke into a run.

"Take left!"

Carl fixed his eyes on the targets to the right as he came to the end of the path. He brought his weapon up and fired two rounds into the chest of the man leaning against the boat. The man on the hatch had only enough time to glance at Carl before he took a bullet in the stomach. Carl kept running. Never lowering his gun, he put a second bullet in the man's throat.

Jerry had the easiest shot. The man in the engine compartment raised his head, and the big man just shattered it like a watermelon.

Six down, fourteen to go.

Jumping onto the boat, Carl saw that both engines were disassembled, with parts lying all over. They would not be able to use the boat to get out of there—but neither could anyone else. He leaped back onto the mudbank.

"Call Leroy and Corvalán," ordered Carl. "Tell them we have Harding . . . Tell them to prepare to engage at the mouth of the tributary . . . but to stay hidden. They are not to attack except on my order. Then tell Bosco our situation. Stay here . . . I'll be right back."

Jerry passed Carl's instructions to the others. Carl ran back up the path to get Harding. He stopped just before the clearing.

Harding was not in the clearing. Carl raised his pistol and walked slowly toward the tent, scanning for targets as he went.

"American coming in!"

He threw open the tent flap. No Harding! *Where the hell did he go?*

Carl initiated a circle search, starting at the edge of the clearing and working into the jungle stillness. He was now sorry he had given Harding his weapon. It would be a real shame, he thought, to lose the guy he was trying to save.

"Harding!" He was shouting now as he crashed through the foliage. "Harding . . . come out of there . . . I'm taking you home, damn it!"

Carl stepped around the trunk of a large tree and found himself staring down the barrel of his own submachine gun!

Harding was sitting on the ground, hyperventilating at the other end of Malinowski's weapon. The barrel was just beyond Carl's reach; he didn't even have time to cringe as he watched the ambassador squeeze the trigger!

If it hadn't happened in slow motion, Carl would not have remembered it later. There was no flash and no sound. The pain he expected did not come. He was not blasted into failure and oblivion.

Harding had forgotten to disengage the safety.

Carl sprang at the ambassador like a cat. Before landing on his prey, he extended his left hand and grabbed the business end of the weapon. He slammed the pistol in his right hand into Harding's chin. The MP5 was knocked to the ground, along with Harding.

"You idiot!" shouted Carl into the babbling face. "If you want to live, you do exactly what I say . . . You got that?" Now it was Carl's turn to hyperventilate.

"S-sorry," wheezed Harding through broken teeth. "I thought you . . . you were going to kill me."

"If you fuck up again, sir . . . I will!"

Half dragging the ambassador, Carl rejoined Jerry at the landing and got some news he didn't need.

"Bosco says the bad guys are coming back from Maldonado in the other go-fasts . . . two of 'em. Corvalán is ready to fight it out on the river. Whaddaya wanna do?"

Carl's mind raced as he tried to digest the information. He needed time to search the second compound. Corvalán would have to destroy the go-fasts. The American punitive raid, no matter what form it took, would be in the air by now. Headed his way!

"Tell Leroy that Corvalán must let the go-fast boats into the tributary. Let them *into* the tributary, but do not let them out. Repeat, do not let them out. Then tell Leroy to call Robinson again. If there's anything General Stewart can do for us . . . now would be the time."

Carl assessed the ambassador's condition. The man would be a huge burden. An unpredictable huge burden. If Carl hadn't realized that CIA wanted Harding dead, he would have been tempted to shoot the guy himself. *Now there's a thought!*

He decided to keep Harding alive and deal with Jeff later.

"Butkus . . . take this guy and don't let him out of your sight!" Carl angrily shoved Harding at Jerry and refocused on the trail connecting them with the lab. Jerry Tompkins introduced himself by extending his enormous hand and grabbing the ambassador by the back of the neck.

"You heard the man, sir . . . let's go." Jerry pushed Harding into the jungle.

"Bosco, Carlos . . . we have the hostage." Carl took one deliberate deep breath, which he desperately needed. "The go-fast over here is down hard. Where are the other go-fasts now?"

"Carlos, Bosco . . . about even with us, headed toward Leroy."

"Can you see how many bad guys are on board?"

Jose took a minute to respond. "I see two in each boat. Total of four."

"OK. We took out six so far. The rest are in the lab buildings farther down the trail. They still don't know we're here. Ask Tinker to come on the line. I need some ideas at this end."

Billy Joe had been listening on his own squad radio.

"Carlos, Tinker . . . they got a fuel farm over there? If you still have a soap dish, slap it on and use the explosion to drive the rest of the bad guys to me and Bosco."

"We haven't found any fuel drums . . . What do you recommend?"

"Go ahead and lay the demo on the hull of the boat . . . the fuel tank is just forward of the engine compartment . . . It pro'lly still has enough fumes in it to make major fireworks."

"Got it, Tinker . . . You and Bosco stay put . . . Wait till they bunch up at the river."

"Leroy, Carlos . . . did you copy my last with Tinker?"

"Carlos, Leroy . . . got it, Boss. We're standing by to engage the other boats when they try and come out of the tributary."

Carl was thinking at a rate of speed not humanly possible under conditions short of life and death. Luckily for him, the rest of the team was thinking just as fast. Too fast to call it thinking at all. Teamwork on a subconscious level. Pickup basketball. A mysterious energy sustained Carl. It was like this every time: the closer he was to death, the more alive he felt.

They all held their positions and waited. Ten minutes seemed like ten hours.

"Carlos, Leroy . . . the go-fasts are turning into the tributary, moving slowly. Lucho and I are across from the confluence, ready to pounce."

"Leroy, Carlos . . . got it . . . Stand by."

Carl reached into his leg pocket and extracted an olive-drab box the size of a cigarette pack. He ran to the side of the racing boat and placed the soap dish charge outboard of the fuel tank. He initiated the glue pot mechanism and set the fuse. No more than ten seconds later, he and Jerry were herding the ambassador down the trail into the forest. What remained of the daylight now worked in their favor; the remaining targets were easier to see. But so were Carl and his men. They had to maintain surprise.

There was a split-second delay between the initiation of the fuse and the thundering explosion. Fumes in the gas tank, combined with the C-4 plastic and aluminum powder, created an explosion of volcanic proportions. In a flash of yellow, the boat was lifted completely out of the water, its carcass tumbling through the air. What remained of the hull came down right in front of the approaching go-fast boats. The young man in the starched khakis began an emergency maneuver to turn the lead boat around in the narrow stream. The second boat collided with the first. With panicked shouting and furious gear shifting, it took several minutes for the boats to reverse course.

Only two men at the laboratory ran toward the explosion. Carl, running ahead of Jerry, took them both out without slowing down. As Jerry pushed the ambassador past the bleeding bodies, Harding started whimpering.

"Just like my Marines!" he wailed. "What have I done?"

"Gotten a whole lotta people killed," snapped Jerry, pushing harder. "Now shut the fuck up!"

Carl and Jerry got to the lab compound and found it deserted.

"Bosco, Butkus . . . looks like a lot of 'em headed your way . . . All hostile . . . Repeat, all hostile!"

Carl looked at the five flimsy buildings in front of them. There was no alternative but to search all of them. He had to make sure they'd flushed everyone to the river.

At that moment, the distinctive sound of M60 machine guns erupted at the mouth of the tributary. Dozier and Corvalán were engaged. Carl and Jerry got to work again.

"Ambassador Harding . . . you have to sit and wait for us to search these buildings," burst Carl, talking as fast as the machine guns in the distance. There was no response. Harding just sat there like a drunk. Carl grabbed the man's tattered shirt and shook him violently. "Harding! Sit down and stay *right here* . . . Do you understand me?"

Harding nodded his head but said nothing. Jerry laid one hand on the ambassador's shoulder and pushed him to the jungle floor at the base of a large tree.

"If you try and run, sir, I will shoot you," said the big man, straining to keep his finger off the trigger. "We'll be right back."

This time, Harding did not get a weapon.

With Carl on point again, they ran to the first door. Carl kicked the plywood off its rope hinges and stepped in with his MP5 shouldered. Jerry was right behind him as they divided fields of fire. Scanning rapidly with their eyes and muzzles, they moved quickly through the empty bunks, tables, and chairs. There was no one in the building.

One down, four to go.

As they prepared to kick the next door, the heart-stopping percussion of a close firefight arrived from the direction of Billy Joe and Jose. Carl turned to Jerry and quickly told him what to say. Jerry immediately passed it to Dozier.

"Leroy, Butkus . . . get your ass upriver as soon as you break contact. Tinker and Bosco are in a dick dragger and will need fire support. Carlos wants everyone to rally on the riverbank when it's over . . . Bosco, do you copy?"

Jose came on the line. "Yeah . . . I count eight of 'em. They came in two groups . . . and we opened up on the first one. We got the second one pinned down, but they have AKs and we don't. Just hurry!"

Carl and Jerry ran to the second door and smashed through it. Nothing.

They moved quickly to the right and kicked the third door. As they crashed into the small room, Jerry knocked over a steel drum filled with acid. The caustic liquid spilled onto his leg up to the knee. He was so focused that he didn't feel the burn. All he saw was an empty room. No targets.

Time to move again.

They needed to move faster! Abandoning his training and instinct, Carl sent Jerry into the fourth building alone and took the fifth one himself. Just before he kicked down door number five, he listened to an exchange of gunfire next door. Then the chilling sound of someone dying. He wasn't absolutely sure Butkus had taken the man out; there was a small chance the man had killed Jerry. Carl didn't have time to analyze it further than that. He just trusted the big man to be alive, ready to back him up.

Number five was the smallest of the hootches. From their surveillance, he knew it was the quarters of the woman they had watched from the OP. The one who seemed to be in charge. He would have been surprised to find her still there, but he thought he might uncover some important documents. Documents with his name on them! Perhaps the video he wanted.

He did not expect to find the woman sprawled on her back with a bullet through her chest!

Carl stared at the dead woman for a moment. A moment he didn't have! To his utter astonishment, he had seen her before. He didn't have to think very long to remember her as the beautiful young lover lying next to Jorge Mena when they'd snatched him from his bed.

How did she *get here?*

He glanced quickly around the room, squatted in front of the body, and went through the pockets of her jungle fatigues. The videotape was still there. He knew what it was, and he knew what he would do with it. He didn't have time to search for documents, so he pulled another soap dish charge from his leg pocket and pulled the fuse. Dropping the device in the middle of the room, Carl ran from the building and grabbed Harding.

"Let's move," he shouted, looking up to see Jerry Tompkins charging toward him, changing magazines on the run. Nobody can kill Tompkins, thought Carl with a surge of pride. "Butkus . . . go to the river . . . I got Harding . . . We'll be right behind you."

Carl hated to wear the radio earphone, often relying on Jerry to be his radio operator. Just like the old days. He had taken the earphone out again.

"Carlos, Bosco . . . Tinker's down! He's not moving! I'm hangin' on, but there's two more I can't get . . . in between you and me. I'll shift fire when you come down the trail."

"Keep your head down, Bosco . . . Butkus here . . . On the way." As he hurried off to rescue Jose, Jerry didn't have time to tell Carl about Billy Joe.

Jerry sprinted along the winding path, looking for two targets. The enemy would have to be at, or near, the end of the trail. The big man slowed to a fast walk and shouldered his weapon, scanning left and right.

He found them with their backs to him, on the wrong side of an enormous tree trunk. Two more easy kills. Faceless, final, and clean.

But too late for Billy Joe.

"Butkus, Bosco . . . I think you got the last of 'em . . . I'm going to try and save Tinker."

Jose crawled over to Billy Joe while Jerry ran the rest of the way. Suddenly, more bullets were thudding into trees on either side of them. Jose ignored the incoming fire as he checked Billy Joe for vital signs. Jerry spun around and returned fire, protecting the medic and his patient. One of the traffickers had climbed into a tree, and Jerry couldn't find him. If the guy had a lot of ammunition, they could be in big trouble. More trouble than they already had.

Carl was coming down the trail with Harding!

Jose found no vital signs.

Jerry dragged Billy Joe's body behind a tree and got on the radio.

Just then, the laboratory went up in an ear-splitting cloud of smoke and fire.

"Carlos, Butkus . . . I hope that was your way of saying goodbye . . . We got a guy in a tree over here . . . Stay put till I get him down."

Carl was up on the radio again. "Got it . . . We're about fifty meters back from your position."

"Leroy, Butkus . . . where the hell *are* you?"

Dozier and Corvalán had won the river fight within a few minutes. The go-fasts had more power, but they were no match for the Piranhas in battle. The Colombian Marines had laid a perfect ambush at the mouth of the tributary, using 40-millimeter grenade launchers to destroy both racing boats. Two of the crewmen had been killed in a hail of machine gunfire; the other two were treading water next to the sinking boats.

"Butkus, Leroy . . . five minutes out!"

Luis Corvalán held up his left hand as the Colombian gunners were about to take out the men in the water.

"Leave this to me!" commanded the major.

Lucho shouldered an M16 and put one 5.56-millimeter round through the head of the man on the left.

"Por mi madre."

He put a bullet through the other head without taking his weapon down.

"Por mi padre."

Corvalán turned to his crews, and to the American. There were tears in his eyes.

"Vamos!"

The Piranhas raced upriver to deliver the fire support Jerry so desperately needed.

"Butkus, Leroy . . . closing on your position now."

Corvalán slowed and moved the lead boat along the bank, while Jerry directed its M60 fire at the trafficker in the canopy. Carl was now monitoring the battle from his position on the trail. Harding was still a zombie.

"Butkus, Carlos . . . what's going on down there?"

Jerry hesitated, not because he was busy directing fire support, but to try and control his choking voice.

"Corvalán is trying to take out a sniper at the riverbank." He drew another breath. "Tinker's down, Carl . . . Jose couldn't bring him back . . . He's dead."

Carl's somber reaction came quickly. "Shit." There was a short moment of silence. Carl spoke again, as Jerry found the trafficker in the tree with his laser aimer, marking it for the gunner. "Now we have to get him home, Jerry, where we can honor him properly." Then he added, "You and I both know this is how he always wanted to die."

The sniper fell from the tree and into the river. Corvalán maneuvered the Piranhas to the rally point on the bank. Harding in hand and twenty KIA, it was time to get far away from the grid coordinates Carl had given his employers—the government that now wanted them all dead.

Carl dragged Harding out of the forest and almost threw him to the ground. He ran to where Jose knelt over Billy Joe's lifeless body. Jose looked up and nodded. No words were exchanged. As a medic, he knew there was nothing he could have done. Grieving would come later. "Sleep well, my friend." He reached over and closed the young eyes that had seen so much.

Dozier jumped off the boat and hoisted Billy Joe over his shoulder. Blood poured from the dead man's mouth. Much later, when stories were told, they would all say that Billy Joe Barnes had been smiling when he died. The reality they would never forget was somewhat different. Billy Joe had died painfully.

Carl waited until the body was safely aboard, then Harding, then Jose, and then Jerry. He looked around at the scene of the battle, thinking the rest of them might actually get out of this situation alive. He loved the smell of spent gunpowder, but this time it was the residue of his friend's death.

He just wanted to go home.

Victor Ozal picked up the phone and called the president on his secure private line. He did not usually initiate his own phone calls, but this one required absolute secrecy. It was almost five o'clock in the afternoon, and it had been a long day. Even so, the time had passed too quickly.

"Ferguson."

"Mr. President," Ozal began. "We launched the stealth fighters a few hours ago. They are over the Pacific, headed south. They should be hitting the tanker just about now. After topping off, the planes will enter Colombian airspace just north of Tumaco. It will be dark by then. They will go through the mountains and follow the Putumayo River east to the target . . ."

"Good," interrupted the president.

"Not necessarily, sir," replied Ozal. "I just got a frantic phone call from a brigadier general in Panama who claims Harding is still alive . . . and that there are five more Americans with him." He waited for Ferguson's reaction before going further.

"That can't be right, Victor. I have received assurances from William that both his sources are Colombian, and that they are actually *with* the mob that killed Harding. We have eyes on the target, Vic. There can't be any mistake."

"Sir," said Ozal, a little less gently. "You have information that conflicts with mine. The general says he is in contact with the same sources Randolph told you about . . . but that they are Americans."

"Who is this general?"

"His name is Reginald Stewart, sir. He commands our special operations forces in Latin America. Not exactly a crackpot."

"Victor," said the president in a relaxed tone meant to soothe himself as well as the SECDEF. "He can't possibly have troops down there . . . or CIA would know."

"He says they're not his troops . . . They're civilians."

"Civilians? In the jungles of southern Colombia? Really, Vic . . . I don't think so."

"Mr. President . . . I don't think we should proceed with this operation."

"Nonsense, Victor!" The president did not want to challenge his CIA director, and he did not want to deal with another political crisis. Robert Harding had caused enough trouble for Ferguson during his stormy tenure as ambassador. The president wanted to put the Harding affair behind him. There was an election coming up. He was secretly glad that Harding had been killed. It was easier for everyone, except, of course, Harding.

"Sir . . .," stammered Ozal, "are you telling me to ignore Stewart?" Ozal was talking to the taping system he knew the president used for the purpose of recording history. The SECDEF wanted history to show that he had tried to stop the mission.

Just in case Stewart was right.

"Yes, Victor." The president paused. "I am. The general is mistaken, and we don't have time to delay this thing."

Ozal didn't really want to rock the boat. He liked his job too much. Allen Ferguson had fired more than a few of his cabinet officers for not listening to him. Having flourished in Washington, Victor Ozal did not want to go back to Tampa. And he didn't want to go back to the House of Representatives. He needed to maintain his perfect record of performance.

And he wanted a shot at the Senate.

"I must tell you, sir . . . I don't believe it either. My intel folks have nothing to substantiate what Stewart is saying. But I wanted to check with you before we lay ordnance on the camp."

"It's OK, Vic . . . William's people have been following the Harding case from the beginning. Tell Stewart to back off. I appreciate your calling me on this. Anything else?"

"No, sir. Time on target is 1900 hours. They won't miss."

Corvalán guided the Piranhas upriver. He had discarded the canoe in an effort to increase speed against the current. Tipishca was a long way ahead. The sun raced for the short horizon in front of them. It would be dark in less than an hour, and the so-called rescue force would be advancing on the ruins of the camp. Carl and his men would be well to the west by the time they got there, disappearing into the rhythm of the river.

The Colombians manned their machine guns while the Americans rested. Carl and Jerry sat in the lead boat. Harding lay on the deck, still barely aware of what was happening. Dozier and Jose were in the cover boat with the body of Billy Joe, wrapped in a poncho and secured with bungee cords.

"What did you find in the last building, Boss?" asked Jerry. As they shouted over the noise of the engines, he and Carl kept their eyes on the jungle racing by.

"Something you'll find hard to believe," said Carl.

"It must have been something worth destroying . . . I've never seen you destroy anything without a reason."

Carl raised his eyebrows and looked at his friend. "Remember when you lifted Mena out of that bed down in Brazil?"

"Yeah . . . he was a heavy son of a bitch!"

"Remember the woman next to him in the bed?"

"Do I? I'll never forget her, Boss. She was beautiful."

"That woman was in the fifth building."

"You're shitting me! The woman we saw making the video?" Jerry looked down and lowered his voice. "Did you have to . . . kill her?"

"No," said Carl firmly. "She was already dead . . . gunshot wound to the chest."

"That's good," said Jerry, nodding up and down. "It would have been tough to shoot someone like that."

213

"Apparently, it wasn't too tough for *somebody*."

"I can't believe a woman like her would sleep with a creep like Mena. She could have slept with any man on the planet!"

"You can imagine how good she looked when she charmed Harding out of his senses . . . an explanation, not an excuse."

"So why *did* you torch the camp, Carl?"

"I just felt like it."

They were all experiencing the exhaustion that comes after a close encounter with death. But Carl's men felt it more than Corvalán's. Having had no real sleep in three full days, they were muddy, wet, and numb. Without the Colombians, the Americans would have had to lay up somewhere and rest, hiding for their survival. And how would they have gotten out of there?

Your security will be the responsibility of the Colombian Marine Corps.

With the Colombians manning the throttles and guns, this was basically a taxi ride back to Tipishca. Gradually, they drifted into a zombie state between sharpness and sleep.

No one noticed the men hidden on the north bank of the river, as the Piranhas followed a forty-five-degree bend to the left.

One minute later, the river ahead of them was suddenly filled with canoes about four hundred meters out. War canoes! The boats, filled with angry people waving long guns, formed a skirmish line most of the way across the Putumayo. Peering into the waning light, Carl was jolted back to reality. Corvalán slowed the Piranhas and directed his crews to get ready for action. Then he turned to Carl.

"Carlos . . . we can go through them . . . but it will be expensive. I cannot get all of them with the machine guns before they get some of us. What do you want me to do?"

If he'd had the time, Carl would have reflected on the trade-off the Americans had made in the design of the Piranha class craft they'd given the Colombians: more speed or more armor. They had chosen speed.

"We could retreat to a thousand meters and pick them off with the M60s. They cannot hit with accuracy that far out . . . What do you think?"

"That works," said the Colombian, already turning the boats around.

At that moment, gunfire erupted from the north bank, just a hundred meters out. The FARC—it had to be the FARC—had laid an L-shaped ambush with firepower from two directions!

Jerry was the first to be hit. A hot slug slammed into his thigh, right in front of Harding's head. Bullets whizzed by Carl's ear as he fell, instinctively, on top of the ambassador. The howl of a Colombian crewman, hit in the stomach, added to the chaos. Jerry pulled a large bandage out of his other leg pocket and tied it tightly around the wound. The femur did not seem broken; the bleeding was serious but steady rather than pulsating. He had been lucky, but the leg would slow him up.

The Marine gunners raked the edge of the forest with all four M60s as the Piranhas raced out of the kill zone. The boats kept racing, and the guerrillas kept firing.

It was a long kill zone.

And then Carl's worst nightmare unfolded. Just as they were coming to what seemed like the end of the gauntlet, a 7.62-millimeter round went through both engines on the second Piranha. Without warning, the boat went from 40 knots to 0 knots. In an instant, Dozier, Jose, and the Colombian crew sat rocking back and forth in the middle of the river, several hundred yards behind Carl and the others.

The gunfire that had tapered off began picking up again as the guerrillas on the bank passed the word, running ahead to stay even. The stricken boat returned fire, but they were sitting ducks. The bow gun was out of ammunition. Dozier was focused on the riverbank. Jose and the Colombians watched as the skirmish line of canoes advanced from upstream.

"They're closing on us!" shouted Jose. He picked up an M16 and started firing at the flotilla, armed with AK-47s. It was not a contest; the AKs delivered a heavier slug with more range. His MP5 and Sig Sauer were useless—at least until the enemy got a lot closer. The rear gunner continued to rake the shoreline, but he too was running low on ammo. They were outgunned on both sides of the L.

The coxswain was busy trying to restart one of the engines. Jose put down the M16 and grabbed an M79. As the canoes came closer, he fired off forty-millimeter high explosive rounds as fast as he could. That slowed them down but did not stop them.

Dozier's forward gunner, now firing forty-millimeters, took a round in the shoulder that knocked him down. In the next instant, a rocket-propelled grenade impacted just in front of the boat with a huge splash.

"Carlos, Leroy . . . you guys OK?" Carl was astonished that Dozier had beaten him to the radio.

"Yeah . . . Butkus is hit . . . and one Marine . . . Coming your way, fast . . . Casualties?"

"One Marine wounded . . . not life-threatening . . . but they have RPGs . . . and they have us bracketed! Forward gun is out of ammo . . . You engage the enemy on the bank . . . We'll take the canoes."

"Got it," replied Carl, as the lead boat raced to the rescue.

One minute later, Dozier called him back. "Carlos . . . I just got a transmission from Robinson . . . He's inbound!"

"Robinson! *Himself?* Inbound? In what?"

"That's affirm . . . I just gave him our revised position . . . He'll be overhead in five minutes . . . in a Chinook!"

Carl shook his head with disbelief. "Are you *sure?* How did he get all the way down here without telling us?"

"He doesn't have authorization for this mission. According to Washington, General Stewart's gone rogue. He was afraid they would stop him, so he went low-level and radio-silent . . . straight across Colombia!"

Carl could hear the rate of fire on Dozier's boat diminish from automatic to single shot. Corvalán still had both M60s firing as they paralleled the riverbank. But he was running low on ammunition too! He pulled alongside Dozier and began firing both ways—the forward gunner still raking the bank, the rear gunner blasting canoes out of the water as they came closer. Carl was able to make brief eye contact with Lucho. They agreed without saying it: there was not going to be enough ammo to get them out of this.

The Piranhas were fighting side by side now. Carl and Dozier were off the radio and shouting. "Leroy . . . tell Robinson to come in with door guns blazing. He won't be able to pick us up until the enemy breaks off . . . Got that?"

"Yep . . . I'll tell him fire support is job one." Dozier relayed Carl's request to Stewart and looked at his teammate again. "The general says it's *stealth fighters* coming in to waste the camp . . . not Army Rangers. Can you believe that?"

"Wow!" replied Carl at the top of his lungs. "I'm just glad we're out of there . . . and I can't wait to get out of *here*!"

The pilots would never know that Carl had gotten to the camp first . . . that there was nothing left to bomb. Carl had always preferred to put his hands on the things he destroyed. That way, he could destroy only what needed to be destroyed.

If he felt like it.

The pilots would just release their bombs and go home. They would be at the officer's club at Holloman before Carl and his men got to Panama.

If they made it off the river.

The Piranhas continued to pick off individual canoes, but the firing from the north bank did not abate. Dozier's boat was still dead in the water. It was almost dark. As he stood up to see better, Jose took a flesh wound in the shoulder. Ignoring the pain and the blood, he picked up his MP5 and started delivering close fire support to the crew. *Very* close. Soon, the Americans would be drawing their pistols. It was just a matter of time.

Suddenly—over the din of the firefight—they heard it. The MH-47 Chinook was coming to get them! Dozier, working the radio in one hand and his weapon in the other, called on the big chopper to suppress enemy fire along the north bank. The Chinook swooped in, parallel to the water's edge, and tore up the tree line with machine gunfire. The effect was immediate. The enemy rate of fire was cut in half, and some of the guerrillas began jumping into the river. With his men firing the last of what they had, Carl watched the helo come back for a second run, this time firing into the river as well as into the trees. The FARC who were not already dead ran for their lives. This time, into the forest.

The canoes broke off their attack and started running upstream toward the Peruvian side of the river.

"Leroy . . . bring the helo in right *here!*" Carl was already bending over to put on his fins. Corvalán bent over with him.

"Carlos . . . how do you plan to get from this boat into that helicopter? There are no landing zones anywhere near here!"

"The river itself is a landing zone, Lucho." He was smiling. "We didn't teach you *everything!*" He stood up and looked his friend in the eye. "You and your men want a free ride to Panama?" He shouted over the sound of the approaching helicopter.

"First tell me about the river as a landing zone."

"The Chinook, with its two large rotors, can hover low enough to drop its tail ramp and wheels into the water. All we have to do is swim into the back end, sit down, and hang on."

Corvalán looked at his mentor with serious doubt. "*Loco . . . completamente loco!*" The Colombian leveled his dark eyes at Carl. "I could not bring my men with you . . . even if you had a magic carpet. We are not finished with this war. You have won your battle, but we have many more still to fight." Lucho held Carl by the arm as he spoke, bracing against the wind, now gusting over the deck.

"We haven't won this battle *yet*," replied Carl, looking up at the descending machine. He grabbed his friend by the shoulders and looked him straight in the eye. "Your war is also our war. I am confident we will win it, Lucho."

"I am very sorry for Tinker," said the Colombian. "He was my friend, too. I would like to go back and tell his family how brave he was. Please tell them for me." Carl nodded. "We have too much to do here," continued the major. "My role in this will not cause us harm . . . Indeed, our reputation will be strengthened. I will take my boats to El Encanto. We can resupply there and return home in a few days. My wounded will not die."

"Watch out for the FARC!"

Luis Corvalán looked at his mentor with tears in his eyes. "I do not think you will be back, my friend. Am I correct?"

"You are correct, Lucho . . . I will not be back . . . at least not as a warrior." The emotion of bidding goodbye to his friend superimposed itself on his elation to be alive. Before tears could betray him, Carl looked up at the chopper.

The Chinook descended from the jungle sky like a bird of prey. The boats were floating together in the steady current. The water lathered into white foam as the helo came lower. Carl had done what they called the Chinook squat many times, but he had never done it in the middle of a flowing river! He was glad he didn't have to fly the machine. All he had to do was swim.

Jerry, literally laughing at the pain, pulled a life jacket out of his rucksack and threw it over Harding's head.

"We're going for a swim, sir . . . I don't care if you know how or not! Just let me carry you across the chest . . . I used to be a lifeguard!"

The big man adjusted his battle dressing, slowing the leakage of blood soaking into his pant leg. He pulled his fins over his boots and jumped into the river. He knew that shock would soon overwhelm him, but he needed to delay it just long enough to get Harding into the helicopter. Jerry Tompkins knew where his limits were; he pushed himself toward them.

Jose put a life jacket on Billy Joe and inflated it. With Carl's help, he got in the water with the corpse. This would be, thought Carl, the last swim of a great frogman. Unless Billy Joe's parents wanted him buried at sea.

On Carl's signal, Ron Dozier jumped into the river and swam toward the tailgate. The helicopter's wheels were now wet, and Carl knew the pilot would not be able to hold the airframe in the water for long. His men moved out together, Jerry Tompkins dragging the ambassador as if the man were a teenage girl.

"Goodbye, Lucho," Carl shouted over the punishing beat of the Chinook's twin blades. He gave the Colombian a bear hug. "*Gracias por todo.*"

"*Buena suerte, amigo* . . . I will see you again . . . some day . . . in some place."

Carl jumped into the water and stroked easily to the ramp. He held the video cassette in a plastic sac above his head. The prop wash that usually bothered him on this evolution did not even faze him. This would be his last evolution. And it struck him—there in the froth of the Putumayo—what a funny word "evolution" was to use for such an extraordinary act. *A civilian wouldn't talk like that.* And he looked forward to becoming a real civilian.

An ordinary life.

Reginald Stewart, shin deep in river water, was on the ramp to assist him. Personally. Carl Malinowski looked at his mentor and felt the brotherhood of the armed forces well up in him one more time.

"You must be tired of pullin' my ass out of the fire by now, General!" This time, the fire was in Carl's eyes as he grabbed the thick black hand.

"Don't you ever call me general again, Carl!" Stewart was smiling at the friend he thought he might never see again. "What else can I do for you men?"

"Give Dozier a medal, sir. A big one! We wouldn't be here without him."

"Done. That will be my last act as the commander of SOCSOUTH."

The pilot slowly lifted the airframe clear of the river. Carl had to hang on tightly to keep from rushing off the end of the tailgate along with the water. He had one hand on a strut and the other clasped to Stewart's iron grip. Army crewmen pulled the others farther into the bird. They placed Billy Joe's body, still wrapped in a poncho, gently on the floor. As they strapped it down, everyone hesitated in a quick moment of silence. Very quick.

Carl smiled at the man who had just saved them all. "You're still a general, sir . . . I can't call you Reggie."

"I won't be a general when we get back, Carl. I signed my retirement from the Army right before getting on this bird. I won't serve a government that would do this. I went all the way to SECDEF to try and find out what was happening. Nothing! Then I had to piece it together myself. I'm a rogue general working for a rogue government. We're even . . . and the ministry calls. It's time to serve God."

Carl stood up as the helicopter gained altitude. He stumbled to the canvas bench lining the cargo compartment and sat down next to the general. The increasing g-force pressed him back against the bulkhead as the pilot banked to the left.

Toward Panama.

Carl found the seat belt and braced himself for a long, bumpy, low-level flight. Still breathing hard, he leaned closer to Stewart.

"When you told me they play by jungle rules," he shouted, "I thought you were talking about the narcos and the guerrillas . . . not Washington!"

"I was, Carl . . . I was."

"You'll make a great civilian, Reggie . . . I want you to be my best man."

Chapter 13

Redfish Pass

C arl waited in the darkness before dawn for a man he had never met. It had been eight months since the Putumayo mission. A lot had happened since then, and time had slipped away almost unnoticed. The ordinary life he had once dreaded was treating him well. He was not a religious person, but he had developed a workable spirituality. More importantly, a moral code. He believed the good things he had done in his life were judged to have outweighed the bad. He felt he had been rewarded for the balance. That reward had come in many forms, beginning with his own survival. This day, his reward took the form of a subtropical sunrise and a morning of good fishing.

He was proud to be a fisherman. Not a struggling fisherman like his father had been, but a fishing guide. He wore a permanent tan and a smile that never seemed to go away. The tan came from being in the sun most of the time; the smile came from his surprise at how much fun an ordinary life could be. Carl's search for meaning had taken him to the southwest coast of Florida. There, in the warm water of the barrier islands, he had settled down in a small beach house on Captiva, not far from where they had spread Billy Joe Barnes's ashes on the Gulf of Mexico. He sat in his office, a twenty-six-foot Mako with Bimini top, as it rested temporarily on its mooring lines in the still water.

A heavyset man came wandering down the rickety wooden planks, looking back and forth. He carried a spinning rod and a cooler as he searched for the boat he had chartered. The *Madrugada*. A strange name, the man thought again, as he narrowly avoided the indignity of falling into the water. He stopped and surveyed a cluster of boats. Then he saw the Mako, by itself at the end of the dock. An athletic-looking middle-aged man, wearing a Boston Red Sox baseball cap, was waving to him.

"Carl Barnes?"

"That's me," said the man in the baseball cap, standing up. "Good morning!" He extended his hand and helped the man aboard. The Mako gave in to the extra weight and gently rocked away the disturbance.

"Victor Santanelli," said the man, extending his meaty hand. "Nice to meet you . . . Looks like it's gonna be a be-yootiful day!" said his companion for the morning. Mixed with his Brooklyn drawl, the fat man had an Italian accent that sounded to Carl like music.

"Every day's a beautiful day in paradise," said Carl without losing his smile. "Have a seat, and we'll be on our way." He fired up the large outboard engines. "Sun should be up soon, but it won't get hot for a few hours." Carl cast off the lines and idled the Mako into the channel.

Santanelli sat next to him on the bench seat behind the wheel. He studied Carl's boat with a critical eye. It wasn't a specialized flats boat like most inshore fishing guides used, but a general-purpose shallow V-hull craft, capable of taking visitors on a variety of trips. If his client had asked about why he chose the boat, Carl would have told him that he was just as happy taking a family shelling on the world-class beaches of the outer islands as he was taking people fishing in the shallow water. The Mako also made a good platform for scuba diving, a habit Carl had never broken.

"Nice boat ya got here, Carl. I've been wondering about the name. It's unusual . . . and a good business decision on your part. It got my attention on the Internet, but I don't think I can pronounce it. What does it mean?"

Carl nudged up the throttles a bit and made sure the boat was in between the wooden channel markers. "*La Madrugada* is a Spanish word. It describes the early morning, like now, just when it starts to get light."

"Makes sense for someone in your business."

"Yeah," replied Carl, "but that's not the only reason I chose the name."

"What else could it be?"

"The early morning has always been the luckiest time of day for me."

"I hope that luck applies to fishing," quipped the Italian.

"I can assure you that it does, Vic . . . Your friends call you Vic?"

"If I *had* any friends, yeah, they would call me Vic," he joked. "You look Italian, Carl . . . How'd ya get a name like Barnes?"

"My mother was Italian." He lost his smile, just for a moment. Then it was back. "I got her genes."

"You speak any Italian?"

"*Si!*" said Carl, tempted to continue. "But I'm a little rusty." The truth was that Carl was trying to learn a fourth language, not at all close to Italian.

He pushed the throttles a little more and got the Mako on step. "We'll start on the other side of the pass, just inside the flats," shouted the guide. "The tide is coming in, and the fish should be feeding there for a few hours."

Santanelli nodded as Carl adjusted the outboards again, bringing them to full power. In seconds, they were racing over the bay at close to forty knots. He thought of Lucho Corvalán and felt a surge of emotion as nostalgia swept over him like a wave.

The humid air rushing past was already warm against his face. It was best to reminisce at high speed, he told himself. Especially about people he missed. Tears dried quickly at forty knots. His tears for Billy Joe always came mixed with anger for what his country had tried to do to them. But all the negative feelings could not diminish the pride he still carried with him. A sense of accomplishment that would sustain Carl for the rest of his life.

His ordinary life.

"This your first trip to Florida?" asked Carl at the top of his lungs.

"No . . . I usually fish the Keys, but I wanted to try something different."

"This is the best inshore fishing I know of," said Carl, keeping one hand on the wheel and gesturing—like an Italian—with the other. "The islands around us provide the perfect habitat for many types of game fish . . . and the environment is so clean, you can actually eat what you catch!" He held out his hand as if to introduce his guest to the mangrove trees, now emerging in the dawn. "This is my living room."

"I already like it better than Islamorada," said Vic. "It's not as crowded . . . and a lot greener."

Redfish Pass separated Captiva from the island of North Captiva. Until a hurricane cut the pass in 1921, the two islands had been one. Carl loved the north island because the only way you could get there was by boat or small plane. He drove the Mako across the entrance to the pass and bled off speed as he moved out of the channel. He let the boat drift into the flats, tilting the big engines just far enough out of the water to avoid damage. Santanelli took a position on the bow of the boat and waited. Carl took a long metal push pole from under the gunwale and thrust it into the water.

"Take this one to start, Vic," instructed Carl, reaching around the console. "Just cast it to starboard and drag it slowly along the bottom. It's a plastic shrimp . . . let it stir the mud."

As he poled the boat along the edge of the mudflat, Carl treated himself to a binocular-assisted look at two tricolored herons in the mangrove to his left. He wished he could catch fish as easily as they did. The birds were canopy feeding, holding their wings over the surface of the water to form shadows, and then picking off the small fish taking shelter there. *Now* those *are jungle rules!*

With one eye on the herons and the other on his client, his thoughts turned to Reggie Stewart. Now that his Article 32 hearing was over and his Baptist minister's life on track, the general was about to fulfill a longtime promise to visit. Carl had testified for Stewart on videotape (with his face blurred), describing the events of his Putumayo mission to a closed session. His testimony was more than enough to have Stewart's case dismissed. Instead of a dishonorable discharge, the Army had given Reggie a Silver Star for bravery.

A Silver Star he richly deserved.

Had Carl executed the mission while on active duty, he would have gotten a Silver Star as well. Instead, he had been forced to take measures to protect himself and his wife for the rest of their lives—from his own government, and from any surviving cartel members who might want revenge. He had destroyed the documents at the jungle lab, but he understood there might be other papers out there with his name on them. He had taken Billy Joe's last name as an additional insurance policy. It was a very light cover, but it made him feel better.

The sound of Santanelli's reel brought him back. By the time Carl turned his head, the light rod was doubled over against the brightening sky, straining against the pull of a strong fish. Displaying his experience, the Italian held the rod high and let the fish run. Carl didn't have to do anything but keep the bow of the boat to the left of the action. And enjoy the show.

"Yeah!" Vic sounded like a kid with a new toy. "This is great! He's gonna take most of my line!" The fat man was leaning over the starboard side of the Mako, and Carl chuckled at the thought that the guy might fall in. The water was only two feet deep, but there was plenty of room for the fish to run. The smile on his client's face told Carl he was in the right business.

A few minutes later, he reached for the net. "Bring his head this way . . . That's it, Vic." Carl slid the net under the exhausted redfish and lifted it over the rail. "Good catch!"

"Eight pounds?"

"That's about right . . . That's as big a red as they let you keep around here."

"You mean there's bigger ones out there?"

"They get up to twenty-five pounds, Vic . . . I shit you not."

"They any good to eat?"

"My personal favorite," responded the captain. "Not like your average Islamorada bonefish."

"I like that!" said the Italian, smiling.

"Great. Let's keep this one and release the rest . . . OK?"

"Sounds good to me, Carl. I'm not a meat fisherman anymore. You can have a filet . . . I can't eat a whole fish by myself, and I don't want to freeze it."

"Deal . . . Now get that shrimp back in the water!" Carl gave the lure back to Vic and put the fish in the box. "It's only a half-day charter, but you'll be tired by lunchtime at this rate."

"I hear ya, Captain . . . This is the life!"

Yes, this is the life!

Jerry Tompkins had written to him from Wyoming the week before. The big man had gone back to his roots on the range near Laramie. His leg had healed completely, but he was still bitter about what had happened to them. He had never understood the rules. In Jerry's world, everything was supposed to be fair. Good guys were rewarded; bad guys were punished. Nobody fell in between the cracks. Carl had told him about the Stewart hearing and given him Jose's new address. Jerry had promised to stay in touch, and Carl knew he would. Butkus would always be there for him.

Jose had called him every few weeks since the mission. Like Jerry and Carl, he needed to talk about Billy Joe. You can't lose someone that close to you, thought Carl, without losing a piece of yourself. As team leader, he felt the loss even more than the others. He was happy that Jose had decided to become a paramedic. Lots of action, even in Virginia Beach, and nobody shooting at him. Despite the bad memories, Jose was noticeably happier. He was engaged to an EMT colleague named Ana. Carl had promised to take him fishing as soon as he could get to Florida for a visit.

So much for his old friends. He was making new friends so fast, he had trouble keeping track. Carl Malinowski, the loner, had become Carl Barnes, everyone's candidate for mayor. As for family, he had paid off his father's debts and gotten Uncle Jerzy off his back. A new lease on life all around.

"Have you always been a fisherman?" asked Vic, casting again.

"In my heart, yes," said Carl. "But I spent some time in the Navy."

"What did you do in the Navy?"

"I was a gunner's mate."

"Did ya get to 'Nam?"

"No, I didn't . . . I'm not as old as I look!" Carl was laughing now. He actually liked lying about his past.

"Gulf War?"

"Nope . . . missed that one too."

"I hope the Navy wasn't too boring," said the Italian, chuckling.

"I managed to find some interesting things to do," said Carl, savoring the understatement. "But I grew up in a fishing family. This is where I belong . . . What business are you in, Vic?"

"I import olive oil."

Before Carl could respond, another fish took Vic's line across the flats. The details of Santanelli's business were left unstated. Carl chose not to speculate on what else the man might be importing. He hoped it was all legal. He assumed it was. He wanted Victor Santanelli to come back and fish with him next year.

A few minutes later they had netted and released another redfish. A ten-pound specimen to dream about for next time. Santanelli was happy. Happy enough to come back.

"Whaddaya think of the president's resignation?" Carl felt a bolt of electricity surge through his body as Vic continued. "I mean, ya gotta ask yourself how someone that powerful could be that *stupid*! Ya know what I'm sayin'?"

"To be honest, Vic, I haven't had time to follow it too closely."

Carl, of course, had followed the news of the last month more closely than almost anyone. He had, in fact, contributed directly to Ferguson's political demise, probably more than anyone except Robert Harding, the president's principal accuser, who had agreed to make sure Carl's role was never made public. Harding had been rehabilitated and was about to be appointed undersecretary of state. He was still married to Norma.

President Ferguson was not the only casualty of the Harding affair. William Randolph, claiming to the end that he hadn't known about the Americans at the jungle laboratory, tried to defend the raid (which—since everyone was already dead—had not killed anyone). He couldn't. Randolph lost his job, and his reputation.

Jeff Girardin lost more than his job. The proof-of-life video—bearing a date and time—constituted hard evidence that Robert Harding had been alive after Jeff reported his death. Subsequent testimony, some of it from Carl, had resulted in the arrogant young man's incarceration. For thirty years to life.

Victor Ozal—another immigrant named Victor, thought Carl, watching Santanelli retrieving his lure again—had escaped with his reputation intact. Like Harding, Ozal had come out of the situation stronger than he'd gone in. What had saved him were the White House tapes that became key pieces of evidence in the investigation of what was to be forever known as Colombia-gate. Ozal was still the secretary of defense, and he still had a shot at the Senate.

Jorge Mena Velasquez was back in Colombia, and the justice department was quietly returning his two sons. The Ferguson administration, trying hard to cover up their crimes, hadn't been able to come up with a credible explanation for having Mena in custody. They had arranged for a ship to Cartagena and simply sent him home. Carl had understood their reasoning, but he wasn't happy about it. Mena was certainly better off. Ironically, so was Carl.

"I guess fishing is more fun," Vic continued. "I mean, more fun than listening to the most powerful man in the world trying to explain how he authorized *framing* the president of another country! I just don't get it." The Italian was speaking more with his hands than any other part of his anatomy. He spoke with enough passion to give Carl the impression his client had some experience in the art of framing.

"Neither do I, Vic . . . neither do I," said Carl, shaking his head for effect. He scanned the sky for ospreys and found three. One bird had a small fish in its talons. Nature, he reminded himself, was a blend of beauty and brutality. The trick, which Carl had mastered, was to stay at the top of the food chain. On the Putumayo, Carl had felt like the fish; here, he felt like the osprey. He had complete control of his life, and he would never again let anyone take it away from him.

"Wanna catch a snook?"

"Sure!" said Vic. And he forgot all about the president's stupidity.

"We can't keep snook this time of year, but they're a lot of fun to catch," announced Carl as he polled the boat over to the edge of the mangrove forest. He dropped the anchor, and they began casting live bait. Carl, now using his own fishing rod, kept the conversation on fish, marine mammals, and birds. It was easy to stay off politics, thanks to the snook slamming their bait for the rest of the morning. Between the two of them, ten more fish came to the side of the *Madrugada*. But it wasn't just the fish that captured their attention. Carl handed the binoculars to Vic often; he felt joy every time the man marveled at the wildlife dancing all around the boat. Wildlife the businessman had looked at for fifty years but had never really seen.

Just before noon, they agreed it was time to go back to the dock. It was getting hot, and they were all fished out. The sky was a cauldron of thunderheads. Afternoon showers, as always, would cool things off and set the tone for a romantic evening at home. Carl fired up the outboards and ran for Captiva. Twenty minutes later, he pulled up to the pier and began putting the Mako to bed. While Carl washed the boat, Vic helped him stow the gear and then cleaned his own fish. When he was finished, Santanelli handed him a piece of redfish in a plastic bag and stuck out his hand.

"This the best fishing I've ever had, Carl . . . and thanks for the nature show. You should be on the Discovery Channel, ya know!"

"It was my pleasure, Vic. I can guarantee you that I'll be here for a long time. I hope you decide to come back."

"Count on it," said the client, handing him a fifty-dollar cash tip.

"Thank you, sir!" said Carl.

"I envy you," added Santanelli. "You get to live at the beach . . . I have to go back to the city and sit at a desk! Anyone ever tell you how lucky you are?"

"My wife tells me that all the time! I've been lucky all my life." He couldn't stop smiling as Victor Santanelli turned and walked down the dock to his Cadillac.

Carl snapped the cover on the Mako and checked the mooring lines. He practically ran to the parking lot and jumped in his truck.

With dinner in the cooler and Santana on the stereo, he cruised to the beach house five minutes down the island's only road.

She was not there. But he knew where to find her. He kicked off his shoes and walked out on the beach, carrying a towel. His heart beat faster as she rose from the gulf like a mermaid and ran to him like a young girl. Long hair, wet and straight, framed the face that still took his breath away.

Lucky is not the word.

He ran to the water's edge. She flung her arms around him, soaking his clothes. "You're early, dear . . . I wanted to be in the house when you came through the door!" He wrapped the towel around her glistening shoulders.

"I prefer to meet you here, Mrs. Barnes. This is where you belong."

She turned around and touched the sky with one outstretched hand. "This is where *we* belong, Carl."

"Let's go home," he replied, leading her through the sea oats to their front door.

When they got to the kitchen, there was a package on the counter. As they examined it, Carl could see that it had come from Germany through the military post office. It was a small box, roughly square, addressed to Carl and Gabriele Barnes.

"Any idea who it's from?"

"No, I don't," said Carl, turning the box over again to make sure it wasn't going to explode in his face. "Don't worry . . . It's not lethal! Probably someone I know at the European Command in Stuttgart."

He slid a knife into the seam, broke open the box, and extracted a smaller box. There was a short note taped to the outside. He read it out loud.

> Carl and Gabriele,
> A belated wedding present for the bride of my "sea daddy" (we couldn't think of anything you need, Carl, that you don't already have). The stone reminds my fiancée of a man she wants to forget.

We thought it would be perfect for Gabriele. Enjoy
your new lives. We are enjoying ours!

"Leroy"

He opened the box. They both gasped at the huge emerald
inside. For different reasons. Gabriele had never held a precious stone
that large; Carl recognized it immediately as the pendant Laura had
worn to dinner the night after Gabriele left him. His suspicion that
Harding had given it to her was now confirmed. It made sense—
more than Ron Dozier knew—to give it to Gabriele. Carl knew his
wife would never be fully aware of the irony. And that was just fine
with him.

"Carl! I love it! It's so beautiful!"

"Turn around, honey . . . I want you to wear it for the rest of the
day." He fastened the chain behind her neck and watched her spin
like a ballerina to face him. He took her in his arms.

"You're the most beautiful woman ever to wear an emerald like
this."

They kissed like new lovers as she pulled him back outside.
They ran to the water's edge, Carl still in his fishing clothes and
Gaby in her Speedo. They splashed forward until the warm water
was waist-high. There in the gentle surf, he put his arm around her.

"Who's Leroy?" she asked without taking her head off his
shoulder.

"He's a friend from the field," said Carl, gazing out at the gulf.
"I'll probably never see him again, but I'll never forget him. He saved
my life."

"That makes two of us saved by your friends from the field."

"That Forshay's a piece of work, isn't he?"

"Before he rescued me, I was preparing to go back to Germany."

"I would have followed you."

"I would have wanted you to."

"Now that I have you back, Gabriele, I will always protect you."
With his free hand, he swept the rumbling horizon in front of them.

"You're right, *querida* . . . This is where we belong."

About the Author

P aul Shemella lives with his wife in California, finally settled after traveling on behalf of the US government for more than forty years. He has written academic books on terrorism, maritime security, and African governance. *Jungle Rules* is his first novel.